DOWN IN THE DEVIL'S HOLE

ISABEL CARTER

Published by VenX Publishing
PO Box 780, Edgecliff NSW 2027 AUSTRALIA
www.venx.com.au

First published in Australia 2017
This edition published 2024

Cover design, typesetting: WorkingType (www.workingtype.com.au)

This book is a work of fiction. Any similarities to that of
people living or dead are purely coincidental.

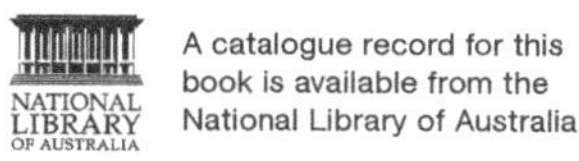
A catalogue record for this
book is available from the
National Library of Australia

A CIP catalogue record for this title is available from the British Library.

ISBN: 978-1-922923-12-7

VenX Publishing acknowledges the Traditional Owners of the country on which we work, the Gadigal people of the Eora nation and recognises their continuing connection to the land, waters and culture. We pay our respects to their Elders past, present and emerging.

ABOUT THE AUTHOR

Isabel Carter, originally from the Kingdom of Fife in Scotland, now resides in the picturesque coastal town of Batemans Bay in New South Wales, Australia.

Isabel is a Registered nurse and a university tutor for nursing students at the University of Wollongong.

She is the proud mother of three grown sons and a passionate poker player who has secured victories in several local tournaments.

Isabel has recently ventured into the world of crime fiction, and her debut novel is the first in the *Macgregor Murder Mystery* series. She is currently hard at work on the next installment.

The book has now been adapted to an award winning podcast starring Iain Glen from Game Of Thrones fame:

www.voyagemedia.fm/show/pulp-fever-dreams/ down-in-the-devils-hole/

ACKNOWLEDGEMENTS

I am grateful for the generosity of time and guidance from my dear friend Sarah Veitch, who was very helpful with editing and reading dialogue out loud with me. Along the way, I received invaluable input and feedback from friend, and experienced police officer, Dave Craker. Longtime friend and poker buddy Dr Doug Gock was also an invaluable source of knowledge. Thanks also go to Drew Lipinski for the 'male perspective'. Love and gratitude to my beautiful niece Laura Gilks for her help and encouragement.

Thank you Gavin Lee for taking time to read and review the manuscript. Special thanks also to Ian Stokes for his friendship and guidance.

Special mention to my friend and colleague Dr Sanjay Singh, for inspiring me to create a character. However, Dr Singh is a wonderful, kind humanitarian and a brilliant surgeon who would never play a part in the nefarious deeds the character undertakes within the novel.

Thanks also to my lovely mum and lastly, to my three gorgeous sons Elliot, Laurence, and Cameron, who have always been my mainstay and have given me so much joy and love.

CHAPTER ONE

The air was thick, the fog hung like a great cloak stretching across the quiet calm of the bay. The South Coast landscape was now preparing for winter; frost had begun to take hold among the shaded undergrowth of hedgerows along roads untouched by the warming rays of the sun. Fields stood stiff, crisp and motionless, Mother Nature's winter sieve covering them in a blanket of tiny, white, shimmering crystals.

Only months earlier, these fields had been bone dry. Parchments of land, widening dusty cracks, scorched from the ruthless intensity of the sun, awaited the relief of life breathing rain.

This small coastal town – known as the Bay to locals, and Batemans Bay to the flocks of tourists that descend every summer – weathers the cold like a comfortable old slipper while the summer warmth fades into memory.

Jennifer Jones took her usual walk not far from her home in Surfside, a quiet coastal suburb. Despite the winter it was fairly busy at this early hour. She nodded and smiled as she passed the early parade of joggers. As she walked by the cafe, she inhaled the welcome aroma of freshly brewed coffee, thinking to herself she would stop and grab one later, after her walk.

She paused as she approached the wooden steps over the beach embankment to take in the view. She looked out towards the estuary, the water flowing down through the mountains to the widening creek where the famous Batemans Bay bridge spanned the pristine Clyde River. The bridge, a steel vertical lift truss bridge had been operating for over sixty years, opening twice a day, it allowed larger vessels to pass underneath. It was fascinating to watch and drew a crowd at busy times. Sixty years old, it was now showing its age, needing frequent maintenance and repairs. The workers happily claimed double and sometimes triple time for their efforts. All too often, following these repairs, it would break down, stuck halfway up or down, leaving frustrated motorists stranded for long periods of time on either side. This usually occurred at the most inopportune moments when the massing tribes were arriving for the holiday season, resulting in queues stretching for many kilometres along the Kings and the Princes highways.

Jennifer turned and watched as black swans glided along the misty river; the swans regally joining others along the sloping sides of wet sand carved out by the king tide coming in the night before.

Seaweed left in the tide's wake saw fishing tackle snagged around the fallen whitewashed branches. Trees bleached and starved of life, long dead, remnants of the winter night's activities.

The steel grey water slowly ebbed back from the Clyde

River, receding to the depths of the sea, eager to join the heavy force that was the Pacific Ocean. Mist slowly dissipated as the sun began to breach the horizon over the water.

Surfside Beach allowed her the freedom to walk her dog, Digger, a young Labrador. He tugged on his lead, jerking her arm in eager anticipation.

Although it was called Surfside the water appeared calm and had minimal waves. It certainly misled some tourists, and often they were looking for the walkway towards the northern end of the beach. It comprised a boardwalk that meandered along Cullendulla Creek. Conservation authorities had mapped out a pathway, with wooden signposts giving directions. The posts had carved images of hikers with distances in kilometres indicating the time it would take for the round trip. The boardwalk was positioned through mangrove bushes and afforded breathtaking views of the Bay and the small coastal towns in the distance.

Heading along the boardwalk and past the headland to a quieter beach, the one most tourists were yet to discover, Jennifer could allow Digger the freedom to run. She knew dogs were not given access on this beach due to strict conservation restrictions, but she also knew that no one would be around at this early hour.

She breathed deeply, filling her lungs with the fresh sea air, easing and stretching her neck, trying to relieve the tension and stress she had been feeling. She tugged her coat tighter around her, feeling the dampness of the salty cool mist cling to her face and hair. It was markedly colder than it had been a few weeks earlier. She unclipped the leash from Digger's collar.

Caw, caw, caw.

Looking up, she saw several black crows circling above as she heard their familiar cry.

Eager to be free from his constraints, Digger tore along the shore, in and out of the waves, exploring and sniffing at everything he found. She followed him – but even watching his excitement and delight on the shore, she couldn't push the nagging frustration of last night's conversation from her thoughts. Her partner, Jack, had made some suggestions about their upcoming trip to the UK. She didn't want to spend two weeks with his snobbish sister in London. Why couldn't they take a week in the Cotswold's and relax instead? Perhaps travel around all the beautiful villages with their pretty gardens and sandstone walls. She'd had a restless night contemplating all the travel arrangements, prompting her to get up and take the dog out earlier than usual.

Excited growls from Digger drew Jennifer's attention. He tugged at a long lump of wood with pink netting-like material wrapped around it. The pink material flapped in the breeze and then flopped to the dog's feet. She groaned at the thought of him, yet again, burying his nose in something stinky, an old fish or rotten seagull. He'd need a bath when he got home.

'Digger! Come on boy.' He ignored her. Instead, he dug deeper into the sand before continuing to sniff and tug.

'Digger, come here right now!' He looked up at her, barked and bit into part of whatever he had found in his mouth. Heading towards the dog, she quickened her pace, picking up a stick to distract him from his new conquest and prize.

The crows circled, agitated, swooping and diving towards

the dog as another chorus of caws and cries began.

As she drew closer she was able to get a better view of what Digger was playing with. She stopped.

Her body stiffened as she became acutely aware of the shape that was before her. Paralysed in disbelief, she almost lost her footing.

The grotesquely distorted, half-naked, body of a woman, golden hair, sand encrusted with twigs and entwined with seaweed, lay face down in a tangled mass. A pink dress, torn and twisted, wrapped tightly around her waist. She wore no underwear and the dress had snagged on a dead tree lying close by. The hem had pulled up at one side, revealing her naked buttocks and thighs. Still, cold, dead, soaked limbs, bloated with strangely mottled skin.

It was indecent. Obscene. Jennifer let out a shocked gasp. 'Oh, oh, no ...' Raising her hand to her mouth as her breathing quickened. Refusing to give up his prize, Digger started to tear into an arm of the body. Sharp incisors ripping into the waterlogged flesh, pieces of putrid muscle shedding easily from the bone; it reminded her of the boiled tripe her father used to cook when she was a child. She hated the smell and look of it when it had gone cold.

She hesitated, frozen to the spot before reality kicked in. Adrenaline coursing through her veins, her heart was now racing, sharp intakes of cool air filling her lungs which were squeezed with anxiety.

She grabbed Digger's collar and tried to attach his leash, her hands shaking, cold fingers fumbling for the metal catch. His wet, sand-covered fur made it difficult to grasp. Finally it attached, as he strained at the leash to get back to his prize.

Bile rose in her throat, bitter and fiery as it invaded her mouth. Retching, she heaved the yellow fluid from her stomach, no breakfast to bring back up, thank God. The bitterness in her mouth caused her to heave again, rasping as she coughed, putting a strain on her muscles and diaphragm. Sweat forming on her forehead mingled with the mist as she pulled off her coat and covered the body. Her cries of help were faint and feeble.

She turned back towards the path and called out, loudly now, for anyone to help ... but no one was around to hear. Only the caws of the crows cut through the silence.

CHAPTER TWO

Police taped off the access to the beach. A couple of uniforms were in place to stop onlookers and bystanders from entering. The last body to be washed ashore was six months ago. An Indian tourist washed off the rocks while fishing. Why did they always ignore the warnings? The police were discussing this as the medical examiner, a local GP, packed away her black medical bag after certifying the body.

A Land Cruiser pulled up alongside several of the parked police vehicles. The Detective Chief Inspector jumped out. John Macgregor strode over towards the uniformed officers. Tall, middle-aged and a bit dishevelled; he wore shoes that were down at heel. His jacket had seen better days, frayed at the cuffs, the elbows shiny from wear. Pushing a mass of black, greying, curly hair from his face, he was interrupted by the local doctor approaching.

'Good morning, Doctor. Detective John Macgregor,' he said as he offered his hand.

'It's a young woman, Caucasian, in her twenties I'd say,' the

GP replied. 'Autopsy will give more details, but at first glance, I don't think she drowned. It appears to be more than that. Somebody's been creative.'

She cocked her head to one side in anticipation of Macgregor's response, still failing to accept and shake his hand as she placed her medical bag into the back of her car.

Macgregor pulled his hand back and dug it deep into his pocket.

'Very good, Doctor. Now I'd like to get on and see for myself,' he replied with a smirk, ignoring her comments as he headed over to where the body lay. Yes, well lassie, you're only here to certify the death, maybe leave the investigating to me, he thought sarcastically.

Macgregor ran a hand across tired blue eyes that offset a rugged face. Still handsome for his years, he had a face which was now more lived in. Weathered by the many years of murders, suicides and assaults; dealing with psychopaths, narcissists, the downright insane, and the ones that were just not wired right in the head. The victims and their families were etched on every craggy line.

He had been seconded to the coastal town but had lived in Sydney for the previous twenty years; he hated this quiet backwater and missed the high-profile pressures of the city. Two years was enough. He wanted to get back to Sydney and hoped a replacement could soon be found.

'Inspector Macgregor?' He was jolted out of his thoughts by a voice that he judged to belong to an experienced officer.

'Aye that's me,' he replied in his soft Scottish brogue. He knew many of the uniformed officers by sight but had no idea of this constable's name. Still, he quickly took charge of the situation.

'Show me the location, laddie,' he ordered. The officer nodded and led him over to the cordon. He lifted it for Macgregor to bend under and get through. As the constable had been first on the scene, it was 'his' case and he took pride in leading Macgregor to the body.

Nothing unusual in finding a corpse on the beach. Macgregor had seen quite a few in his time, not so bad before the flies got to them. The body lay on the edge of the outgoing tide, small ripples of water lapped around her legs and tangled garments.

This one had no ID, and there was no one reported missing locally.

The pathologist was kneeling by the body. Dr Douglas Solomon had not long arrived; he had been brought down from Wollongong because of the case's suspicious circumstances. He was a small, thin, balding man with round glasses perched on the end of his nose; over his clothes he wore a white all-in-one jumpsuit with an attached hood, and blue latex gloves. He was deep in his work as he carefully took scrapings and samples. Forensics had finished taking photos of the body in situ and nearby there was body bag waiting on a gurney.

Solomon stood and introduced himself. The two men nodded in lieu of a handshake as they looked on at the corpse.

'Another new pathologist ... Wonder how long he'll last,' Macgregor murmured, sizing up the man before him. 'Anything unusual or untoward here, pal?' he asked as he grabbed some blue latex gloves from a box next to the gurney and pulled them on. He knelt next to Solomon and the body, carefully lifting hair and clothes, looking for any form of identification.

'Not easy to say really, with the water logging, bloating and damage to the head from the rocks. And the dog. I would say she's been in the water for about three days.' He began to roll the body over so that her face, what was left of it, was visible. The forensic photographer leant in to take a shot.

With precision, Solomon started to cut her tangled clothes from the tree branches using sharp scissors. As he did, the body made a popping noise; the pressure from the tangled garments released some gas and the bitterly pungent smell hovered over them.

'No jewellery or watch, aged anywhere between twenty and thirty-five, judging by her hair, teeth and style of clothes. Nothing's washed up around her,' Solomon noted. He was used to such smells and kept on at his task.

Macgregor turned his head and took deep breaths through his mouth trying to avoid the putrid stench that he'd never been able to stomach.

'I'll know more once I get her to the morgue and we do a full investigation and a post-mortem,' Solomon continued, echoing the GP's sentiments, as he beckoned over a uniform for help to place the corpse into the body bag.

'You have my number, give me a call as soon as anything comes up,' Macgregor said, peeling off the gloves and standing up from his knees.

He glanced towards the far side of the beach, people going about their everyday lives, not tainted with the rancid decay of death.

He looked back at the corpse as the zipper was closed and the body lifted up on to the gurney. A small piece of pink clothing was flapping in the breeze, still tangled on the branch, the only sign of a life once lived. The forensic officer noticed it flapping. Using tweezers, he removed it and placed it into a plastic bag marked 'Evidence'. Macgregor stood and turned his back to the water, wondering who this young woman was and how and why had she died.

A large black crow landed by the spot where the body had been. Picking at the sand, a small black eye careful not to lose sight of the man in front of it. Macgregor thought how quickly the cycle of life resumes.

As for this young woman's death, it would reveal itself, it always did, in time ...

CHAPTER THREE

Memories still haunted him.

A small boy, hungry, scavenging through rubbish, living in putrid conditions in the Dharavi slums, the poorest area in the Indian city of Mumbai.

Over 600,000 people crammed into a space just under two kilometres wide, with one toilet to serve over 1000 residents and severe sanitary deprivation, resulting in rat infested and disease-ridden middens.

Now, he was an eminent surgeon with status, a fleet of classic cars, enormous wealth, several properties in Sydney and on the coast. He also owned a flash, new, day surgery and clinic in Batemans Bay. He kept feeding the desire – his appetite to rid himself of poverty and so many childhood fears and struggles – but it never seemed enough.

Showering up to four times a day was his way to remove the past. The clean, pure water was cleansing, but not enough to wash away the ingrained filth.

His colour was still the same. No matter how often he tried to assimilate with other Australian surgeons, he always felt inferior. His trophy, model girlfriend was a recent addition to his collection. This afforded him some acceptance but she wasn't very bright and often let him down when conversing with the other surgeons' wives.

The anger simmered, the waves of revulsion sank deeper in his psyche.

He hated the wealthy clients in the local community; they repulsed him, those who had given him his lifestyle. They owned him, but he would greet them warmly in his resplendent office with its typically English style furnishings. His smile was perfectly practised, his hair perfectly groomed, his clean nails manicured. He dressed in tailored Armani suits. He liked only the best. Smelling sweet with cologne ... he was always overdoing it, as if to make it last longer. Or, was it to totally overwhelm the utter self-loathing that was stagnating beneath his skin?

Paranjoy Panngesh. His name was given to him from his father, it meant 'King of Serpents and Conqueror of Life'.

He liked to think his name symbolised all he stood for; the medical logo, the serpents entwined around the staff; a healer, he who provides medical help.

His art with the scalpel was impressive. He could wound or heal with the knife and he could bring about death as easily as he could save life. This gave him an unadulterated sense of power. Dr Paranjoy Panngesh – he did not adopt the practice of a surgeon being called 'Mr' – it was Dr Panngesh, 'Mr' just sounded so average.

'Dr Panngesh?' Ms Roseberry, his secretary and personal assistant – an attractive, tall blonde with steel-grey eyes

– waltzed into his office. Always flawless in her make-up, dressed in Chanel. She smiled impeccably.

'Excuse the intrusion, Dr Panngesh, there is a Dr Patel in the foyer wishing to see you. I did ask him whether he had an appointment but he seemed rather insistent that you see him now.' She stood in apprehension of his response.

He glanced up from his laptop. 'Show him in,' he said with the crisp cultured ring of Oxford English. He liked to hear his own voice. He had taken such care to practice and nurture that well-versed English. He never tired of admiring it. Ms Roseberry clipped her beautiful Prada heels together and nodded, her slim neck and slicked back blonde hair remaining in place. In one graceful movement, she closed the door behind her.

She came back within a few moments with the visitor; she afforded him her smile, the one she used on all potential business associates, and offered him a choice of refreshment.

The visitor refused and with a wave of his hand dismissed her from the room. She looked for support from her employer. He seemed surprised by the appearance of the man and did not look up to see her slightly annoyed expression. Lips now pursed and defiant, she hated not to be noticed or acknowledged; she pulled the door shut a little too hard behind her.

Both men emerged some time later and headed out to the car park. Dr Panngesh shook hands with Dr Patel and then proceeded to his own vehicle, a sleek, silver Mercedes sports car with personalised plates 'PP 6'.

He drove out of the car park heading north along the Princes Highway. The four-hour drive to Sydney gave him time to think, to plan, to bathe in the deepest mires of his mind, with his car and his body on cruise control.

The opportunity was exquisite. How could he resist ... the thankfulness, the adulation that awaited him? The fantasies grew: images in his mind of their acceptance of him, of the deep appreciation for him from those well-respected pillars of society. The smile formed around his capped and whitened teeth and he pushed the pedal of the accelerator a little harder.

CHAPTER FOUR

Glenn Miller's 'String of Pearls' was playing on the record player. Macgregor sat in the uncomfortable armchair, sideways across the chair so his legs hung over the arm. He lay back humming along to the tune, bourbon on the rocks in hand – his favourite drink. He was always asked why he didn't drink scotch, being a Scotsman. But he remembered those childhood days of hot toddies, given to him by his Ma at the least onset of a sniffle or sore throat. He had disliked the taste intensely and it had put him off ever wanting to drink scotch again. However, a bourbon with ice ... ah ... that sated the thirst.

His record collection was impressive, with the likes of Cole Porter, Ella Fitzgerald, Duke Ellington, Louis Armstrong, and one of his most favourite, Billie Holliday. The sound of her earthy, husky tones relaxed and calmed his often-frenzied mind. He was proud of his almost mint condition vinyl records, taking care to keep them stacked upright and carefully replacing them in their plastic sleeves.

Macgregor had grown up listening to big band music at home.

His parents were also the reason he joined the police force, his mother watched every Humphrey Bogart movie ever produced. Macgregor was born on Christmas Day, a birthday he shared with Bogart.

Phillip Marlowe inspired him. He loved the one-liners, the clothes and the dames that entered the office seeking revenge on unfaithful or wayward husbands. His favourite movies were The Maltese Falcon and The Big Sleep. He had fallen in love with Lauren Bacall as an impressionable young boy. It affected the way he chose his women, to his detriment at times.

Black and white silhouettes of long forgotten stars, heroes of their day. He had some old movie posters somewhere, always planning to frame them but never getting around to it.

He was originally from Edinburgh, and along with many other families in the seventies, his had emigrated and settled in Sydney. He was a teenager when they had endured those first few hard years, learning to adjust and acquire Australian mannerisms and ways. Never losing his accent and proud of his heritage, he had gone to the police academy a hopeful young man. Keen to do the 'right thing', to serve and protect the people.

Years of futile injustices to innocents had taken their toll on Macgregor. He was tired of it all. Fighting the cause, endless long nights, piecing together fragments, and re-building jigsaws of lives torn and shattered by brutality.

With every new case, he grew more sour at the inhumane callousness of mankind. 'Kind'. That was an oxymoron: there was no kindness in most of the scenes he had dealt with. But still, he would persist to bring these brutes to trial; to bring some closure to those bereft families whose lives had been changed forever by heinous acts.

Stoicism had been born into him from many generations of Highlanders, battling with the elements and the hardships of the land. Joining the force had been the making of Macgregor according to his proud parents. His father was gone, passed from a stroke. Nearly ten years later and he still missed him. His mother lived alone in a small unit, the shine and light gone from her eyes. Losing her darling husband had withered her body and soul.

He got up to refill his glass and opened the freezer. It was empty apart from some ice cubes and a McCain frozen roast-beef dinner, with one edge stuck fast to the side of the freezer wall and about an inch of ice on top. He retrieved ice from the tray and filled his glass with more of that warming golden liquid.

He remembered his father's stories from the old days. Stories of King Robert the Bruce and the spider. The 'Bruce' had watched the spider in a cave while hiding from the English. Time after time, the spider tried to make its web, failing, and eventually succeeding. This gave the 'Bruce' the fortitude to go on and endure for his people and country.

With this in mind, Macgregor recalled his father's family motto: 'If at first you don't succeed, try, try and try again'. He used this stoicism zealously; it had seen him through many a hard case. He never gave up.

He finished his drink and looked around the apartment leased to him for his stay. It was seventies style, if you could call that style. Fake-wood panelling on the walls; orange,

Formica, kitchen benchtops; furniture with wooden arms. The sort that you can't get comfortable in. You end up removing the cushions and sitting on the floor.

He thought about the past, when he had a real home. When he was married to Fiona. How house-proud she was. He could never wear his shoes inside. She scrubbed and cleaned, eventually scrubbing him into a corner with no way out. They had been happy in the beginning, and then the boys came, three of them, each two years apart. He could never please her, and as he had admitted later to her, he spent way too much time at work rather than at home with her and the boys. The revulsion she felt towards him had increased over the years. She wanted the family but didn't really want him. After ten years of loveless, disparaging looks, rolling of eyes, attempts at intimacy rebuked, separate beds, but keeping up appearances for the neighbours and gossipy school mums, they eventually divorced. She remarried an accountant in what became a very materialistic co-dependent relationship – both were greedy for bigger and better things. This had glued them together.

The boys were all grown up. Now men, working and living their own lives. He called them when he remembered and sent cards for birthdays and Christmas.

His phone rang. He put down the drink and grabbed his jacket, which was hanging over the back of the chair, to retrieve it from his inside pocket.

'Macgregor,' he answered, picking up his glass for another sip. Solomon was in his office putting together a report for the coroner and had decided to call before he emailed it to the Sydney head office.

'Douglas Solomon here. Thought you might be interested with the findings on our Lady of the Bay.'

'Go on,' said Macgregor.

'There was not much left of her fingers, so fingerprints are out. A DNA sample has been sent to the lab with her dental X-rays so we may get some leads from those. It appears that our young lady had recently been depleted of her right kidney, clean incision, with no sutures to the wound.

'Someone knew what they were doing. They must have had some clinical knowledge of the body.

'She was dead before she entered the water. The cause of death appears to be strangulation, by what appears to be a thick-set rope with a rough surface. There were small scratches consistent with rope around her neck and forensics found traces of fibre. Blood loss was significant , analysis also revealed ketamine in the blood.

'Levels were extremely high. It's used in sedation and in anaesthesia and some addicts also ingest it orally but mostly it's given intravenously. It's used to spike drinks by unscrupulous men wanting to take advantage of unsuspecting girls. It had been administered through a vein on her right arm.'

Yes, thought Macgregor, rolling his eyes irritably and taking another gulp of bourbon, I do happen to know what ketamine is and how and why it's used. There have been so many young rape victims where it was the attacker's drug of choice.

'So you'll confirm she was dead before she hit the water, and she'd been drugged?' he asked.

'That is exactly what I'm saying.' The pathologist paused.

'Interesting also to note that someone took the time to re-dress her, no signs of any blood or other contaminants on her clothing. You have a murder on your hands, Detective. A very cold, calculated killing.'

'Can you send me a copy of that report? And get the dental report from forensics sent to me as soon as possible. It may give us a lead to identifying her,' Macgregor said, staring into the bottom of his glass.

'Already copied you in. One more thing that's interesting … she was eight weeks pregnant.'

The phone clicked off and Macgregor gulped down the rest of the bourbon, almost immediately regretting it. The fire in his belly ignited into pain as the liquor's flames spread up to the back of his throat. He quickly searched for the pills his GP had given him and took one with some tap water. He was reading the instructions on the bottle, 'Full strength. To be taken one hour before meals. Avoid alcohol.' Fuck! He was getting old!

CHAPTER FIVE

His office was as small as a broom cupboard but it gave Macgregor solace to think and review the information from the post-mortem report now in his hands. Batemans Bay police station was a far cry from a slick city edifice. This building was about forty years old, a concrete block with narrow slits for windows, dreadful architecture for such a pretty town. Slap bang in the middle of the main street, right next door to the ANZ bank and across from the Subway fast-food outlet. The station had four cells and about ten constables that worked on rotating shifts. At any time, four were in operation to man the desk, main office, phone and emergency lines, while another two were on patrol cruising the main streets and beach side suburbs. It was fairly quiet until holiday time. The summer holiday period was very busy, especially with Christmas peaking the season. Extra police were brought in to deal with the drunken tourists and the carnage of drivers heading over the Clyde Mountain from Canberra, a hazardous two-hour drive on hairpin bends and uneven gradients that usually saw fatalities each year.

Being a coastal precinct, the station also had the water police, a two-man crew that would patrol the river and inlets along the coastline, checking licences, safety equipment, and controlling the increasingly popular displays of jet skis, high-speed boats, water skiers and water bikes. There were horrible endings for some tourists. A decapitation last year saw the river closed for days to watercraft while police divers searched for the deceased's missing head.

Macgregor was reading the findings of Solomon's report and making notes when Sergeant Cameron Fowler knocked and came in. He was a smart young man of twenty-four; tall, blond, with a permanent grin and smiling eyes. His fitness was on display, broad shoulders with pronounced muscular biceps, stretching the fabric of his white cotton shirt. An iconic Australian, he would have made a good ambassador for Australian tourism. His father was the local magistrate, a big name in the small town. Fowler was a university boy, he had all the knowledge and none of the experience. He had studied and gained a position as a sergeant and, although very green and unworldly, he had the potential to be a great detective. His father had pulled all the strings to get him to the local cop shop and it had not gone unnoticed. The other young constables made derogatory remarks within earshot and references to 'Daddy' were frequent. He got used to the banter, and had gained respect following his investigations into a long stretch of break-ins and assaults that led to a conviction.

Fowler was in awe of John Macgregor and the older detective sensed this. He'd hold on to the detective's every word. Macgregor didn't mind the accolade but it was often to the point of being annoying, sometimes even embarrassing. 'For Christ's sake Fowler, what do you want now?' Macgregor was in no mood for the eager young man's attention. He had a murder, it was pressing, and he needed results.

'Just thought you might want to know, sir, that I have put out a bulletin on the victim's description – well, as much as we have to go on – and contacted Missing Persons in Sydney. I also contacted the local hospitals.' He stood, smiling, obviously pleased with himself, that he did not have to be asked.

'And?' Macgregor stated, puffing out the word with solemnity.

'The hospitals – they've not had anything unusual, all surgical patients from the admissions register are accounted for. From all three public hospitals within the local area.'

'All three? What about the private hospitals and day surgeries?' Macgregor asked, taking another antacid tablet while gulping the last of his coffee.

'Well, sir, that's not really been part of the investigation. We don't have any private hospitals and only one privately owned day surgery. And given the fact that it's a day surgery, no one stays overnight; they only do minor procedures, so I didn't think it necessary.' He now stood looking a little uncomfortable.

Macgregor noted that he kept looking at his shoes as though hoping he hadn't stepped out of line.

'Do they now! Well, laddie, any operating room that has equipment that can put you to sleep, in my book, has the potential to do whatever surgery they like, when they like. Day or night.' He screwed up the paper cup in his hand and threw it into the waste bin below the desk. 'And I want you to get over there and talk to the staff and the director of this facility. I want an account of all recent patients, and staff, that have been there in the last few weeks, okay?'

Fowler nodded. Head down, he made his way to the main desk. Macgregor overheard him giving orders to the desk uniform to call him as soon as the info came through from Missing Persons.

He now had some calls to make and he was going to have to pull in some favours.

CHAPTER SIX

Detective Inspector Laurence Hargraves picked up the phone at the Surry Hills Police Station.

'Laurie, John Macgregor here, I need a favour. Do you still have contacts at the Cross?' Macgregor asked his old friend. Hargraves had been his partner in the nineties. They had shared many long nights working at Kings Cross, Sydney's red-light district. In those days, it was rough and you had to harden up quickly or perish. Hargraves and Macgregor had gotten to know the brothels, the pimps, the kids on the streets and of course, the girls. They knew them by name and by which street they worked.

They worked many a vice case together, and had covered for one another. They had busted drug rings, druglords of crack, cocaine and heroin. They had witnessed kids as young as thirteen overdose and lie in their own vomit. The seedy side of life. Drug crime now had become more sophisticated. The dealers were wealthy corporate businessmen, and international syndicates had more elaborate methods of getting the stuff into the country than ever before.

Hargraves had taken the position at Surry Hills as Detective Inspector more as a desk job; this was evident from his ever-increasing waistline. He loved his food. While once he could eat huge portions and work it off, it had now decided to take up residence around his middle. He missed the old ways; it was all IT generated information these days, no more legwork, digging, building up a trust with the cons ... that was all gone. History.

'John, how goes it in Hicksville? Caught any fish? I hear it's the best place for flathead?' Hargraves cleared his throat. He had a voice that was strong and full of timbre; he laughed and was genuinely pleased to hear from his old pal.

'Ha ha. Very funny. Listen Laurie, we have a bloater, a young female, fresh, three days in the drink, no one local, and she was pregnant. Strange thing is she had a recent date with the scalpel. Missing a kidney. All the local hospitals are clean, and we're checking another private clinic. I need you to ask around the old haunts, ask any of the girls if they know of a worker who came down here for the winter season. I know they come down for the fishermen, plenty of catch, if you'll pardon the pun.'

'I'm not so sure I would know anyone these days, Macca. Long time since I was in that old stomping ground. But leave it with me. I'll ask around.'

The phone clicked off. Macgregor thought about the working girls. They usually came down to the Bay during the summer holiday period and would place ads in the local press letting the punters know where they would be in town and for how long. There were the regulars, girls and clients, a feeding ground for the girls with tourists, men away from their families on 'fishing trips', lads from Canberra after heavy drinking sessions daring each other to pay for prostitutes. The newbies, one-offs, frustrated and starved of touch, all ready to part with their cash for a quickie.

Macgregor stood up, stretched and retrieved his jacket from the back of the door; he would go and talk to the local press, see if any ads had been placed recently.

As he approached the Land Cruiser in the car park at the back of the police station, he could see journalists waiting by the locked iron gates. So, the news was out about the girl's death. They saw him too and started to ask questions.

'Inspector? Can you tell us any news on the identity of the girl? Was she local?' He ignored them and turned back towards the building. He decided to walk out the front entrance and head straight to the Bay Press, five minutes' walking distance.

Good, he thought. I shall have no problems going straight into the wolves' den, seeing as most of the pack are here.

CHAPTER SEVEN

Cameron Fowler parked his car next to the sleek silver Mercedes Benz gleaming in the sunlight, looking as though it came straight out of the showroom. His own RAV4 was a bit worse for wear and even though his father had offered to buy him a new one he had declined. He needed to be his own man, stand on his own two feet. He locked the car and stood in front of the day surgery, a new building, only a year old, built by the owner and director, Dr Paranjoy Panngesh.

It symbolised opulence. The foyer was grand as you entered from the sweeping driveway, its elevated roof giving the feeling of a five-star hotel rather than a clinic. No wonder local wags dubbed it the Taj Mahal.

Local, Indigenous and some well-known artworks graced the walls. Impressive sculptures also filled the foyer. Soothing hues of aquamarine coloured the vast entrance, giving an air of serenity, not of a busy day surgery. People were quietly sitting reading the latest magazines, unlike his GP's waiting room with its Anglers' Monthly from five years ago and some very old National Geographics.

He walked up to the reception desk. Ms Roseberry was instructing the receptionist that it was time to finalise the doctors' invoices for the week. Fowler could not help but notice the very attractive, smart, blonde woman.

'Good morning. I'm here on police business and I would like to speak to the owner of this facility,' said Fowler, directing his question to the girl seated at the desk.

Ms Roseberry noted his official ID, and was having none of him dealing with a junior staff member.

'I am sorry,' she said, taking charge and intercepting the card he offered to the girl. 'Have you an appointment? Dr Panngesh is the owner and director of Panngesh Day Surgery and he is indisposed at present.

'Shall I make an appointment for you to speak with him?' Her steely gaze gave nothing away and Fowler could see her loyalty went very deep.

'I noticed his car in the car park so I presumed he was here. I'll wait.' He turned as if to look for a seat.

Ms Roseberry immediately replied. 'Dr Panngesh is in surgery and will be all day. He is a very busy man. I am his personal assistant, is there something I may help you with?'

'Can I speak to you in private?' Ms Roseberry nodded and gestured for him to follow her to a small office near the building's entrance.

'Ms ... Roseberry,' he began, peering at her name badge, 'we're investigating a murder, a young woman whose body was washed up on the beach in Surfside. And we need to examine some of your records and speak with your staff, including Dr Panngesh ... to assist our investigation. I would like to see the admissions register for all patients from the last month and theatre operation register, also, for the last month. Could that be arranged?'

'Murder! And you think she had surgery here?' She spoke in a hushed whisper – heaven forbid that patients and other staff members should hear the conversation.

She hastily pressed a button on the phone and was put through to Dr Panngesh in the operating room. She chewed her lip and went on to explain to her boss the situation as Fowler watched her intently.

'He won't come back later, he wishes to see the registers and the staff now!' She frowned as she replied. A crease formed on her forehead. She glanced up at Fowler as she put down the phone. 'Dr Panngesh would be happy to cooperate with the police investigation,' she said, in a clipped tone. 'I shall get the registers and information you require, but it will take me at least an hour.'

'Would you also get me a list of employees? I'd like to interview the staff that have been working for the last four weeks.'

She put her finely manicured hand to her throat and thought carefully before replying.

'Sergeant Fowler, I will have to clear this with the practice manager and director of nursing. The staff are busy. Does this include all nursing staff as well?'

'Yes. All staff, then we can begin to eliminate this facility from our enquiries,' he confirmed.

She made a few calls to members of staff in other departments, then organised one of the available consulting rooms for him to use for the interviews. Her priority was to act as though nothing was wrong, to keep any intrusions away from the clientele. Smiling and acting as though nothing was untoward, she passed the waiting room tidying magazines and placing them neatly into piles on the tabletop, as she led Fowler up the staircase to the second floor.

He looked around the room, a smaller consulting suite used by visiting surgeons. It was elegant, again with a feeling of opulence. Chesterfield couches in a deep burgundy colour of leather sat facing one another; and there was a sleek, pale wood, designer desk towards the back wall. Elegant, gold-and-burgundy striped chairs faced the desk where Fowler placed his laptop.

Above him hung a large watercolour painting of a sailing ship in stormy seas, huge waves breaking over the bow. The room had the smell of new carpets and polished wood, with a large window overlooking the well-kept gardens below. He took out his notebook and phone from his pocket and placed them on the desk. Three missed calls, two from the station and one from Macgregor.

He decided to quickly listen to the messages as Ms Roseberry came in with a list of staff who had worked over the last six weeks. She waited until he was finished with his calls. 'I have consulted with Dr Panngesh. He is making time available for you at 2:30, at the end of his theatre list. Does that suit you, Sergeant Fowler?' He looked at his watch, 12:15. 'That sounds fine Ms Roseberry, and if you would kindly start sending in the staff that are available for interview? It'll only take a few moments to speak with them, and, oh, do you have those admissions and operations registers?'

'They're being retrieved now by the reception staff,' she replied briskly.

As she finished speaking, a young girl of about twenty with glasses and mousey brown short hair came in with the ledgers and placed them on the desk. She hesitated before Ms Roseberry dismissed her. Ms Roseberry then turned and left the room placing a stray lock of hair behind her ear, hair that had dared to come loose. She appeared flustered and made mutterings of being 'so busy' under her breath.

Fowler listened to the desk uniform's message and noted the dot points on a pad.

Three women had recently gone missing but none from this area.

A sixteen-year-old girl from Melbourne was last seen leaving her work from a store in a shopping centre in Chadstone, the mother thought she may have gone off with the boyfriend as he was also missing.

Second missing person: a twenty-two-year-old woman from Dubbo who had not been seen for the last three days, her parents very distressed as it's not like her to not call them. She was last seen taking a bus from Dubbo to Canberra to spend the weekend with her girlfriend, the girlfriend said she never arrived.

Third missing woman: a twenty-eight-year-old from Newcastle who was last seen working in a pub in Swansea. She had finished her shift at midnight, closed the pub and waited for a taxi outside the premises but it had not turned up. Witnesses said that over four weeks ago they saw her getting into an old Kombi van that was outside the pub. The local police were making enquiries.

He went on to listen to Macgregor's message that he'd gone to the Bay Press offices to speak with the editor, Isabella Kowowski. He would be back at the station sometime after four to meet with him.

Fowler sighed. He knew it was going to be a long day. He had wanted to take his girlfriend to Canberra that evening. It was their one year anniversary and although he did not place much sentiment on the occasion, he knew she would. They would have to leave early in the afternoon if they were to make it in time over the Clyde Mountain on the Kings Highway. A new band, The Dog Heads, were playing at The George, an English style pub on the north side of Canberra; they usually had good gigs on the weekend. Fowler played guitar himself and had been in a band at university. One of his old student friends had given him tickets for the gig. He started to formulate the discussion in his mind before calling Hannah, hoping she would be happy with a candlelit dinner at The Pier instead, an upmarket restaurant on the waterfront. He would get flowers and book a table on the way home, that should do it, as long as Macgregor let him leave on time. He made the call. Hannah was the recently appointed junior accountant in a small firm of chartered accountants. Positions like this were hard to come by and she was happy to comply with her bosses even if she did get all the menial tasks. Fowler charmingly asked how her day had been and told her how much he missed her, coyly making declarations of love and backtracking his way out of the trip. He mentioned the restaurant and she happily agreed, responding, as he had hoped, with excitement.

He smiled to himself – he always had a way with words. Since childhood, he was able to get away with most things just by being pleasant and articulate. He turned his phone off and placed it back into his pocket.

Opening the registers, he started to look for specific dates in relation to the victim's death and up to four weeks previous. The theatre registers were all in order, all patients had been discharged on the day of surgery, most were elderly, only a couple of patients under the age of forty had been admitted, both male patients. No young females. At least, not registered on the admissions ledger ... as far as he could see.

The first knock on the door came just as he was closing the last of the registers and making notes on his laptop. He called for the interviewee to enter and a short, overweight, middle-aged woman came in. Mrs Rita Summerville had medium length reddish hair, permed and scrunched into shape with copious amounts of product; it barely moved. Even when she put her hand through the fringe, it stayed hard and well controlled.

She told him straight away that she was an enrolled nurse. It seemed to Fowler that she hoped this meant he didn't expect too much from her. She seemed very uncomfortable, chewing her nails and nervously looking around the room with brown, beady eyes. He beckoned her to sit down in the elegant striped chair across the desk from him. The climb up the stairs had left her breathless and sweating. He noted she looked uncertain being in his presence. He'd seen it before. Police made people nervous if they had something to hide, but it seemed odd for her to behave that way. Maybe she was just rattled at being interviewed.

She said she was very busy, explaining she had left the theatre during an anaesthetic and had only a few minutes to spare. He acknowledged this with a smile, thanked her for coming, and reassured her that he would only take few minutes of her time. She relaxed a little as she settled more comfortably in the chair. He began with his questions. She gave some thought to each one, pausing and being very careful with her answers.

Another twenty interviews to go, he thought, as he sat looking out past her, through the window. The sky was grey and black clouds loomed above the small town.

A storm was on its way, Fowler could hear the distant thunder. A storm – and not just with the weather. He sensed that his town was holding secrets and was about to erupt.

The last on his list – Dr Panngesh – had requested that Fowler interview him in his private office. Having concluded the staff interviews, Fowler gathered his papers and headed back downstairs.

Dr Panngesh was waiting in his office, still wearing his royal blue surgical scrubs.

Fowler knocked and entered. So, he wants the upper hand, Fowler thought, make me sit in front of his desk. He knows the game. Fowler gave him a firm handshake and sat in an elegant armchair. The suite was impressive; it was filled with antique furniture, all very stylish, with an attractive painting in oil of the coastal landscape dominant behind the large oak desk. His diplomas, doctorates and certificates covered one wall. Each one was mounted and framed in a golden wooden architrave.

'Sergeant Fowler. Do make yourself comfortable. Have you had any refreshments yet? I can ask Ms Roseberry to organise coffee. Tea perhaps?' Fowler noted that he was pleasant and polite with a practiced smile. One obviously reserved for his wealthy clients.

'No thank you, Dr Panngesh. I had a coffee and a sandwich earlier when I popped into town.

'I appreciate you are a very busy man but I do need to ask you some questions. As you may be aware, an as yet unidentified woman's body recently washed up on a stretch of beach in Surfside. We would like to thank you for your cooperation with our enquiries.' Fowler retrieved his notebook from his computer satchel, bending under the chair without losing eye contact.

'Yes, fine. I did hear,' replied the surgeon. 'I was very upset, such a young woman, a tragedy. Yes. But how can we help you? My staff and I had nothing to do with this terrible loss of life. I thought maybe she fell off a boat or swam into a rip. Just how does this concern my facility and my staff?'

'Well, Dr Panngesh. The interesting part is that her right kidney had been removed, possibly surgically, and there was a large amount of ketamine in her blood. I have spoken to your anaesthetic nurse … Rita Summerville … and she said that you do use and keep a stock of ketamine in the drug cupboard. It's used in anaesthesia particularly if someone has an allergy to the standard Midazolam. So I was informed by Mrs Summerville earlier today.'

'Yes we do, but so do all the other hospitals and clinics in the area. We are a day surgery, Sergeant Fowler. We do mostly plastic surgery, small corrections for people that want to improve upon nature. Fine. We do not do urology or any of the major surgery here,' he answered. Fowler could hear the nervousness in his voice. It jarred with the tone he had spoken with only moments earlier, the slip back to the Indian accent that contrasted with the impeccable Oxford English of before. Fowler paused and thought, He's trying very hard to cover his background. I wonder what else he's hiding?

He went on, 'Dr Panngesh, you have the equipment, the staff and the drugs that are capable of doing that type of surgical procedure, is that correct?'

'Well yes, fine, but you can check my records. We have not had any one here for that procedure.'

'I've gone over your registers and operation notes and, yes, it all appears to be in order. But as you can appreciate, Dr Panngesh, we must eliminate you and the other local hospitals from our enquiries.'

Fowler was sure Panngesh was keeping something from him, he was well trained in detecting nervous flustering beneath a calm exterior. But did not want to push the matter any further. He stood and thanked him for his cooperation and time. Fowler saw a composed smile fill the doctor's face, his change in posture.

He stood taller, 'Anything to help with your enquiry, Sergeant Fowler. I am at your service,' Panngesh replied.

CHAPTER EIGHT

sabella Kowowski rose from her desk; beautiful, tall, alluring; dark hair pulled back into a ponytail. With deep blue eyes that conveyed a keen intelligence, and fine features, she oozed sex appeal and elegance as she bestowed her smile upon the detective. She held out a well-manicured hand, with tidy, shiny nails, to shake his.

'Won't you sit down?' she asked in her sultry tone.

Isabella was a Polish immigrant, arriving with her family at a very young age. Although now in her twenties, she had poured out thousands of stories and media releases and was always at the cutting edge. She was editor of the Bay Press, a local rag – it was simply a stepping stone to greater things. Isabella knew what she needed to do to get ahead and more so, how to use and manipulate people and situations when she had to.

She liked the look of John Macgregor. The rugged face, slightly greying at the temples, a little older than she fancied and in need of a haircut. She had entertained thoughts of sleeping with him. For one thing, he was smart. Men like him didn't become experts in their field unless they had the mind and conviction to achieve results. It turned her on. She was single after all, never liked to date or be in committed relationships. That would be too stifling and controlling for her. She had casual sex if and when she needed to.

'So, Detective Chief Inspector, what can I do for you?' she said, leaning over the desk so that just enough ample cleavage was at his eye level. 'I believe I sent some reporters to find you and ask you some questions at the police station and yet here you are.' She paused then licked her bottom lip and sat down at her desk.

'Ms Kowowski, the pleasure is all mine,' he answered.

'Isabella, please Inspector' she said. She saw his eyes glide to her breasts and it made her tingle. She knew the game, and just how to land this fish.

'I'm here to ask a favour, it's in connection with the recent recovery of a woman's body from Surfside, as you are well aware – and no, I don't know who she is.' He swallowed then went on.

'I need to look back through the classifieds from the last couple of months, working girls from Sydney, just to see if any chose to come down for the winter. I need to eliminate any possibilities that the lass was one of them. Is that okay with you?'

'Well. That depends on the story you're giving me once she's identified.' She was quick with her answer and ready to be aggressive if she had to be ... anything for the paper, for her future, and her career.

'I can get my sergeant to wade through reams of old

newspapers if I have to, Isabella.' He paused and looked her in the eye. 'I would rather you helped me with this request and do your community a service.'

She leaned back in her chair, enjoying the moment as she carefully crossed her long, well-defined legs. She saw his eyes dart, taking in the move. She hesitated for a moment and then asked over the intercom for an assistant to come through.

'Kayla, please assist Detective Inspector Macgregor with any requests he has, and perhaps offer him a coffee.'

Kayla acknowledged the request and held the door open for him. She was young and attractive, a recent school leaver, eager to please, with a pretty face and long brown hair held to the side with a clip in the shape of a frangipani flower. She smiled sweetly at him and headed towards the reading room.

'Oh ... and John,' Isabella purred, standing in the doorway. 'You don't mind if I call you John? How about a drink later, say six at the golf club? You can let me know how you ... went.' He turned and nodded, following the girl through to the viewing room. Kayla turned back towards the staff room and returned some five minutes later with a mug of black coffee.

CHAPTER NINE

Macgregor was standing at the front desk of the police station when Fowler returned, just before five.

'Where the bloody hell have you been, Fowler? I asked you to interview them, not book in for a bloody operation.' He noted the startled reaction from the desk uniform, Janette Green, and winked at her to show he wasn't really serious. She managed a half-smile back as he and Fowler headed towards Macgregor's office.

Macgregor sat in his chair. Fowler remained standing, notebook in hand.

'Well laddie, what's the story? Was there anything for us to go on?'

'Sir, all the records and registers were fine and in order, the staff were efficient and answered all my questions. Dr Panngesh's personal assistant, Ms Roseberry, runs very deep and she's a bit too protective of her boss. She's Ms Roseberry to everyone, I had to dig deep to find out her first name is Alison.

'And as for Dr Panngesh, what a smooth operator he is, very slick. The place is like a five-star hotel, the equipment they have could run a major hospital, all brand new and top notch. I spoke with an anaesthetic nurse,' he quickly thumbed through his notebook, 'Rita Summerville, she said that they keep the standard drugs locked in the drug cupboard. And one of those drugs is ketamine, used for sedation.

'I have the feeling the good doctor is hiding something though. He was arrogant and seemed very prepared, couldn't wait to get me out of the place once our interview was over.'

'Is that so?' Macgregor said, leaning back. 'Well, I might want to have a few words with him myself.' He paused and looked out the window.

'On another note, did you get the call about the missing girls?' Macgregor asked, getting out of his chair.

'Yes,' Fowler replied. 'Any of them fit the description of the victim?'

Fowler put his notebook back into the side pocket of his computer satchel as Macgregor retrieved a missing person case file from the top of the filing cabinet.

'Unfortunately, yes. A young lass from Dubbo missing for just over three days now, the parents are frantic. Detective Inspector Mike Willoughby is coming to the Bay tomorrow with them. He's sure the description fits and thinks they'll be able to make a positive ID. Apparently, she had a distinctive mark on the base of her hairline, a sort of birthmark.'

Macgregor turned and handed Fowler the file as he grabbed his jacket from the back of the door. 'Be here early tomorrow, it's going to be a long day. And I don't want the press involved, so mum's the word on this. The less they know, the better.

'Have Janette Green available to be with them at the

morgue, and call Douglas Solomon. I want him present, not some lackey.' He put on his jacket, walking out from his office. 'And, Fowler,' he said, tapping his fingers on the file, 'have a report written up tonight. I want it all tidy for the morning.' Fowler sighed: so much for a candlelit dinner! He would take Hannah on the weekend ... he started to make the call, hoping she would understand.

Macgregor was perched on a stool at the bar in the large green trophy room of the golf club when Isabella Kowowski found him. He was drinking his usual bourbon with ice as she sidled up to him and smiled. She had pulled her hair out from the confines of its tight band and it fell around her shoulders with a slight wave where it had been secured ... she was stunning and she knew it, in her black, tight-fitting, jersey dress with long, black, leather boots that came up over her knees to meet the end of her dress. Glimpses of black stockings shimmered as she sat on the stool next to him and pulled one long leg up across the other.

'What are you having?' he asked.

'May I have champagne?' she trilled, tilting her head to the side. She placed her bag down by her feet and perused the room. It was empty save for a couple of elderly golfers sitting in the corner near the window, reliving the game they had just played, blow by blow accounts with arms swinging and animation in their voices.

'French?' he asked, as if he didn't know.

'Moët, of course.' He raised his eyebrow at the barman, who shrugged and pulled a full-sized bottle from the depths of the fridge. It had been there for some time.

'That will be one hundred and fifty dollars, sir,' the barman declared loudly, causing the two golfers to pause in their conversation and watch what was happening. Isabella smiled prettily and nodded her consent as Macgregor sighed and reached for his wallet.

The barman smirked as he gathered an ice bucket and single glass, ready to loosen the cork. This was the best entertainment he'd had all day.

Isabella plucked a piece of fluff from Macgregor's collar as the cash was handed across the bar. She knew that interesting men were hard to find at the best of times, but even more so in this small town.

The barman winked at her as he poured her champagne with a flourish. It was his way to acknowledge that she had power – and she used it in every smile and flash of those deep blue eyes.

Macgregor asked if she would like to move to a more comfortable chair with a table. She nodded and picked up her bag. Awkwardly, he picked up his drink, her glass and the bottle in its ice bucket. They sat in a quieter area, away from the bar.

'Walls have ears around here,' he said, as he placed her drink carefully on the table.

She sat down in a fluid motion. 'So, John, did you find what you were looking for?' She asked casually as she crossed her legs and lifted her glass to her lips.

'Well, it was certainly useful in the elimination process, but no. All leads accounted for, so our Lady of the Bay was not a hooker. At least not one that had placed a personal ad.' He sipped his own drink and placed it on the table, looking her in the eye.

'So, what's a beautiful young lady doing asking an old croak like me out for a drink?'

She laughed. 'Well. I've wanted to have a drink with you for a while and at last the opportunity came up. And I thought, what the hell, why not? We both know what I want ...' She tailed off with a wicked grin and started to circle the top of the glass with her right index finger. Her fingers then reached over towards his hand, which was wrapped firmly around his glass.

'Isabella I could be your father the age I am. I'm flattered. And don't get me wrong, I've thought about it myself. You're beautiful and desirable, very sure of yourself and your needs.' He hesitated. 'But not tonight.'

She laughed and threw back her head, 'Am I being knocked back?' she spluttered, her mouth full of champagne.

'Not for the reason you think, lassie. But tonight I have a poker game that I cannae get out of, it's a monthly ritual with some old poker cronies. It's taken very seriously, without me they'll be a man down, it's taken me months to be a part of that group and I have to be there. I love the game.' He looked into her eyes, 'Can I take a rain check on us?'

'How can I possibly compete with a poker game,' she said sarcastically, opening her arms widely and thrusting out her breasts. She downed the rest of her glass, reached for her bag and checked her make-up using the compact that was in a side pocket. After applying lipstick, she stood up, bent and kissed him on the forehead. 'Bye daddy,' she whispered.

Chuckling, she elegantly crossed the room, all eyes from the bar watching every long stride. He waved and sat for a moment thinking about what he had just turned down. He shook his head and thought he must be going senile to turn down that vixen, although she's more trouble than I need at the moment.

He gulped down his drink and stood to leave. The three-quarters full bottle of Moët dripped condensation from the ice bucket onto the table.

'Christ. I wonder if they'll give me the bloody cork. Apparently, it's wide open for me 'to thrust it in there,' he muttered under his breath.

Crossing the floor and noticing a smudge of vivid red lipstick across his forehead in the bar mirror, he casually wiped it away with the back of his hand.

Poker was calling and it was his night for a win.

CHAPTER TEN

Sitting on the bed, she glanced around the room.

It had recently been redecorated. Soft-pink painted walls, a white, crisp, cotton bed cover with pink silk cushions on top. Posters adorned the walls – unicorns, dolphins, Lord of the Rings, The Hobbit – and the shelves were full of cuddly toys, mostly animals.

They had lived here all their married life, and had been a happy close family.

Clutching a soft, cuddly tiger in her hands, she bent her head to smell the toy. Tears welled up in her eyes, the room belonged to her daughter Danielle, missing for nearly four days now. Only two months before, she had been celebrating her twenty-second birthday, how could this be happening to them ... she was now losing hope ... Danielle would always come home. Why not this time? A model student at school, kind, sweet and obedient, she loved animals – always wanting to bring home strays or abandoned cats or dogs, she was training to be a veterinary nurse at a local veterinary surgery in Dubbo and loved her job.

A tear fell on the tiger's soft fur. She let out a gut-wrenching sob ... her baby was gone ... you read about this happening to other people ... not to her own family. It had all been surreal over the last few days. The phone calls, neighbours coming in, the press, police, some very cold and hurtful questions. She knew they were only doing their job, but they were relentless. She gave the same reply every time, as far as she knew Danielle had gone on the bus to Canberra to see her friend Alicia. She had never arrived. Alicia had not been aware of her plans and had not spoken to Danielle for at least a week before she left on the 9:15 from the bus station in Dubbo.

Danielle's phone went unanswered. Hundreds of messages left on it, the recorded message said 'Message box full, please send text message'. The police had taken Danielle's laptop and a journal for investigation. She had been feeling angry about that, she wanted everything to be in its place for Danielle when she got home ... those thoughts now empty ... even her bones felt heavy and numb. She had not eaten in three days and as time went on, so did the anguish and distress. Her husband, Andy, had pleaded with her to stay strong and eat the meals he prepared every day. How could he not feel the same way? She was numb, her hair unwashed, no make-up, clothes sagging from thin limbs. The thin veneer of vanity shed like a skin to reveal this vulnerable tortured soul. She was wearing her daughter's jumper and refused to wash it, it had been in the laundry hamper waiting to be cleaned ... the last article of clothing Danielle had worn before changing to go to Canberra. Pleading ... Please God ... please let her be safe, let my only child be safe and bring her home, she prayed, clutching the toy to her breast.

Andy came in to the room, his head bent, unshaven, he looked grey and his face was frozen in a tight grimace. He hesitated and cleared his throat. 'That was the police on the phone, Barbara. A woman's body has been washed up on the coast ... Surfside Beach ... Batemans Bay.' He hardly believed the words coming out of his mouth, he cleared his throat again trying to sound stronger. 'They want us to go and see if it's Danielle.'

He raised his hand, pulling back his hair from his forehead, he looked drained, unbelieving and in shock. He sat next to her, went to hold her hand and searched her face for some reassurance.

'NO!' she screamed. 'Danielle was nowhere near the beach. It must be someone else ... tell them it's a mistake, it's not our girl ... it's not our baby girl!' Gripping the toy harder in her hands, an overwhelming ache squeezed at her heart, she held her breath and fell back on to the bed. She pulled her knees up towards her chin, lying on her side, a groan came from a place so deep it sounded unworldly and strange ... he lay down next to her holding her as she rocked back and forth sobbing into the pillow ... still clutching at the toy.

CHAPTER ELEVEN

t was well after two in the morning when Macgregor got back to his unit. He drove more slowly on the way home, recounting hand by hand the poker game and also trying to avoid the many kangaroos and wombats on that particular stretch of road, on the Princes Highway north of the Bay. The last time he drove home from the game it had cost him over $500 getting the front of his car fixed. Kangaroos can make a hell of a mess if you hit one, especially the Eastern Grey males – they stand more than six feet tall.

Texas Hold'em poker suited Macgregor. You go hard, you go easy, you bluff, you learn to read tells. Just like real life, or his life at least.

The game had been played at Frank and Flora Davies' home. Both retired and in their seventies, they lived in a large farmhouse north of the Bay, about twenty-five minutes' drive away. Frank had been a bank manager and was a great poker player; he held a game at his home once a month. He had overcome cancer twice and although overweight and very unfit, he was still smoking and drinking. Ignoring his doctor's advice, he continued to eat all the wrong foods and had supplied plenty of food and drink for the get-together. The usual players were there: Kelly in her late forties, the only daughter of Frank and Flora, wild red hair, clothes that were always too loud, freckles, and a laugh like a kookaburra bringing forth the dawn on a summer's morning. She had just been promoted to school principal at the local primary. The kids loved her free spirit and she dressed like she was at Woodstock attending the Jimi Hendrix concert. Her ex-partner, Bryan Johnston, was a cabinetmaker and all-round handyman nearing his sixties. He was tall and thin, wiry but fit. He wore a woolly jumper that had been knitted by Kelly with a large smiley face in the middle, giving more bulk to his slim frame and an insincere look of happiness to his appearance. He rarely smiled but he was pleasant enough, willing to do any of the practical jobs that most of us put off.

Lorna Paterson worked as a registered nurse. She had recently started working at the day surgery for Dr Panngesh. She was his scrub sister; tall, slim, mid-length auburn hair and green eyes. In her mid-forties, she had aristocratic features; finely chiselled cheekbones gave her an air of superiority but she had an infectious grin featuring a small gap in her front teeth. She was very animated and warm. Macgregor could well see how she could be an asset for the surgeon: intelligent, attractive and well-groomed with a caring nature. Lorna was divorced. It was almost six months since her last child had left home and she was now getting out more, socialising and having fun.

Macgregor had grown fond of her and was at the point of asking her out on a date. This had been her third game of poker at the Davies' home. She'd only recently started playing and having known the Davies for a while they had encouraged her to come along.

She had been out more in the last six months with her girlfriends than ever before. Some were married, escaping their husbands for the night; others were widowed or divorced, or had simply given up on men altogether. But that didn't stop them going out and having fun.

Graham Paxton worked as a local GP. He was in his early fifties, Jewish-looking, but held no religious beliefs. His long, thin face showed dark brown eyes; his short dark hair was balding on top, and he appeared rather nervous. He was married to Virginia, with three teenage children at home. She was a little mousey wife with a small pointy nose, they reminded Macgregor of two lab mice, both nervous and scurrying about, always making themselves busy. Virginia never played but sometimes sat in the corner watching, ready to jump up and make tea or refresh drinks for the players. The last player to make the eight needed for the table was Danny Smith, a plumber, local jack the lad in his day, now semi-retired and playing more golf than making trouble. Although well into his sixties, he still had contacts with an old bikie gang, the Skull Brothers, but had kept his nose clean for the last few years, only occasionally dealing with dodgy goods. He didn't trust Macgregor and the feeling was mutual – they kept their distance politely.

Macgregor had been heads up with Frank. The players had battled it down to the last two players over nearly six hours. Frank had more chips than Macgregor by 10,000.

Macgregor dealt the cards. He looked down at a pair of kings, and he raised to 10,000. The blind, the minimum bet, was 2,000. Frank called. Macgregor dealt the flop, three cards in the middle of the table. On the flop came king of diamonds, seven of clubs, five of spades. He checked it down hoping to raise the bet on the next card if Frank checked too – one sure way to build the pot was to slow play, to not give anything away to your opponent, to make them believe you have nothing. Nine of hearts. Well, thought Macgregor, no flush. He had 'trips' – three of a kind – so he raised another 10,000 in chips. Frank called. The 'river' card was seven of diamonds.

Macgregor pushed all in; he had a full house and knew it was a winner. Frank called, putting all his chips into the middle of the table. He turned over his cards – pocket sevens – giving him four of a kind to beat Macgregor's full house. Frank laughed a huge deep roar; he had been a smoker all his life and sounded as though he had gravel stuck in his throat. He puffed on his cigar and blew out a big ring of smoke above the cards. Macgregor sat, stunned.

'Well done boy,' Frank roared, 'but when you've played as many games as I have and get to my age, then you might beat me! Get your first thousand games out of the way then you might begin to play poker.' Frank finished his merlot and dropped the glass accidentally, missing the small table at the side of the chair with the drinks, nibbles and ashtray that Flora had placed there earlier.

'Shit!' he said as he floundered, trying to catch it before it smashed to the floor on the slate tiles. They played at the back of the house in a rumpus room-cum-pool table-games room. It was large and open and wide windows covered three quarters of the walls; several heaters kept the room warm and cosy. Flora rushed over with a small broom and quickly swept up the pieces carefully into newspaper. She tutted to him as ash flicked and mingled with the broken glass on the floor.

Macgregor helped them clear away the chairs and glasses and said goodnight. He shook hands with Frank and Bryan, kissed Flora and Kelly on the cheek and smiled as Lorna came forward for a hug. Frank called out to him as he was leaving, 'Same time next month then John? God willing if I'm still breathing,' he laughed, coughing as the cool night air entered his lungs.

Waving goodbye, Macgregor reached his car parked just off the side of the property near the entrance gates. It was very dark and he had to use the glow from his phone to find the key and unlock the door. He could still hear them laughing and Frank's coughing as he shut the door, started the engine and drove home.

He wasn't quite ready to go to bed. The day had been long and the case of the murdered girl was on his mind. He turned on the television, flicking through the channels as he reached for the bourbon, the glass still on the table from the night before.

Washing up was very rarely done. Cups and glasses actually needed to have life forms growing in them for him to give them a scrub; mostly he rinsed under the tap and let them sit till dry. Tomorrow would be a difficult day with the dead girl's parents from Dubbo, but it had to be done. He hoped for the parents' sake, it was a mistake and that their daughter was off cavorting somewhere, maybe with a boyfriend. He tried to switch off. He focused on the poker game. Four bloody sevens – that was luck, not skill. But it had been a good game; he enjoyed these nights, stress free. It was good for him just to think about the next play, the next card, rather than the next day.

He thought about Lorna Paterson. He knew she liked him. He'd given her his mobile number, and she had taken it as she hugged him and smiled. She kissed him briefly on the lips before Flora had come in to the room with his overcoat. It had been raining when he arrived and he had left it hanging in the warm conservatory at the back of the house to dry.

He imagined a different life where he could be happy, spending his days and nights with someone like Lorna, being normal, not thinking of death and always being suspicious of others.

He finished the drink and closed his eyes, half listening to the news channel, voices drifting in and out of a hazy dream.

CHAPTER TWELVE

Cameron Fowler was waiting at the morgue for Macgregor to arrive.

It was cold and the wind was biting. Three black crows were sitting on the fence that wrapped itself around the outside of the small courtyard at the hospital entrance, giving him a cold stare as he walked swiftly past, heading to the rear of the hospital where the morgue was.

He decided to go into the building, an annex that hadn't been updated when the rest of the hospital had been refurbished. It was forgotten, unseen, unworthy of the cost the government would have to fork out. It was old and had few windows. There were two main rooms and a small office as you entered, painted in standard pale green with worn furniture and a wooden bench seat. The refrigeration room was tucked away at the back of the building; it had nine compartments and could store bodies for several weeks. The medical pathologist worked here and when special investigations were required, they brought in forensic pathologists such as Douglas Solomon from Wollongong.

Fowler rang the bell, a button on the main desk, and Dr

Joseph Kelly came out from his office, eating a doughnut. A tall, slightly built man, he was in his late fifties with a long chin and small eyes, his hair fair and fine. Clear-rimmed glasses perched on his nose, he wore a white lab coat and thick woollen jumper underneath, with brown corduroy pants. On his feet, he wore trainers with blue overshoe covers.

He quickly wiped away the sugar crumbs from his mouth with the back of his hand and smiled at Fowler, a slightly sinister grimace. 'Hi. Awfully sorry about that, didn't get time to have brekkie what with the early start. Joe Kelly.' He held out his hand, now cleaned from the doughnut crumbs. 'Is the Chief Inspector here yet?'

'Good morning, ah, no not yet, but the parents are arriving in about twenty minutes so I hope he gets here soon.' They shook hands; Fowler knew his palm was damp from apprehension.

'Sit down Sergeant, can I get you some coffee?' he replied casually.

'That would be good, thanks. White, one sugar.' They proceeded through to a very small kitchenette at the side of his office; the kettle was already steaming and he reached for another mug from the cupboard.

'It's getting very chilly now in the mornings,' Kelly remarked. 'It was frosty when I went out to the car at my place.'

Fowler relaxed just a bit. He loved the cold weather, it meant ski season. He was a great snowboarder, reaching instructor level, and he went every year down to the Snowy Mountains.

The two men sat in silence as they sipped mugs of hot coffee. 'Must be very lonely doing this sort of work,' Fowler said, breaking the silence.

'No. Not really. I have a morgue technician. And detectives from all over the place come and investigate the interesting ones, plus there are doctors in and out all the time, and cops, of course, they follow the deceased from car crashes and stuff. Pick-ups from the funeral homes as well, you know, when Aunt Beryl gets laid to rest.

'And if I want female companionship there's usually a couple of good-looking ones lying in the back.' He laughed a snorty laugh. Fowler started, not quite sure if he was kidding. Kelly placed his mug on the desk; it was very tidy and he made sure that he placed his mug on the coaster. The file of the dead girl lay neatly on the top of the desk; it was open, showing photos of the girl as she had been found at the beach.

This brought back the reality of his visit … Fowler's heart rate increased. He had never actually been in this situation before, dealing with the family of the deceased at the identification, and he was nervous. He had hardly slept, the report had taken up most of the evening and he had not been able to take his girlfriend to dinner after all.

The bell rang from the main desk. It had a shrill sound and made Fowler jump, shaking his hand and spilling some of the coffee. Kelly saw this and was swift to grab a tissue from a box on the shelf behind him.

'Ah, must be the Chief Inspector now,' he said as he made his way to the front desk. 'Unless it's another delivery.' He snorted his laugh again, his eyes crinkling behind his glasses.

Macgregor was standing at the desk with Janette Green, the local officer who had experience in, and a natural ability for, grief counselling; she'd always accompanied detectives on these assignments in her previous posting in Coffs Harbour. She had built a reputation based on her kindness and empathy. She knew she could make the experience a lot smoother for the relatives, and for Macgregor. She wore a thick, red, woollen jacket and a black beanie with a matching scarf pulled up around her face so all that was visible was her nose and eyes.

She pulled off her gloves and unwound her scarf. 'Good morning Sergeant Fowler, I see you have the coffee sorted,' she said pleasantly. She could sense his nervousness and wanted to make a good impression on Macgregor in the hope that he would allow her to continue in the role and assist in these matters in the future.

Fowler smiled back, relieved, and with a nod from Kelly, he showed her to the kitchenette so she could make coffee for her and Macgregor. She got to it and quickly had them both a drink.

Macgregor turned to Kelly. 'The parents are on their way. A Mr Andrew Dickson and his wife Barbara. They'll be accompanied by Detective Inspector Mike Willoughby from Dubbo. They should be here very soon, expected at 7:30.

'Forensics have confirmed that the dental records are a match so we are quite sure it is their daughter. Danielle.

'Officer Green, you have the leaflets and forms for them and you know the drill. Sergeant Fowler, when we go back to the station I want you to lead the interview of the parents. You can get the file from Willoughby. Have a good read while we're in the identification room, okay, and let me know what you find.' Fowler nodded and put down the mug, now drained of its contents, relieved that he would not have to deal with the family's grief as they identify their daughter. Macgregor turned to Kelly.

'Doug Solomon not here yet? So Joseph, how are things with you? Been busy with this cold front?'

'Dr Solomon had an interesting suicide in Wollongong to see to. So he's unable to attend. As for me, I've got two from that head-on yesterday, a cot death, and two old dears, one with a stroke and the other cancer, and of course, your young lady.

'So enough new friends to keep me out of trouble,' he replied matter-of-factly.

The shrill of the buzzer was heard again, and voices coming from the main desk. Kelly and Macgregor looked at each other then headed out to the entrance. Willoughby was standing at the desk with the Dicksons – they were both ashen-faced and had dark circles under their eyes. Mrs Dickson looked frozen in body and soul.

Without hesitation, Green came forward from the little office where she had been waiting to greet them She introduced herself and offered them something to drink but they both declined.

Macgregor leaned forward with an outstretched hand and introduced himself. 'Mr and Mrs Dickson, thank you for coming. If you could both please come with me, we should like to get this matter dealt with.' He saw the pain in their eyes and added, 'I know it's very difficult for you both but we do need you to identify this girl, and if it is your daughter, we can start finding out what happened. You need closure and I need identification.'

About as subtle as vicar in a sex shop thought Willoughby,

his short stocky frame filling the foyer in his long, black, woollen overcoat. He still wore his black leather gloves. With his shaved head he gave the appearance of a bouncer at a nightclub rather than a detective. Willoughby had a history with Macgregor. Twenty years before, Macgregor had been sent down from Sydney to Dubbo, to be put in charge of a case that was getting nowhere, involving a killer who was on the run. Macgregor had successfully tracked and flushed him out. The killer was tried, convicted, and put in jail, the judge sentencing him to twenty years. Macgregor had gained a lot of media attention and almost hero status with the locals, which had put Willoughby's nose out of joint at the time, but they soon developed a mutual respect and friendship.

He gave a short sigh and cleared his throat in the hope of getting Macgregor's attention, and having achieved it, rolled his eyes in a disparaging glare that said, What the fuck are you saying, mate?

Macgregor ignored the stare and continued on, turning to lead them through to the viewing room.

'We understand, Inspector. It's just so unreal and final. We do want to help, I'm sorry.' And with that final word, Mrs Dickson could no longer hold her tears. Her husband sat her down and comforted her. Green came forward, 'It's all right Mrs Dickson. If you don't want to go in we can take your husband, you can sit here. I'll stay with you,' she said kneeling in front of the older woman and holding her hand.

Mrs Dickson wiped away her tears and looked up at Macgregor. 'NO! I MUST! She is my daughter and if that is her lying in there I want to be able to see her and comfort her. I am okay really. We must do it, Andy,' she said turning from Macgregor to look at her husband her eyes red-rimmed and swollen.

They stood at the door to the identification room, a small side room big enough to house the gurney, a cupboard and a few metal-framed shelves with metal trays, boxes and old files. It was tiled in pale green from floor to ceiling.

Green stood by Mrs Dickson's side, holding her up, her husband on the other side. Macgregor opened the door and Kelly led them through. The body was lying on the gurney covered with a white crisp sheet. The room was cold and had a strange glow from the main light, which gave everything a pale green hue. A strong smell of disinfectant mingled with formaldehyde hung in the air.

Kelly came forward and removed the sheet to reveal the girl's face. Despite his offhand remarks to Fowler, he obviously cared a lot. The body was well presented and he treated Danielle and her parents with utmost respect. He had managed to make the deceased girl look neat and tidy, the sand and twigs had been removed, and her hair had been washed. But despite the grooming, the mottled discoloration and bloated appearance of her face were still very evident.

The parents peered and slowly moved forward, then looked in disbelief.

Mrs Dickson broke down. 'Yes ... yes it's her. I would know my baby anywhere!' She gasped as she raised a tissue to her mouth in horror. Mr Dickson pulled his wife close to his chest, completely distraught but needing to comfort the woman he loved almost as much as he had loved his only child. He held her tightly, not taking his gaze away from the grotesquely distorted face of what was once his daughter.

Macgregor nodded to Willoughby, he then asked the parents to follow him out of the room. Mrs Dickson turned and looked at Macgregor and with pleading eyes said, 'Find the bastard who did this to my girl, Inspector, please!'

And with a last look at her daughter, she went sobbing out of the building, gripping her husband's arm.

CHAPTER THIRTEEN

The call came while he was in the shower.

It had been a long day. The hot water soothed his aching and weary muscles; completely drained and tired, he stayed in for an extra ten minutes, letting the steaming water wash away the remnants of the day.

Macgregor stepped out from the small and narrow tiled recess and tied a towel around his waist. He cleared the mirror from condensation with the edge of it and looked at the unsmiling face staring back. He was nearly fifty and it was showing ... the sagging overhang of his abdomen, the spongy mass of chest hair now greying. He sucked in his stomach and turned sideways, then let it out with a sigh. Well, he wasn't going to start jogging or getting to the gym anytime soon. His middle son had given him a gym membership last Christmas; it lay in the envelope on the dresser. Christ. What the hell, maybe it's time to start!

He walked through to the bedroom and sat on the bed. His phone buzzed alerting him to a missed call. He leaned across to the other nightstand to retrieve it, cramping a muscle in his leg as he did so. Caller ID: Lorna Paterson. He retrieved the message.

'Hi John, look I was wondering if you're not doing anything this evening, well what I mean to say is, I have cooked a very large beef stroganoff and it would be a shame to let it go to waste, oh and there is homemade apple crumble with custard to follow, call me!'

He dialled back, rubbing his left calf as he did so. Three rings later, she answered.

'Well hello, stranger,' she said laughter in her tone.

'Lorna, you do know the way to a man's heart, apple crumble, eh? I cannae turn that down. What time?' He looked over at the gym envelope, the image of a very fit young man peeping through the top, and smiled.

'Seven thirty. Have I caught you at a bad time, you sound a little breathless?'

'No, no, just had a cramp that's all, give me your address and I will see you soon. What do you like to drink?' He said it a bit too keenly and quickly, felt a little foolish as he offered to get some wine on the way. Jesus man. Control yourself, you'd think you were a teenager, it's just a dinner. But his mind was turning to other things ... he made sure he put on his best Y-fronts.

Wearing a black jacket, black t-shirt and very dark jeans, he splashed on some cologne which had been sitting in his toiletry bag for a very long time. It reeked. He quickly went to the sink to wash it off; some had splashed onto his shirt but he decided not to change it. Because nothing else was clean.

Lorna had set the table and gone out to the garden to

find flowers that had survived the frosts over the last few mornings. Lavender and a few sweet-smelling jonquils were all she could find. The candle was lit, she wanted to make an impression.

She was wearing a tight-fitting, green, velvet top that highlighted her eyes and her hair, and low-rise jeans. She looked good and was proud of her figure. Luckily, she had not gone flabby after the children. She had good genes; her mother was also slim and well preserved. She touched up her lipstick and checked herself in the hall mirror, seeing the silhouette of a man at the door. Macgregor stood at the entrance, on the verandah.

She lived in an older, Federation style house. It was well maintained with whitewashed walls and a small garden that she carefully tended, borders to the manicured lawn and a small picket fence edging the property. A large chimney was billowing out grey smoke against the darkened backdrop of the Clyde Mountain. The moon was full and bright, the air was crisp, a million stars shone above him as he knocked on the leadlight door.

Lorna smiled and kissed him on the cheek. The sultry tones of Madeleine Peyroux played in the background as she welcomed him in, breathing in his overwhelming aroma of stale Old Spice aftershave. But he was clean and had shaved and looked happy as he offered two bottles of wine. He had been undecided; he'd picked one of each, a West Australian Margaret River cabernet merlot and its counterpart in white, a chardonnay. The labels had frogs leaping around the bottle and it had made him smile when he saw them, remembering that Lorna had said she collected everything to do with frogs. She looked deliciously sexy as she smiled. She laughed when he handed them to her, and she led him through to the kitchen. The wonderful aromas of beef stew and apple crumble with hints of cinnamon filled the room. An old Aga stove was dominant and impressive, and several pots filled with vegetables bubbled away on top.

She handed him the red wine to open, and busied herself with retrieving the pan from the oven and then taking the vegetables from the stovetop to the sink to drain. The table was set in the kitchen; she said it was more homely and warmer as the Aga was on. Macgregor smiled happily and poured the wine into the two balloon glasses as he sat down.

He woke up at 5:30 as the first rays of light were settling through the fine flimsy curtains. He had not meant to stay so long. She was warm and funny and had made him laugh, the wine had taken over and now here he was, staring at her while she slept. She was beautiful, her skin soft to touch; her hair smelled of lemons and her breath came in small regular sighs. She had wanted him as much as he her, the trail of clothes from living room to bedroom told the story. They had sat for hours, relaxed, talking, discussing anything and everything. Then desire stirred in them. First the touching, then kissing, the need for comfort, release, they could not keep their hunger at bay any longer. They were both craving love, life and a physical connection.

The clock on the nightstand sent a red glowing beam onto the floor. He turned over and very quietly removed his arm that had gone to sleep under her waist; she wriggled but did not wake. He softly kissed her back and pulled the duvet up over her bare shoulder.

Macgregor followed the trail of clothes, picking up items not yet identifiable in this dawn light. Missing a sock, he put on the shoe anyway and quietly crept out of the front door.

A black crow was standing on the fence. It glared at him as he went to the car, trying not to slam the door and wake the neighbourhood. He felt renewed and energised for the first time in a long while, and headed straight out of town.

CHAPTER FOURTEEN

t was midday by the time Macgregor drove through the centre of Dubbo, nearly six hours on the road, a city sometimes known as the crossroads of New South Wales with Brisbane to the north, Sydney to the east, Adelaide to the south, and Broken Hill to the west. Its name comes from the Aboriginal word meaning 'Red Earth'. He could see why, when all around the town, red dirt prevailed. A fine red dust covered the Land Cruiser.

With a population of over 30,000, it had been classified as a city since the nineties. Long, wide streets welcomed him on entering the central business district. Macgregor noticed a cafe on the corner and parked the car. He had enjoyed the drive, listening to Ella Fitzgerald, Satchmo and Cab Calloway. It had given him time to think and go over recent events; he had decided to interview the parents again, in their own surroundings. He thought they might be more relaxed and come up with something new, something he might have missed. He'd also interview Danielle's employer at the animal hospital, then look at some CCTV from the bus-train station and head into the police station in Justice Place, just off Brisbane Street. He could see the new square building, the police headquarters, from where he had parked. Its original, older, Federation style front was still intact and it had been sensitively restored with the main complex at the rear.

The station and bus depot were around the corner on Trafalgar Street. He had called Willoughby and arranged to meet later that afternoon. Willoughby had organised some accommodation for him at the Dubbo RSL on Brisbane Street.

The cafe was warm and cosy, smelling of strong coffee and grilled bacon, with an open fire at the back of the room. He ordered a burger with the lot and a large flat white coffee then picked up the Daily Liberal, a local newspaper lying on the counter, and sat near the fire. The Western Plains could be biting in the winter. A few suits and office workers had started to queue and he was glad that he had been in first for brunch. The local paper was full of news about the girl's death; a happy, sweet-faced girl, smiled at him from the front page. He scanned through the first few pages, statements made by neighbours, her boss, old school friends, all in disbelief. There was a photo of himself in the bottom right-hand corner of the second page, looking old and saggy with unruly hair. He shook his head as he glanced up to see the young man deliver his burger and coffee.

'Thanks laddie,' he said putting the paper to the side of the table, and then asked, 'Would you happen to know where I could find Dr Elliot's Animal Hospital?'

The youth replied. 'Yeah mate, ya have to go down Trafalgar, head to the end, turn right into Fitzroy. You'll see the showground, then about a block along, the vet's on the corner. You'll be right.'

Macgregor nodded his thanks, wolfing into the whole beef patty with egg oozing out from the sides. 'No worries mate,' the youth said clearing the table next to him.

Feeling warmer, with a full belly, and coffee to kickstart him, he went back out to the car.

'Hell! Not a bloody parking ticket,' he said out loud. He had failed to see the sign, 'Please obtain your ticket from machine. $3.00 per hour'. Macgregor stuffed the ticket into his pocket then headed down Trafalgar Street and on to Fitzroy to the animal hospital.

The building had a large sign –'Dr Elliot's Animal Hospital'– below it a picture of a happy smiling snail, and coming out from the snail's shell, a handsome young man, presumably the vet, wearing a white tunic and holding a small poodle in his arms. The building was Californian style, typical in Australia in the thirties and forties, with a wide verandah and large red roof. The car park was full, so Macgregor opted to park on the grassy pavement strip.

The room was full as he entered the reception area; it was warm and bright, very modern and well designed, but had a smell of disinfectant and wet dog hair about it. An array of clientele was sitting in chairs with various cats and dogs in small-wired cages. A large Great Dane sat sprawled on the floor, the owner gently patting its flank and making soothing sounds as he did so. Macgregor had to walk around it towards the desk. He rang the buzzer on the desk and waited until a fresh-faced girl came from the back and asked if she could help. She was wearing a tunic with black and white spotted dalmatians all over it and her nametag said 'Sarah'.

Macgregor pulled out his ID and asked if he could speak with the owner. Sarah looked closely at the ID then at Macgregor. 'Just be a tick, Dr Elliot is in the procedure room, he shouldn't be too long. I'll tell him you're here.'

She had a small cat tucked under her left arm and it squealed as she readjusted her position to give the ID back. Several minutes later, Dr Patrick Elliot appeared – tall, dark short hair, mid-thirties. The handsome tanned face from the sign outside smiled. An open hand came forwards.

'Good to meet you, Chief Inspector, I was wondering when you would call. I presume it's about Danielle?' He half asked, half stated the question.

The office was high-tech and Elliot sat opposite Macgregor behind a large, polyurethane, clear desk. On top it held an assortment of small animal ornaments.

Macgregor felt suddenly conscious of his lack of a sock as he sat on the clear plastic chair. He crossed one foot over the other. Macgregor cleared his throat.

'So, Dr Elliot, you say Danielle was in your employment for the last two years?'

'Yes, a very hardworking, diligent girl, always willing, she often came in on the weekends to help out, without pay. It is so hard to believe that she is gone. She loved her work, the animals,' he said, the handsome face now showing a flicker of grief.

'Can you think of anyone that might have had a reason to hurt her?' Macgregor asked. 'Perhaps a disgruntled customer, a jealous colleague, jealous of her talents? I notice from the corridor wall photos that she was employee of the month three months in a row. 'A rejected boyfriend? Any reason at all, Dr Elliot?'

Elliot was shaking his head, when suddenly 'Scotland the Brave', resounding in full Edinburgh Tattoo force, bagpipes and all, filled the room with noise. Macgregor hastily retrieved his phone from his pocket and saw Laurie Hargraves on caller ID. He touched decline and apologised to the handsome face. 'Sorry about that, bloody thing is so loud, haven't worked out all the bells and whistles yet.'

He placed the phone back into his coat pocket.

'I'm staying in town for a couple of days … if anything comes to mind, even if it sounds insignificant, please call me,' he said, pulling out a card from his wallet and leaving it on the clear desktop.

'Oh one more thing, Dr Elliot. Do you use ketamine on your animals?' He asked, rising from the plastic chair to his feet and leaning across the desk. The handsome face looked perplexed as he answered.

'Yes, frequently. I'm often asked to sedate animals and it's regular stock in our drug cupboard. Sometimes I'm asked to help over at Western Plains Zoo, not far from here, with sedating the bigger animals. Why do you ask, Inspector?' He didn't wait for an answer.

'In fact I'll be there tomorrow, I have to help with checking the teeth of the baby white rhino, it's a big job and it will take a lot of sedation.'

Macgregor was about to speak when Sarah came into

the room, cheerfully telling him his next appointment was waiting. Macgregor decided not to say anything else but put his hand forward to shake the vet's hand. He nodded at the girl as he passed her in the corridor and left the premises.

CHAPTER FIFTEEN

Barbara and Andy Dickson were sitting in their lounge room, waiting. The aftermath of shock, grief and despair had taken its toll. They both looked like they had aged twenty years in the last week since Danielle had gone missing. Photograph albums were littered on the coffee table and on the floor; certificates and merit awards belonging to their daughter, once neatly kept in plastic covered folders, were removed and strewn everywhere.

The doorbell rang.

Mrs Dickson ushered Macgregor into the government leased, three bedroom, red brick house. The stale air hung with the smell of cigarettes and whiskey as they went into the lounge room, a small rectangular shaped room with two blue plush recliners and a matching couch. In the corner, a large television sat on a low-rise unit, and a print of Jesus hung above with a rosary draped across one edge. Prints and photos of their family covered one wall. Mrs Dickson's hair had a large grey streak along the centre parting. Mr Dickson was unshaven and hunched over in his recliner chair and made no effort to get up. She forced a hint of a smile as she led Macgregor through.

Mr Dickson was drinking scotch. The bottle was now nearly empty as he proffered an arm in an attempt to offer one to Macgregor, who declined.

Mrs Dickson shook her head and through red-rimmed eyes pleaded to Macgregor not to judge her husband.

'Chief Inspector, is there any news? Anything at all?' she asked desperately, 'We're in limbo, we can't sleep or eat, we have to get the funeral organised, it's all been so horrible! I'm so angry and there's no one to blame!' She scrunched a tissue in her hand until it fell in bits on to the floor.

'Andy won't stop drinking … and he's all I've got, do you understand Inspector … all I have got!' She walked through to the kitchen and put the kettle on, trying to resume an act of normal behaviour. Macgregor followed.

'Mrs Dickson, Barbara, I'm here to help you. I want to find the bastard that did this, believe me, no stone will go unturned.' He looked over towards her husband in the chair.

'Do you want me to call social services for your husband, not coping too well … is he? He may need some help with grief counselling?

'I can make a call and get someone over here to help you both.' She shook her head and busied herself with making tea.

'Inspector, look, I am sorry but no one's helped, rang or spoken to us. No one!'

'That's why I'm here, Barbara. Please, let's sit down and just talk. Tell me all you know right from the beginning, aye? Come on lass, just sit down.' She started to cry again as he held her hand to lead her through to the blue recliner.

She told him all she knew, that Danielle had been rather excited at the prospect of going to visit and stay with her friend Alicia in Canberra. She had packed an overnight bag, she was going to take the Countrylink bus from the railway station in Dubbo at 9:15 am. Danielle had never arrived in Canberra, her friend knew nothing about her coming to visit or stay.

Macgregor gently asked, 'Did you already know that your wee lassie was pregnant?'

She looked up at him, the pain evident on her face. 'No,' she said slowly and quietly 'That was the biggest shock of all, we never knew, she never said ...'

Macgregor asked as gently as he could, 'Did she talk about anyone? A new boyfriend? Work colleague? Anyone she had met recently?' Her eyes met his.

'No, she never said a thing. She just seemed excited about going away, she bought a new pink dress that week and had her hair done.'

He reached out to her hand. 'Barbara. Would it be possible to have a wee look in her bedroom, would that be okay?' Macgregor, now feeling he had her trust, asked the question while squeezing her hand.

'Yes, yes all right Inspector. I've kept it just as she left it, the police came and took her laptop and some journals, but otherwise it's as it was.' She started to get out of the chair, Macgregor put his hand on her shoulder and said, 'It's okay. I can manage.'

She stared across at her now snoring husband, comatose in

a drunken stupor, escaping to oblivion from the cold reality of despair.

Danielle's bedroom was second on the left-hand side of the narrow corridor. The house was L-shaped with bedrooms and a bathroom that ran along the back, lounge and kitchen forming the smaller part of the L. The room was very typical of a girl her age and Macgregor noticed Cosmopolitan and Total Girl magazines neatly stacked on a dresser along with an assortment of make-up, facial cleansers, hair products, a hair drier, beads, bangles and gaudy rings sitting in a pink-lidded ceramic box.

Posters of Lord of the Rings and The Hobbit were neatly pinned on the walls, with an array of stuffed furry animals on every shelf. Macgregor was looking along one of these when he came across a framed photo of Danielle, possibly three to four years younger, smiling and standing with her arms linked around a red-haired boy of similar age. There was a long-necked giraffe in the centre of the photo between them. Macgregor took the photo down from the shelf and had a closer look at it.

He slipped it into his pocket then went to her cupboard and drawers; nothing unusual, lots of clothes and at least fifteen pairs of shoes. She liked her fashion, he could tell by the number of handbags, scarves and hats. Thumbing through the magazines, he could see where she had circled in pen all the items and clothes she liked. No secret letters were found, he knew nothing had come to light from the diaries and journals that the local police had taken and returned earlier was worth noting.

Macgregor headed back down the corridor and into the lounge room.

Mrs Dickson had made tea and was quietly sipping from a mug. She had laid out a mug for him with two lamington cakes set on a bone china, flower patterned plate.

Macgregor sat down on the couch and sipped the tea, munching on the cake. He wiped the coconut crumbs from his mouth then asked a question.

'Mrs Dickson, Barbara, who is the laddie in the photo with Danielle?' He took it out from his pocket and let her have a look at it. She held it and gazed without speaking then said, 'The boy's name is Ryan Adams, they were the best of friends and she told me he had a crush on her for a while. That's a picture taken from when they worked at the zoo, they used to go after school. Then when they left school, the zoo gave him a traineeship as an animal keeper and she went on to work at the vet's.

'I don't know if they fell out but she hasn't had a lot to do with him for a while now, she said to me once that he needed to 'grow up', that she had out grown him. Ha! Can you believe it ... she was the same age as him.

'My poor baby, now she will never get old ...' The tears welled up again.

'Barbara, is it possible for me to take this photo for a few days? I'll take great care of it and return it soon as I can, is that okay?' She handed it back as he went on to ask, 'Would you know if the laddie is still working at the zoo?' He put the photo back into his pocket.

'Ryan? Yes I think so, we haven't seen him for well over a

year now, but as far as I know he is. Ryan Adams. I wonder why he hasn't called us? He mightn't know what's happened to Danielle. Inspector, will you tell him? I can't bear any more phone calls.'

Macgregor nodded and asked, 'So, Adams you say … and I can contact him at the zoo?'

'Yes. Danielle seemed to think he was still there the last time she spoke about him.'

Macgregor finished his tea and stood up to leave. He glanced over to where her husband was snoring and noticed the bottle completely empty, lying on the floor.

'Inspector, I'll sort him out, it will take time but we'll be okay. You see, Danielle was the light of his life … he loved her so much.' She sighed as she stood and walked him to the front door. Turning to him and touching his arm, she said, 'Please Inspector. Find him. Get the monster who did this!'

CHAPTER SIXTEEN

t was late afternoon and the sun was casting long, low shadows on the Obley Road. Macgregor made his way to the entrance of Western Plains Zoo. He had decided to speak with Ryan Adams and had messaged Willoughby to say he would have a drink with him later at the RSL on his return from the zoo. Although he'd called several times, he was unable to get hold of Hargraves. He'd sent a text message to him giving details of where he would be, asking him to return his call.

The photo was now sitting in the cup holder of the Land Cruiser. He parked as dozens of families and workers were leaving the car park. Macgregor picked up the photo, taking one more look at the red-haired youth, and slipped it into his pocket. The noise from the howler monkeys was quite startling as he got out from the car and checked his watch: five to five. The zoo would close at five, he would have to hurry if he was to catch the lad at work. He made his way over to the ticket booth and pulled his ID from his wallet. A middle-aged Aboriginal woman asked him to speak through the small, half-pane, glass window. She almost filled the booth with her ample size. He said he needed to chat with Ryan Adams and asked where he could find him.

She gave him a quizzical look then proceeded to give him the map indicating the African picnic grounds; she said he would be in the keeper's hut getting the last feed ready before the park closed. He thanked her and made his way to the path.

It was a bit of a hike, at least a kilometre, to the picnic grounds. It was also getting darker and as the sun went down so did the temperature. Macgregor shivered as he pulled his collar up around his neck.

The monkeys' high-pitched whoops and screams filled the air as dusk approached. He quickened his pace as trees and shrubs took on a formidable appearance and dark shadows moved between them. The park seemed to be empty and devoid of people. Dark eerie shadows loomed from thick undergrowth making the pathway difficult to follow and unfamiliar sounds, of growls and snorts, came from fenced paddocks and enclosures. Macgregor became acutely aware of the alien territory he was in; he sensed predatory eyes watching him.

Christ! he thought, I would hate to be left in here for the night. The monkeys started another rousing chorus of whoops and screams, as he felt for his phone in his pocket. 'Damn' he muttered, 'left the bloody thing in the car.' Anxiety started to take hold and his breathing quickened, Macgregor rounded a bend in the path, turning into the African picnic grounds. Ahead was a hut with a light visible. 'Thank Christ for that!' he said out loud as he proceeded to make his way over the grassy knoll towards it.

The blow came from behind ...

Piercing bright flares of light collided and smashed into a thousand sharp needles impacting every deep recess of his brain. He heard the thud as his body crashed to the ground. Incapable of preventing the fall, his limbs became powerless and heavy as his legs gave way. The smell of the earth hit the last of his senses as the cold wet grass met his face, filling his mouth and nostrils. The whooshing in his ears drowned the animal screams. Sharp, blinding pain behind his eyes told him he was slipping into darkness beyond sound and light.

CHAPTER SEVENTEEN

Chandeliers shimmered with beautiful crystals, glittering rainbows reflected upon the highly polished cutlery. Sparkling wine glasses adorned the many white linen laid tables. The Westin's ballroom looked splendid with the annual Sydney Medical Charity Ball in full swing.

The Westin Grand Ballroom, No.1 Martin Place, once the magnificent General Post Office in Sydney's CBD. Built originally in 1866, it was sold in 1966 for refurbishment into exclusive shops and a hotel, tastefully and sensitively restored.

The five-star choice of many stars and sports celebrities, it was also a fitting venue for the prestigious event. Anyone who was anyone attended the annual ball. Beautiful women in Collette Dinnigan, Chanel, Lisa Ho, Prada and other noteworthy designer gowns graciously adorned the room and danced on the parquet floor. The Westin's beautiful clock tower was in full view through the huge, sandstone, arched windows, taking centrestage on the back wall, illuminated with an effervescent glow from the many strategically placed spotlights.

The room was splendid, a magnificent venue. Dr Panngesh

had paid heavily for the tickets, over $2,000 each for him and his blonde, model girlfriend and, on top of that, he had donated way more than was necessary in the hope of securing his place at the most influential and important table.

He was seated next to Professor White, his attractive wife, and other dignitaries including the Lord Mayor of Sydney. Professor White was President, Chair and Council Executive of the Royal College of Surgeons. This was the moment Panngesh had looked forward to his whole career: to be accepted to sit with these dignitaries, dressed in dinner suit and black tie.

His girlfriend had got up to dance with an aspiring actor and was in raptures showing off her beautiful figure in a silver, silk, Yves Saint Laurent gown. Panngesh was relieved, he wanted to talk with Professor White and did not want the intrusion of her simple chatter to distract from his attention.

He approached the professor and in his well-practiced Oxford English said, 'Ah Professor, what a splendid event ... the college should do very well with the contributions and the donations made this evening ...'

He waited for the professor's response knowing that he had given the most money. The professor had had a few too many champagnes and slapped Panngesh on the back saying, 'What, what ... well done Panngesh. You're the sort of chap we need for these dos.'

Panngesh's hand was jerked forward with the slap to his back; he spilt some of the red wine down his front and onto his blue silk cummerbund. He grimaced and removed a pale blue silk handkerchief from his pocket to mop the wine. Composing himself he went on to say, 'Yes, Professor. Fine. I am sure we could get more of these wonderful evenings organised with my help and know-how. I would be very pleased to offer my assistance to support the cause.' He smiled obsequiously, showing perfect white teeth.

'Panngesh, you know I would like to have a chap like you on the board. How about that, old man? Fancy yourself on the board? You give me a call tomorrow, let's see what we can do, eh ...'

Panngesh bent forward and bowed; he headed back to his seat as the professor was whisked off to the dance floor by his tipsy wife.

His name, Dr Panngesh, was written in gold, embellished across a black, table card. He smiled ... to be truly accepted on this night, given the honour of being included, to be offered a seat on the Board of the Fellowship.

The evening had gone very well, it had been successful, that 'other business' with the irksome police sergeant was now being pushed away from this glorious moment, packaged to the back of his mind to be opened later. It had worried him at the time but he now felt his secret was safe, after all, he had got away with it for this long. He just needed to stay calm and not get flustered as he had before, so important for him to get this settled then deal with all the loose ends.

CHAPTER EIGHTEEN

Willoughby had decided to go ahead and watch the CCTV footage of Danielle's last known movements at the bus station in Dubbo on the day that she went missing.

He had received Macgregor's text message earlier that said he was going to the zoo to interview a potential lead. Willoughby had waited patiently and made one more call without success. It was now dark outside as he stood in his office at the Justice Place police station.

He had hoped to go through the tape with Macgregor. He loaded the footage, getting a chair from behind his desk and sitting down to watch as the grainy, black and white image appeared on screen.

The bus station was located directly outside the main railway entrance; the area comprised a long, metal, bench seat with a steel-frame covered roof and glass panels on either side. A CCTV camera gave a clear view of the bench and focused on the doorway of the bus when it was pulling in and out of the station.

The time on the screen was 7 am; he fast-forwarded to 8:30. It was clear and sunny on that day. He watched as dozens of people in fast motion entered the station getting on and off the buses – it was like watching an old movie – until he finally paused and pressed play at the allotted time.

About fifteen minutes of screen time later, Willoughby noticed the deceased girl, Danielle, come into view. She wore a dress, light jacket and flat shoes, and carried a dark-coloured overnight bag. No wheels were visible on the underside of the bag as she carted it over her left shoulder. In her right hand she held her handbag. Neither of these items had come to light yet.

Willoughby remembered the computer that had been taken from her bedroom; they had focused on her Facebook account and emails but nothing untoward or suspicious had been found.

She stood in the centre of the screen. She put down the overnight bag and retrieved her phone from her handbag. Danielle appeared to be texting and was smiling as she did so, on a phone that had never been found. It was difficult to see the type of phone being used; her parents could not confirm the brand when they had been interviewed.

Once it appeared that her text message was complete she glanced around as she sat on the bench. An older Aboriginal woman carrying shopping in Aldi bags came along and sat on the right-hand side of her.

Two young boys around the age of twelve came into view wearing rugby gear with caps and backpacks on their shoulders and sat on the left side of her. A bus pulled in and five people stepped off, then the young boys got on and the bus pulled out. Budding sportsmen thought Willoughby, knowing that the cricket icon, Glen McGrath, had been born in Dubbo and had gone on to become one of Australia's greatest.

Danielle remained seated for the most part. She kept glancing around, standing up a few times to look towards the roadside then sitting back down, checking her phone.

Another bus pulled in five minutes later and the elderly Aboriginal woman with shopping was assisted on to the bus by the driver. Always friendly in the country ... not so in the city ... more likely to be ignored, thought Willoughby.

Still seated, Danielle checked her phone again; slightly off screen a dark car pulled into view. Only the front was visible as the driver appeared, not wanting to block the buses from entering the station. The time on screen said 9:02. Willoughby slowed the tape down, freeze-frame by frame. He watched in slow motion as Danielle looked ahead and started to rise from the bench. She picked up her heavy overnight bag and swung it over her shoulder so that it threw her light frame slightly off balance. She proceeded to walk towards the car and to Willoughby it appeared she got in.

Damn! Willoughby was unable to see the registration or make of the car, a mid-size saloon perhaps, or sedan? The car reversed out of view and the CCTV was unable to show any further images of Danielle, the car, or driver. Willoughby got up from his chair and called through to his sergeant, asking him to get the tape to the IT boffins, to identify as much as possible regarding the overnight bag, the handbag, mobile phone, and especially the car. His sergeant retrieved the tape from the monitor and set about it. Willoughby also wanted the drivers of the buses interviewed from all the runs that morning and organised a couple of uniforms to the task.

Willoughby then headed out to the RSL club on Brisbane Street. Although it was within walking distance, he shrugged on his thick, black, woollen overcoat as the temperature out was almost zero, hoping Macgregor had got the first round in at the bar.

CHAPTER NINETEEN

The jackhammer had been constant throughout the night, ratataddaddaddadda, and now it was finally beginning to subside – along with the intense pain – as he attempted to open his eyes.

Someone was calling his name and, through blurred double vision, he opened his eyes very slowly. The jackhammer was ready to leap up and start again if any sudden moves were attempted. He began to make out the frame of a rather large man.

'John, John, wake up mate, how are you feeling?'

Macgregor recognised the distinctive tone of his old sparring partner, Laurie Hargraves, but did not want to turn his head in fear of awakening the jackhammer. He groaned and cleared his throat in acknowledgement of his pal.

Other voices were close by in the room, talking, he could hear them say his name. Shapes began to form as his vision improved. He was suddenly conscious of a strong smell of disinfectant from the sterile environment in which he now found himself.

He slowly scanned the side of the room he was facing

without turning and saw a tall locker next to him with a jug of water and a tumbler on the top of it, and beyond that, a doorframe with a large window on the right-hand side. He assessed that he was in a room in a hospital; the white wall ahead caught the sunlight streaming through from the window so bright it was blinding to his eyes. It started to awaken the jackhammer, so he quickly closed them. His mind was searching, trying to recall … how and why was he here? His memory banks were frozen and it hurt too much to even try to think, so he lay still and quiet.

A nurse had entered the room. He could smell her, a mixture of cheap perfume and antiseptic as she came close to his bed to take his blood pressure and pulse. He could hear the steady ping of the monitor from the ECG as it recorded heart activity and other observations. She opened his left eye and shone a bright torch directly onto his pupil. He moaned and squeezed it shut.

'Good. He's improving. Now gentlemen, he needs some rest. I want to change a dressing so you can both please leave the room,' she commanded. Hargraves gave the nod to Willoughby and they both headed towards the door. The nurse drew the curtain around the bed as they stood in full view, by the door, staring into Macgregor's room.

'Thank God he'll be okay,' said Willoughby, pulling his phone from his pocket to check for messages.

'Good thing you called me, Mike,' said Hargraves. 'I'd tried several times to let him know Gunner Adams was on the loose, that fucking psychotic bastard, the leader of the Skull Brothers. He killed those kids in '93, you remember? The five- and three-year-old sisters that were found in a fucking suitcase, strangled and mutilated, lying together, floating down the Macquarie River, out west of Dubbo. It was a terrible case. You remember Macgregor was there?'

Willoughby did. 'I'll never forget that one. Macgregor was brought in by our department from Sydney, we hated that: having the big city hot shot on our patch, but I have to say he tracked the bastard down and had him put away for life.'

'Except he isn't now is he! He's out! And I have my suspicions he could have clocked Macgregor at the zoo,' Hargraves said as the colour rose in his face.

'Yeah? But how would he know Macgregor was even here?'

'Doesn't take much in a small town for the word to get around. You should know that, you live here. Gunner's got family. They helped him before, and that's the first place he would go to. Better get some uniforms out there and start looking.'

'Already on it, some uniforms went out there last night. They questioned some of Gunner's family. They live out on a property near Devil's Hole Reserve.'

'Who found him?' Hargraves asked, changing the subject in a concerned tone.

'A young guy at the zoo, an animal keeper, he was finishing up for the day. He gave his statement to us last night, he practically stumbled on top of him when he was leaving.

'I'm on my way to the station now, do you need a lift? I know you came with the uniforms this morning; it's been a long night, you must have been up since before dawn on that early flight from Sydney. I could drop you at the station or in town?'

Still deep in thought, Hargraves replied.

'Err ... no thanks, I'll stick around here for a while ... wait till he wakes up. We've been mates for a long time, I'd like to make sure the old bastard is okay, but thanks anyway. Keep me posted.'

Willoughby headed down the long corridor of the surgical wing of the hospital, out into the cold, late-afternoon sunshine to the awaiting car.

Hargraves stood at the window to Macgregor's room and rubbed his eyes. It had been a long day. He had a good growth of stubble on his chin and his stomach was growling. He decided to find the nearest vending machine for a snack and a coffee. He felt relieved now, knowing his old friend was going to be okay. Let's face it, he thought, it would take a hell of a lot more than a blow to the head to get through that thick Scottish skull.

He chuckled as he went in search of sustenance.

CHAPTER TWENTY

The red-haired boy was angry, always being picked on at school with names that hounded him daily ... carrot top, red, ginger, blue, ranga. Australian colloquialism at its worst with associated jibes in reference to baboons and other primates. He was fair skinned, freckled and poor-looking; he never went in the sun as it made his face very red, drawing more attention to his appearance. He stayed away from the playground and sat by himself. Pale, alone and angry. The red-haired boy was never invited into their games and playtime frivolity. He sat alone under the trees, kicking at the stones and dirt beneath his worn boots. Watching.

He hated going home after school. Home was a dive, a pit of mounting scrap metal, rusty cars and piling rubbish in an overgrown yard; a ramshackle hut held together with corrugated iron and rotting wood. No maintenance or upkeep to the place; he had never brought a friend home, he was ashamed; his so-called family, eight of them; six kids, three older brothers and two sisters, who were now 'on the game' although still in their early teens. Even if he had a friend, he wouldn't take them home.

A teacher had once taken an interest in him with his remedial reading and had appeared at his home one sunny afternoon after school with some extra books she had found for him. She had been greeted at the door by his drunk and abusive father, who had attempted to molest the pretty teacher. When she had started to cry out and refused his advances, he had punched her in the face while screaming absurdities at her. The police had been called and his father arrested and jailed for three months. The teacher left the school and the town where she'd once lived happily. The red-haired boy had liked the pretty, young teacher, she had laughed with him, not at him.

The father's abuse was not only kept for pretty, female teachers. The red-haired boy was regularly beaten, by his older brothers but mostly by his father, his mother giving no protection, ignoring his existence. She appeared to be devoid of love for him, no tenderness, no waiting at the school gates like the other mums with a treat, a cuddle and a smile as the kids came out from class. The red-haired boy walked past them, head down, kicking at the dirt with worn boots and unwashed clothes. Holes widening under the soles of his boots, allowing the small gravel stones to enter his sweaty, naked feet – angry now from the irritation it caused, giving rise to small red blisters. He shuffled on, using the pain to fuel his anger.

He never knew how his father and mother would react; it seemed to him his whole young life that he walked on eggshells around them. He kept himself seen and not heard. To avoid the beatings, most nights he would hide, waiting until his parents and brothers became comatose from alcohol. He'd then sneak into the hovel of a kitchen, looking for scraps of food before finding a safe place to sleep and curling up in a ball, still wearing his clothes, until morning. He would then get up and walk to school without breakfast or any food for lunch.

The school had a breakfast program run by the government and a few children would arrive with empty bellies waiting for a bowl of cereal and a glass of milk. The rest of the time he would steal other kids' lunches and snacks and feel the churning hatred towards them deep in his belly. A belly empty of food, but full of resentment and fuelled by a hunger to lash out and hurt them.

He wanted to rub their smiling faces and clean shiny hair in the dirt. Make them the same as him, then they would see, and maybe then understand.

The Department of Child Services had been called several times by anxious neighbours and school teachers; attempts were made to place him with foster parents but nothing ever seemed to last.

The red-haired boy had been taken into foster care a couple of times, only to stay a few weeks before his carers called the department with concerns that he wasn't fitting in and had caused problems within the families. Even seasoned foster parents were reluctant to have him now.

One family persisted for two months with his antisocial behaviour and lack of discipline; organising child psychologists' and counsellors' appointments every week for him. He sat in their offices, arms folded, nonverbal; once defecating on his chair deliberately, laughing when he got the reaction he craved. The counsellor ordered him out of the room to the bathroom calling him 'disgusting' and a 'little shit'.

He ran away returning to the only life he knew ... with his family. A family that was abusive, violent and neglectful. He punched walls and broke windows, venting anger. It was never enough ...

It seemed he was always angry. He could never escape the abuse, the family, his small size, his hair colour.

Hungry, hungry, hungry.

Why was he so small? Why did his head hurt?

The first time he hurt the cat it felt good ... power over the defenceless animal made him feel strong, in control, and a little excited. The cat's demise was slow and painful, hanging from the door handle of the shed by fishing line, squealing and wriggling for its dear life.

He watched as it slowly stopped wriggling and squealing, its little tongue turning a strange blue colour. The cat dangled lifelessly, its small blue eyes staring blankly at him. The fear gone. An emptiness. He liked the calmness. No more squirming or meowing. Silence.

He poked at it with his thin little finger. The kitten rocked back and forwards. He liked this game. The red-haired boy poked the kitten again. It made him laugh.

He laughed out loud ... it felt good to laugh ... and he laughed again ...

CHAPTER TWENTY-ONE

Isabella Kowowski sat by the bed. She'd had news from the local command police HQ of the escaped convict and of Macgregor's attack. She wanted the scoop for the Bay Press and had decided to make the trip to Dubbo herself.

Her beautiful black shiny hair was piled on top of her head, held in place with a silver comb, her long elegant legs crossed at the knee. She wore a grey pantsuit, pink silk blouse unbuttoned, revealing hints of black lingerie, and on her feet, black patent leather ankle boots, very businesslike. Her computer bag lay by her feet and she had her phone in her hand. She had been linking in with the staff back at the Bay, keeping her finger on the paper's pulse.

She stared at Macgregor as he slept. She was not usually a bedside vigil kind of girl but this was different. First hand news.

She thought about Gunner Adam's history. It had been a savage attack on the little girls, a neighbour's children living on the property not far from where the killer lived, nearly twenty years ago now. She had been a child herself at the time and remembered the look of horror on her mother's face as she read the story in the paper out loud to her father, whose English was limited.

Gunner Adams had been caught several weeks later, on the run and hiding out in the bush, stealing food from nearby farms and homes.

His family had kept quiet at the time, refusing to give any information to the police – which was to be expected given the kind of family they were, members of a local, outlawed bikie gang, the Skull Brothers, renowned for destruction of property, illegal guns, violence and thieving. Drug dealing was their main source of income. Gunner, their leader, had a long history of violence. It was later found that the family and gang members had aided his escape by providing cash, clothes and a rifle. It was big news at the time and sold many papers. She had her eye on the prize; this scoop could be the big one.

Gunner's long history of violence had made Isabella quickly put two and two together: he probably did attack Macgregor two days before at the zoo. But who helped him escape from Goulburn Correctional Facility? It was one of the most secure jails in the country, with super-maximum status – some of Australia's worst and notorious criminals were held there. He had been on the run for three days now and it's more than likely he would still have connections and family in the area. But then Macgregor was onto a lead with the Danielle Dickson case ... perhaps ... Her thoughts were interrupted with Macgregor's slight moans as he awoke.

She watched as he stirred and opened his eyes. He had recovered quite well but appeared to have no energy and would fall asleep quickly. The doctors told her it was the brain's way of dealing with the trauma; the brain wanted to heal and sleep was the only option. His CT scans were all good, and although he had suffered a severe concussion and hairline skull fracture, he had no sensory or physical impairment. They said he could be discharged in a day or two.

Macgregor cleared his throat. 'Well hello. Fancy seeing your lovely face at my hospital bed.' He turned to sit up slowly; his head still hurt but moving was getting easier now. Isabella came forward to assist him and plumped up his pillows. 'Why, you're quite the attentive nurse,' he said grinning ironically.

'I'm mortally wounded – don't you suppose I care? And have concern for your welfare?' she crooned, lips pouting as she gently stroked his hair. She disdainfully avoided the dressing, which was still in place at the back of his head.

He let the last comment go – if anyone was wounded, it certainly wasn't that tough young broad.

'Are those for me?' he asked, looking across at the large bowl full of mixed, fresh and juicy grapes. He knew why she was here but all the same he might get some mileage out of it, too.

Isabella bent over and kissed him on the forehead, allowing some cleavage to nestle in his face. He could smell Chanel Nº5, the perfume she always wore; it would linger in the room long after she had gone.

Macgregor moaned a little, a mixture of pain and pleasure, but the pain in his head took over.

She wanted to ask questions and probe him for information but even she could see he was in no state for the sort of interrogation she had planned. She pulled back and stood in front of him.

'You're still in pain and tired, I'll come back later when you're more up to talking. I have a few … ah … interviews in town to attend to,' she purred, retrieving her computer bag from the floor. As she headed towards the door, it opened.

Lorna Paterson stood in the doorframe, full of smiles; arms laden with flowers, fruit and a couple of crime novels.

'Hey,' she began, entering the room and speaking softly to Macgregor – until she noticed the glamorous woman in front of her and was caught off guard. She hesitated.

'Bye darling. See you later,' Isabella trilled, flashing a beautiful smile Lorna's way. With an air of arrogance, Isabella strutted out the door, blowing a soft kiss from her hand back to Macgregor.

Macgregor smiled and waved a pathetic goodbye. Sensing tension, so thick in the room you could cut it with a knife, he groaned. He laid his head down, feigning pain – which had recently been relieved by the Endone pill, a powerful, morphine-based painkiller that the duty nurse had given him earlier.

Lorna tried to retain her smile but her eyes were giving her away – green, and not just in colour. She banged down the goodies she had bought on top of the locker and turned towards Macgregor.

'Who was she, John?' Like most people in the Bay area, she knew full well who 'she' was. She avoided Macgregor's eyes as he replied.

'The editor of the Bay Press, Isabella Kowowski. She came

to get a story, she's an old friend.' Even in his groggy state, he knew as he said it that she wasn't buying it.

Lorna tried to keep her voice steady as she plucked from her handbag the black sock he had left at her place.

'Missing something?' she asked, busying herself with arranging flowers in the vase.

'Ahh ... my old friend. I cannae believe you would put that in your bag. It wasn't clean, you know.' He grimaced as he placed the sock in the drawer of the locker. 'The only thing I've been missing is you,' he said, smiling as he looked up into her face. She looked good in her black leggings and thick, woollen, red jumper, a dark-green silk scarf tied to one side around her shoulders. Her hair was glossy and recently cut, styled into a long bob. It suited her small face and it gave her a pixie-elfish look.

Macgregor noticed her new 'do' and gently touched her hair in approval. She started to babble.

'I was so worried about you, when I hadn't heard from you, I called so many times and texted and when Sergeant Fowler called me and said you'd been attacked I had to come and see for myself. We'd had such a lovely evening together I thought maybe you didn't want to see me again ...' Macgregor listened, stroking her hair. His tender touch and smile helped reassure her of his feelings. The jealousy subsided; she still wanted to know more about Madame Kowowski, but she let it go. For now.

Taking a step back, Lorna went into nurse mode, checked his wounds and then his charts. She fussed around, instinctively pouring fresh water into the tumbler sitting empty on top of the locker.

'Someone tried to kill you John ... I'm scared! Will they come back?' she said, concern in her voice as her lip quivered, reflecting her growing feelings for him.

'It's not the first time, Lorna,' Macgregor sighed, as she rearranged his pillows, 'I can't remember much ... didnae get a look at him, he got me from behind. I think he was a big guy, he made little effort in hitting me. I've been going over it again and again in my mind. My colleagues Har ... Hargraves and Willoughby, seem to think it's an old con. Gunner Adams ...

'I put him away for murdering two little girls over twenty years ago. He's been on the run now for a few days. God only knows how he managed to get out of Goulburn and where he is now ... but I have my suspicions. I'm not so sure it was him ...'

CHAPTER TWENTY-TWO

For three long days, Macgregor had been recovering, resting, sleeping.

He was now much improved – apart from a stiff neck, the occasional headache and bruising. The hospital physician told him he could be discharged on the condition that he take it easy and continue with the painkillers. He was to rest up and return for the removal of sutures from his scalp in a few days. Hargraves returned to Sydney, relieved to know his friend was okay. He was eager to get back to the hustle and bustle of Surry Hills Police Station; the countryside did not suit him or his lifestyle. 'Too much bloody dirt and dust,' were his parting words to Macgregor as he made his way to the airport for the Sydney flight.

Willoughby insisted Macgregor stay with him and his family to recuperate, as he was certainly in no condition to drive or travel just yet.

Willoughby's home was a two-storey, a relatively new, large brick-and-tile house. It was built on a crescent of similar properties in a quiet suburb, not far from Dubbo's CBD, and was to be a sanctuary for Macgregor's recovery. Its neat and well-maintained garden featured a large fish pond in the centre, home to large koi.

The family made him comfortable, offering him the spare room, a small attic with a modest bed. An electric blanket gave extra warmth to the chilly night air.

New pyjamas, socks and jocks were duly bought from the local Target department store.

Lots of homemade soups and broths saw him respond and heal quickly. His wound now felt itchy and with no dressing in place he started to scratch at it only to remove a large, dried, blood-encrusted scab. It had the pungent smell of iron as he sniffed at it. He had been advised not to get the wound wet. But bugger it ... when the family were all out mid-morning, he headed for the shower and gently washed around the scabby area. Washing away the dried blood from his hair made him feel like a new man.

He was not used to being fussed over. Macgregor had protested at first but then submitted to the care and attention from Hilary, Willoughby's wife – a large, motherly, wholesome, countrywoman. They had four teenage children; twin boys aged sixteen and two younger girls. Macgregor was thankful for their kindness but was now bored to tears.

He dressed and made his way to Justice Place Police Station.

Fortunately, he could walk the distance, a couple of kilometres from Willoughby's home. It would give him time to think, reflect, and get back into gear with the case. It was still quite cold outside with temperatures barely getting above three to four degrees Celsius. As he headed to the front door he grabbed a thick overcoat belonging to Willoughby that was hanging on the coat stand in the hallway.

No one was home when he left and the polite thing to do was to leave a note for the chatty and warm-hearted Hilary, adding that he would come home with Willoughby later that day. He placed the note on the kitchen benchtop where he was sure it could be seen when she returned from her shopping trip.

Macgregor had been kept up to date logging into Willoughby's laptop computer and reading the papers, including the Bay Press. Isabella had gone to town capturing the public's attention with sensational headlines: 'Cop Clobbered in Wildlife Park, Left for Dead!' with pictures of himself, head bandaged, lying listless in a hospital bed. She must have taken them when I was out cold he thought to himself. 'Mmmhh.' Stories of the missing prisoner Gunner Adams were also featured, with links to old pictures from twenty years ago, in which Macgregor also appeared.

Fowler had called every day, updating him with the Batemans Bay police' side of things; he particularly wanted to follow up on a lead he had, involving Dr Panngesh. He didn't give too many details, but requested permission to make some international calls to Mumbai. Macgregor had agreed, more interested in the recent CCTV footage involving Danielle's disappearance into the dark-coloured vehicle. Dubbo uniforms had been interviewing the bus drivers and had a couple of promising results.

It was puzzling to him as to how Gunner Adams had managed to escape the maximum-security prison. Macgregor was determined to get the details, although very little information about the escape had been made public, with only brief reports in the news and on TV. There wasn't a lot on the police HQ website either.

It felt like there was something missing ... details about the man ... but not the escape. Macgregor knew that feeling in his gut, the one that would not settle when undercurrents were in play. He needed to investigate more.

Isabella had been to Willoughby's house several times to see how Macgregor was. Oozing charm and flattery, she had been causing havoc in the household with Willoughby's twin teenage boys, who found it difficult to stop leering at her; their jaws dropping every time she appeared at the door; pushing and shoving one another to offer assistance in getting her a chair or coffee. One twin had severe acne the other was slightly taller and with a clearer complexion. Long lank hair hung, curtain-like over one side of their faces; they followed the fashion of young males with the obligatory pants that hung way below the buttock cleft, revealing boxer shorts, the pants having frayed hems from constant dragging along the ground. The twins' voices alternated minute to minute, from high to low octaves, testosterone playing havoc, with every hormone on high alert. Difficult stage, thought Macgregor, as he smiled, remembering his own boys at that age.

Fluttering beautiful long lashes and smiling, Isabella had been delighted when he had agreed to give her 'the exclusive'. It had taken persuasion and coaxing on her part, but he had promised the story to her when he was in the hospital. He needed her to be on his side, as in return he may need a favour from her someday.

So with great interest she sat, dictaphone in hand getting the scoop.

Lorna had stayed in Dubbo until she was satisfied that her patient was stable, comfortable, and settled at Willoughby's house, and thank God thought Macgregor, she had managed to miss Isabella's visits, relieving him of the little zigzags of embarrassment that had caused such angst at the hospital. It had all gone rather well. Lorna didn't mention her name again. Before making the trip back to Batemans Bay she left wound-care instructions and information regarding any possible complications with Hilary.

Macgregor entered the police station, and making his way through to the incident room, walked in on a rousing chorus of whoops and cheers from detectives and uniforms. This was totally unexpected and caught him off guard; he kept walking, feeling embarrassed. He raised his hand in an effort to calm them and keep the noise down. He had not expected this comradeship, especially as it wasn't his patch. He was the outsider. It cheered him and he gave a small bow.

Willoughby sat at his desk, his left hand poised as though holding a cigarette, although smoking was a habit he'd abandoned many years before. His bulky frame crowded the desk as he studied reports in front of him. Macgregor glanced at the large whiteboard on the back wall of the incident room as he walked through to Willoughby's office. It was now covered with photos and names, arrows connecting leads to the Danielle Dickson murder case.

Willoughby looked up on hearing the din in the hallway and saw Macgregor walking towards him.

'Should you be here?' More a command than a question. Macgregor cleared his throat, strode into the office, made for the opposite chair and sat down. He was feeling dizzy and thought maybe he had overdone it with the exercise from walking.

He began to remove the thick jacket, small beads of sweat now appearing on his brow. Willoughby recognised his coat and started to say so, then decided to let it pass. He could see how Macgregor had struggled to get to the station and admired his stoicism.

'I'm fine, Mike, but going a little stir crazy,' he said, steadying himself. 'I'm really grateful and your wife has been wonderful to me, but I can't sit about any more. I need to know what's happening and I need to get back on the case. So many pieces don't fit. I have to know what's been done.' Willoughby could see there was determination in his glare.

Willoughby stood and called through to a uniform who was walking past his office and asked him to get some coffee; he looked towards Macgregor, who turned and nodded in agreement. 'Make that two, both white and one with sugar.' He turned back to Macgregor and picked up a file, tucked it under his arm, and reached for his pen from the desk. He walked through to the incident room and beckoned Macgregor to follow.

'Well, as you know, Macca,' he began, pointing with the pen to a name on the incident board, 'we're following up on the bus driver from the CCTV footage the morning Danielle disappeared, the bus that was pulling out as the car pulled in.' Macgregor sat on a nearby chair in front of the board, his hands gripping the sides of the chair as he tried desperately to focus. 'And we've had a couple of new developments.'

Willoughby took the file that had been under his arm, opened it and laid it on a desk in front of Macgregor so he could look at it.

Macgregor picked up the report, which he attempted to read, but the words appeared to move and jump about on the paper. He put it back down on top of the desk, concentrating on sitting upright, the dizziness now overwhelming him. He held on, knuckles going white, seeking equilibrium; he closed his eyes hoping the room would stop spinning.

Willoughby continued. 'Danielle's overnight bag has been found, it was picked up by some kids near Macquarie River, they had rifled through it, not finding anything worth keeping. They dumped it on the side of the road, just off Brisbane Street.' They were interrupted as the uniform arrived with the coffee. Both men stopped, took a cup, and sipped at the hot steamy liquid; Willoughby swallowed and cleared his throat as he went on.

'A taxi driver passing at that time saw them run off and decided to stop and inspect the bag, he read the name on the tag and recognised it, so came to the station and brought it in. He doesn't know any more than that.

'It's at forensics now and I'm waiting for the findings. It was only found this morning.'

Macgregor opened his eyes wide on hearing this news, and feeling steadier from the coffee, he released his grip.

He leant forwards, pulling the chair closer to the desk, leaning on his elbows and resting his chin on his hands, intently listening to what Willoughby was saying while scanning the reports.

'Another piece of information has come to light,' Willoughby continued. He paused and moved towards the board again, the pen now pointing to an arrow that led to the word 'zoo', with another arrow pointing to the photo of Ryan Adams, a copy of the one that Macgregor had borrowed from Barbara Dickson.

'The kid that gave his statement the night you were bashed at the zoo, Ryan Adams? He's gone AWOL, not been seen since that night, he hasn't shown up for work and as for the family ... well, I think they know something, but they're not playing ball!'

He stared at Macgregor before imparting the next piece of information. Macgregor held his gaze as Willoughby took a deep breath.

This time, he raised the pen to point to a photo of Gunner Adams, with an arrow drawn, connecting him to Ryan Adams. 'It turns out he is the nephew of that bastard Gunner Adams ... mad as a cut snake, him and his family, oh! And one more thing, they live near one another!'

Macgregor cut him off.

'Fuck! Don't tell me! *Devil's Hole Reserve?*'

CHAPTER TWENTY-THREE

He awoke with a start as the rooster regaled him with its ear-piercing screeches. His whole body stiffened as he stared wide-eyed through the narrow wooden slits of the shed he had been hiding out in, an old shed on a cattle-farming property ten kilometres west of Dubbo. He knew the area, he had been there twenty years before and not a lot had changed.

This had been his shelter for the last week. He was aching, cold and damp, and the winter chill had seeped into his bones. His body was now worn and scarred from a lifetime of torturous assaults, beatings and stabbings; every muscle and joint in concentrated pain, sinews held tight with adrenaline.

He stretched out, breathing hard as the icy air hit his lungs; his breath coming in hard gasps with every movement. Twenty years ago, he had done it easily; this time his age and body were not so forgiving.

The moonlight was waning and dawn was approaching. He stared across the paddock, scanning the landscape, searching, always on guard, looking for an exit, a strategy, high on alert, ready to lunge, run or hide.

The mist on the fields hung a few feet from the ground and he could just make out the grainy grey shapes of cattle down on the left side of the paddock by the creek. The sun was on the horizon. He rubbed his eyes and felt the roll of an empty stomach. He was starving. Clutching at the makeshift swag, he rummaged through his dilly, only bread left to find. He had stolen it two days before from a shopping cart in the car park of the little IGA store in a small town. Grabbing what he could, hoping he had not been seen by the woman as she put her kids in her car. In desperation, he had not looked at the items and in his haste had grabbed a bottle of fucking Pine-o-Clean floor cleaner.

'Fuck' he groaned, now only a few slices of the bread left and nothing to drink. Pulling out the last cigarette from the packet, he lit it and took a long drag, coughed, and hocked up some bloodstained phlegm which he spat onto the dirt floor. He cleared his throat, cold and hungry. He sat back against the wooden post, reflecting on the last few days.

A week ago, he had been inside Goulburn prison; he'd been banged up for the last twenty years.

'Fucking cunt Macgregor,' he hissed.

The years had given him time to think, and he had been plotting revenge, simmering hatred, scheming ways to get even with Macgregor.

With bikie-gang mates – the Skull Brothers – on the outside, and a wad of stashed cash, money was no object. He had carefully and methodically planned his escape, waiting for the right fuckwit to come along. It had arrived in the form of a favour owed from another Skull Brother whose lawyer had huge gambling debts and was about as shit scared as Skippy in a bush fire. It was all about to go belly up for him.

It had all gone to plan. 'I paid a FUCKING TRUCK LOAD OF SHIT to that pisspot lawyer,' he growled angrily.

The release papers had been cleverly and sophisticatedly forged by that dodgy lawyer. The documents, with the Chief Justice's signature impeccably forged, were delivered to the governor of the maximum-security prison. No one had questioned the papers; nobody had any reason to stop him as he was led out by the guards and strolled out the front gate.

'Right through the fucking front door,' he laughed. 'That bastard lawyer had promised a car and the rest of me money in the fucking car, fucking bastard,' he snarled, as he recalled waiting for the car for over an hour. When it hadn't shown up he knew if he hung around the guards would be on to him so he had to leg it.

Two hours later, the fraudulence of the documents had been discovered; and questions had been asked of the very embarrassed governor when called to the Chief Justice for answers. Heads would roll from this, but it was all kept hushed up to the public. The press were only told that Gunner had escaped. But not how!

He had hitched a lift to Canberra from Goulburn from a passing truckie who asked no questions. Gunner knew he had two hours of freedom before the alarm bells would go off and the pigs would be after him.

The truck driver had pulled into a gas station to use the men's room and get fuel when Gunner got out. He walked over to the roadside, lit a cigarette and watched as a cab pulled in.

The driver got out and also headed to the men's room. Gunner casually idled towards the cab noticing the keys still in the ignition and slowly made his way inside the car. He pulled the door shut, started the engine, and drove off.

'Stupid fucker left his keys in the ignition,' he spat. It gave Gunner another getaway through the quieter back roads; he had driven the cab as far as Dubbo without being caught and dumped it half a kilometre from the town centre as it ran out of fuel. He had walked the rest of the way.

He had no money or phone, then seeing a sign for the zoo he remembered his nephew worked there. He made his way there hitching another ride.

Gunner had been waiting at the entrance to the zoo and then wandered up to the ticket operator. He asked her about Ryan Adams, where could he find him, and when would he be finishing? The woman told him what she knew.

Walking back towards the main gate to wait, he thought he saw Macgregor, driving an old Land Cruiser that pulled in to park. He couldn't believe it, he stared in disbelief as he watched Macgregor get out of the car and head towards the same booth – he was sure it was Macgregor! Gunner kept out of sight, hiding behind the large entrance sign; he waited and watched as Macgregor made his way towards the park. Gunner smirked at his good fortune – he now knew where his nephew was working and, what was even better, he had found Macgregor!

'Fucking oath!' he said quietly as he followed Macgregor and saw him turn into the African picnic grounds. It was like Christmas ... he couldn't believe his luck!

It was getting dark, the air was filled with the sounds of screeching and howling animals. He kept his distance, several metres behind Macgregor as he approached the turn.

With the cover of dusk and no one around, Gunner took his opportunity.

Reaching down to the ground, he picked up a fallen branch hidden in the undergrowth along the side of the enclosure. He slowly crept up behind Macgregor, then with a ferocious swing, slammed the branch into the back of his head.

Macgregor's knees buckled as he slumped to the ground. Gunner raised the branch again to follow through with a final blow to the skull to finish him off, when he was abruptly jerked backwards.

Ryan Adams pulled his uncle away from Macgregor's head just as the weapon came crashing down to the ground.

Scared and shaking, Ryan had stared at his uncle, fear written across his face, Gunner's mouth a tight grimace, frothy saliva at the corners. Ryan held tight to Gunner's jacket, looking into volatile, dangerous, and glazed, pinpoint pupils. Gunner hissed through gritted teeth, grabbed the kid by the throat and pulled him in close. His fingers tightened on his youthful neck. He felt the urge to squeeze. Hard. His breathing quickened at the thought of watching the colour drain from his face. The struggle as the kid tried to suck in air.

Instead, he released his hold, spitting in his face.

'What the fuck!'Gunner roared.

CHAPTER TWENTY-FOUR

Walking back from interview room four, Macgregor headed for the second floor of the Justice Place police station towards the incident room. He bounded up the highly polished, original, wooden staircase two steps at a time, one hand steady on the rail for balance.

Reprieved from the dizziness and vertigo that he'd been suffering from recently, he stood for a moment with his head down and back bent, leaning on one hand over the banister rail, breathing hard to catch his breath. He was out to prove a point to himself.

'Yes! I'm back,' he said under his breath, feeling more his old self. His heart hammered in his chest, so he waited another minute for it to settle before going through the hallway and past the other officers. Focusing on work had certainly improved his demeanour; he figured he was less cantankerous and more rational to deal with now. The less-senior staff and officers had given him a wide berth since his return to duties. He had barked and growled at them like some crazy rabid dog when they had approached him.

However, this new information had given him a buzz and sparked the old grey cells back to life. Impatiently, he went to Willoughby's office without waiting or knocking and stood over the desk.

Willoughby was labouring over paperwork as he recalled Macgregor's request to have the bus driver interviewed again. He had agreed to it, despite the driver giving detailed statements to the uniformed officers a few days previously. Macgregor had insisted on interviewing the driver himself and Willoughby knew it was futile to argue with him.

The bus driver had arrived earlier at the police station, apprehensive of his second interview. A local man in his sixties, slightly balding, with a deep-set parting where fine dark hair was combed over and given to wearing a small clipped moustache – his likeness to Adolf Hitler didn't go unnoticed.

The driver had worked for the Countrylink bus company for fifteen years without a day's sick leave. Macgregor thought this unusual but creditable, and as such, he saw him as a reliable witness (most blue-collar workers in Australia had regular 'sickies'). The driver had proudly volunteered this information to the uniform at the desk when he had arrived. Nice to have someone keen to oblige.

He sat in the barely furnished interview room on a hard plastic chair behind a black, formica-topped desk. He rested his clasped hands on top of the desk. Quietly spoken, polite, and intimidated by the stark surroundings of interview room four. Giving thoughtful answers to Macgregor's questions, the driver looked up at Macgregor and over to the young female officer standing by the doorway with every answer he gave.

The bus driver confirmed he had witnessed the car seen in the CCTV footage; he had seen it pull out from the bus terminal at Dubbo Railway Station on that fateful morning of Danielle's disappearance.

The information was illuminating to say the least. The driver had remembered the black, shining, new Holden utility truck; as he said, 'I always fancied one meself.'

What he said next was even more revealing.

He had noticed a sticker in the rear window of the ute that showed an image of a round pink shell. Macgregor asked the driver to take a look at a business card he procured from his wallet. The card was from Dr Elliot's Animal Hospital, with the logo of the snail and Elliot's face in the centre of it.

The bus driver wasn't certain but agreed that it looked very similar; he also said that the driver of the ute, wearing dark sunglasses, appeared to be in his mid-thirties with dark hair. He remembered the pretty young girl with her bag as it almost knocked her off balance as she got up to approach the car and get in.

'The driver didn't help her, she got in after heaving her bag onto the back of it. I thought the guy was a dick by not helping her with the bag,' he recalled.

'Do you have any recollection of the ute's number plate?' Macgregor asked.

'No, mate, by that time I was dealing with me passengers and had to collect me fares. It choofed off down the street.'

Macgregor thanked him, finishing the interview by speaking into the electronic recorder sitting on top of the desk. Noting the time and date of the interview recorded, also those present in the room, before removing the three CDs. He placed one in his pocket, handing the other two to the female uniform.

He then asked the female officer present to escort the bus driver back to the reception area.

'I knew it! I bloody knew that handsome, preening prick was hiding something,' spluttered Macgregor still panting slightly from the exertion, thrusting a CD under Willoughby's nose. 'I'm going over there now to squeeze that prick. Let's see how he squirms with this information.

'Listen to this!' he commanded as he pushed the CD into the player on Willoughby's desk, pushing some paperwork out of the way.

Willoughby listened as the dialogue from the interview unfolded. 'You don't know it was him. Don't go off half-cocked. Anyone could have a bloody vet sticker on their car window! They probably give them to all their clients and hope some end up getting stuck onto car bloody windows!'

Macgregor clicked off the player and placed the CD back in his pocket. 'Well I'm going over to see the good Dr Elliot and find out. It's too bloody close to home to be a coincidence!'

Macgregor had checked in to the Dubbo RSL; fully recovered, he did not want to encumber the Willoughby household any further. His new digs were easier for him to work from due to the fact that he often stayed up till the wee hours, restless and agitated with insomnia. Pacing the room or taking a walk in the early hours helped to clear his head. It was a hell of a lot easier to be alone, not to disturb anyone else.

Sightings of a man fitting the description of Gunner Adams

had been reported to the police from a woman, a farmer living ten kilometres west of Dubbo. Uniforms were sent to comb the area, but nothing had come back yet. The young Ryan Adams had not been seen since the evening at the zoo when Macgregor was struck down and Adams's family were not the most helpful people, especially now that Gunner was on the loose. They were tight-lipped and claimed no knowledge of either. Warrants were out for both and searches had been made of the property at Devil's Hole that unearthed several non-licensed guns and a plastic bag with a few kilos of weed that had been stuffed under the floorboards. Enough to have them brought in for questioning.

The drive to Dr Elliot's Animal Hospital was brief, and before he had really got into think mode he was outside the building. He parked the Land Cruiser on the grassy verge. The sky was grey, the sun had gone down, and it was getting chilly – he could see the looming black clouds coming in from the west. Screeching and howling animals from the zoo could be heard in the distance and black crows were circling, cawing in the gum trees above him. He scanned the car park. No sign of a shiny black ute. Nevertheless, he got out, walked over to the gravel path and up to the front entrance, but the sign on the door said 'Closed'. Scanning the rest of the doors and windows of the surgery, he spotted another sign with details of opening hours. He looked at his watch – just missed him by twenty minutes. Bugger!

Macgregor looked at the phone number that was displayed on the sign on the window for after-hours and emergency attention and called it. A voicemail recording – he chose not to leave a message. He tried again, same recording, so he cancelled the call.

Returning to his car to leave, Macgregor saw Elliot's fresh-faced assistant, still wearing the top with dalmatians on it, come out from the rear of the building. 'Hello,' she said, smiling as she pulled on a thick, blue, woollen sweater.

'Hi, Sarah isn't it?' Macgregor replied, closing the car door and walking over to her.

'Yes, are you looking for Dr Elliot?' she asked.

'I am indeed. Can you tell me where he'd be after surgery hours?' Macgregor asked casually. She put on some gloves and slung a multicoloured satchel bag across her shoulder.

'Well, usually he goes to the zoo for an hour or so but I think he said he was going straight home today.' She walked across the gravel driveway, crunching the fine stones underfoot with her shiny black gumboots, and unlocked a bicycle that was leaning against the fence. 'The funeral's tomorrow ... she wasn't that sweet and innocent, you know,' she smirked, putting the bicycle lock in her satchel.

'Why do you say that?' Macgregor enquired walking towards her.

'I knew she was up the duff!' She blustered, her cheeks colouring. She turned her face away from Macgregor as she pulled the bicycle free from its anchor.

'How did you know that, Sarah? Did Danielle tell you?' He asked, turning in to meet her gaze.

'No, but I guessed it. She was chucking up every day and fainting in the surgery. I've seen it before with Kylie.'

'Kylie?' Macgregor repeated.

'Yes, my sister, Kylie, she … ' She hesitated as if to say more but stopped herself. Macgregor knew not to push the point and changed the subject.

'So, lassie, where would Dr Elliot's home be?' Macgregor asked. 'I have to get some documents signed by him, you know, formalities, police work.' He helped steady her bike as she climbed on.

'Dr Elliot lives in the old presbytery, you can't miss it, it's the only house with a walled garden and big gates.' She took off over the gravel path, wobbling on the bicycle until she gained balance and momentum.

'And where would the presbytery be?' Macgregor raised his hands, pointing in both directions as she rode off. She turned her head and called back to him,

'Devil's Hole …'

CHAPTER TWENTY-FIVE

Macgregor drove through the township towards Devil's Hole, skirting along the winding banks of the Macquarie River on the Newell Highway. The river was dull and although fast-flowing it was murky brown from the recent deluge of rain and storm water. Poor visibility gave it a sinister appearance. Macgregor turned into Brisbane Street. The starless sky was now an inky black with heavy dark clouds, rain seemed likely. It had just started to spit. Large drops streaked across the windscreen when a tremendous crack ricocheted across the heavens and an enormous flash of lightening zigzagged its way across the sky, instantly releasing a downpour that lashed at the windscreen.

Macgregor found it difficult to see. His car was old and his wipers squeaked rhythmically, not keeping up with the deluge. He slowed down, as the rivulets of water cascading along the dusty surface made the road difficult to navigate.

Macgregor pulled over to the side of the road in frustration. The noise on the car roof was deafening, but he'd just have to wait it out. Another loud and furious crack careered across the sky, forming a halo around the ominous clouds, giving them an eerie and menacing glow.

Macgregor sat waiting, seeing dim lights in the distance from farms and houses. He wished he had gone back to the RSL hotel; he would have been nursing a bourbon by now instead of sitting out in the dark, in a storm. He decided to put on some music but remembered he'd taken the CDs up to the hotel room. He switched on the radio. The local radio station was playing:

Deep down in the Devil's hole
Sinners burn
Deep down in the Devil's hole
A one way ticket with no return
Oh dear Lord come and save my soul
Once you're down, way down that track
There's no way you're coming back

Deep down in the Devil's hole
Sinners burn
Deep down in the Devil's hole
A one way ticket with no return
Oh dear Lord come and save my soul
He's gonna know you're ready to sell
Way down deep in the fires of hell

Deep down in the Devil's hole
Sinners burn

Macgregor still had his hand on the tuner button, unmoving, gripping as he listened to the unmistakable voice of Buddy Baxter, a voice that sounded like a mixture of gravel with wood shavings, washed down with fine old whiskey. The growling blues singer continued:

Deep down in the Devil's hole
Sinners burn
Deep down in the Devil's hole
A one way ticket with no return
Oh dear Lord come and save my soul
Once you've made that fatal deal
Oh dear Lord there ain't time to heal!
Deep down in the Devil's hole
Sinners burn

Macgregor sat, transfixed, listening to the jazzy blues. 'There is no such thing as coincidence,' he said softly as the song growled on. Thunder rolled into the distance. The rain eased slightly. Switching the engine back on, he slowly eased out from the shoulder, felt the slip of the tyres, heard the thrust of the engine, and pulled out onto the road.

'Gotta catch me a sinner, and drag him out of his hole!' he sang tapping his fingers on the steering wheel, changing the words of the song to suit his purpose.

The huge, Gothic style structure of the presbytery loomed out of the darkness as Macgregor approached the entrance. Two large, impressive, black wrought-iron gates stood ajar as he slowed to turn into the driveway. The walled dwelling silhouetted against the dramatic stormy sky, causing a disturbing feeling in Macgregor's belly. His stomach groaned, acid crept up the back of his throat, burning as it did so. He had forgotten the pills the doctor had given him; the bottle sat, hardly touched, on the kitchen bench back in the Bay.

Macgregor parked at the rear of an outbuilding. It appeared to be an old stable, set along the side of the main house. Rain still poured down. He had no wet-weather gear or umbrella so he resigned himself to getting drenched.

He pulled his collar up around his ears and quickly sprinted from the car to the entrance, sloshing through muddy puddles forming along the path. The puddles were deep and water started to seep through his shoes. He had meant to have them repaired and re-stitched.

Lights glowed from two large bay windows on the ground floor; heavy drapes framed the solid stone features. A large, arched, stone doorframe painted in red stood in an alcove with stone seats either side. At the centre, a solid oak door with a large doorknocker in the shape of lion's head glowered out into the night.

Macgregor approached the door, relieved to be out of the rain. The alcove lit up as he entered it. To his right, he spied an umbrella stand with a metal shoe-scraper in the shape of a smiling gargoyle with clawed hands holding the scraper. A row of shiny gumboots, dark green and black in colour, stood under the seat on the left. Dog leashes and an array of collars hung from a hook above it.

A large straw welcome mat with worn, faded lettering lay at the front of the door. Wiping his muddy shoes on it, he grasped the large iron knocker. Two knocks echoed and vibrated on the heavy wooden door, much louder than he had expected, so he replaced the knob as quietly and softly as he could, and awaited a response from the inhabitants.

The door opened and a very heavily pregnant, short woman answered. Her bulging belly was obviously difficult to cover in the pink fluffy dressing gown she wore. The cord of the gown was stretched around her middle tightly with little excess hanging. On her feet, she wore matching slippers, and she had her hair wrapped in a towel. Macgregor smiled politely, hoping to look friendly given her alarmed expression. He presumed she had just showered. In her hand she was holding a soiled pink towel, streaked with black stains. Her face was round and so were her large eyes. She had a diminished chin and gave the appearance of a chipmunk with her prominent front teeth.

She was startled. 'Oh, I'm sorry, I thought you were my husband,' she squeaked. 'We don't usually get visitors after hours ... err ... what can I do for you?' She went on without stopping, 'Patrick's not here! You might have to catch him on his mobile; you know we don't keep any medical supplies here.' She pulled on the dressing gown cord to tighten it and stepped back a little from the doorway, gripping the solid door handle in her left hand.

'Mrs Elliot? I'm Detective Chief Inspector Macgregor. I did try to call your husband on the after-hours number several times.' He retrieved his soaked wallet from his pocket and pulled out a very limp and soggy card. 'I was hoping to speak to Dr Elliot, I've just come from the surgery and the assistant there said he would be home. I'm sorry if I have caught you at a bad moment,' he continued, glancing at her attire. 'Would you know where he is now?'

Macgregor realised he must look menacing in the dark at night, drenched and sodden from the rain, so he stepped back then went on. 'I apologise if I startled you, but it's important that I speak with him. Will he be back later?'

She shrugged, still gripping the door handle. Macgregor sensed her discomfort.

'Okay, I'll go now. If you could get him to call me in the morning?' He put the wet wallet back into his pocket and turned to go.

'Wait! Detective, why don't you come in out of the rain, I'm sure he won't be too long. As you can see, I'm ready to pop!' She giggled behind her hand. 'Hence my nervousness with strangers at the door.' She relaxed a little more. The centre crease on her forehead dissolved as she stepped back to let him through.

Macgregor squelched through to a large reception room, part office and part lounge, a large Victorian desk with a roller top lid impressively taking centrestage at the window. The room was warm with a large, open fireplace; a great log perched on top of burning embers gave a glow to the dim interior. Musty odours of old church and burning wood filled the air. Piles of books gathered dust on the tightly packed bookcases and tabletops.

'Stay here and give me a few minutes to change, Inspector. Please sit down.'

'Thank you Mrs Elliot, I will. It's a horrible night out there.'

Macgregor walked towards a worn, dark red, leather wing

chair and sat down. A low, wooden coffee table sat in front. 'Please call me Jill – Mrs Elliot sounds so formal. I won't be long,' she said, as she waddled out of the room and through the entrance foyer. Heavy footsteps could be heard as she climbed the stairs, huffing and puffing.

Macgregor waited until he knew she had reached the top of the stairs before he got up and perused the room.

A large winged and horned statue caught his eye – a dragon-like beast that cast eerie shadows in the corner. Its snarling, black marble features mocked him as he walked towards it. He circled the room, noticing more unusual pieces ... ornaments and artifacts of satyrs – a half-man, half-goat; a minotaur, half man and half bull – standing erect with menacing snarls and horns. Daggers with ornate handles in glass cabinets, scrolls and parchments tightly bound with red ribbon and sealed with blood-red wax, sat next to wooden boxes filled with feathers and animal teeth.

He glanced at some of the books on the desktop: *Wiccan Warriors, Natures Angels, The Seven Faces of Darkness*. The pictures that hung upon the walls were similar in appearance. In one, the glowing red eyes of a half-man, half-beast stared at him as he approached; next to it, a picture of a winged human skeleton devouring a beating heart. Christ, he thought, this is very interesting, not quite the clean cut minimalist contours of the animal hospital. What a bloody contrast.

Jill returned as Macgregor was thumbing through a rather thick leather bound volume of The Art of Devil Worship sitting alongside a copy of the Bible. His face gave him away as he quickly returned the book to the table.

'Ah. I see you have realised my husband's passion. I'm afraid Patrick's a collector … he has quite a collection, as you can see … the outer buildings house some of the larger pieces, they're crammed full of the stuff.'

'Hardly light reading,' he murmured, stroking the fine leather of the book cover.

'I can't stand it myself, I have a room in the house that is totally mine, without all this ugly stuff!' She had put on a loose, dark velvet smock that amply covered her full belly and her still-damp blonde hair was piled up and held with a clip. Her pink fluffy slippers protruded from under her long smock. She was wearing a strong perfume that was quite overwhelming as she approached to retrieve the soiled towel which had been thrown on the sofa. 'Bloody hair dye! Why can't he just …' she mumbled.

Macgregor sat forward in his chair as Jill sat opposite.

She offered him a drink and he said 'Aye, thanks' to a bourbon on the rocks.

She sipped some mineral water. 'The baby and all,' she smiled, patting her swollen abdomen.

Macgregor smiled and said, 'First one?'

'Yes, Inspector, we've been trying since we were married, five years ago. And now, just when we started to give up hope it happened. Look, I'm not sure when my husband will be back. He said he was at the surgery, but he may have had a call out to a farm or the zoo. I know you want to talk to him about that poor girl … Danielle. It's her funeral tomorrow, it's going to be so sad, and she was such a sweet and lovely girl.'

'Did you know her well Mrs Elliot … err … Jill?' Macgregor

asked, downing the warm amber liquid, instantly feeling it merge with the acid in his stomach. Then, like a raging fire, a flame rose up the back of his throat, causing him to splutter and draw a deep breath. Gritting his teeth and hoping it would subside, he gripped the empty glass as the fire coursed through his veins. 'Not really well. She was a very good worker, never complained, she often stayed late or gave up her weekends to help out. I used to work at the surgery before all this,' she said, patting her belly again. 'Of course, I don't know the family. I saw the father once, I think – when he came to pick her up – she didn't drive you see and always needed a lift here and there. I think that's why she was so helpful, she was really grateful for all the lifts my husband gave her.' She put her drink down and saw the empty glass Macgregor was holding.

'Another, Inspector?'

Macgregor refused now that the burning inferno in his chest was building. He let out a large belch and apologised. 'Oh, don't worry! I get indigestion all the time since the pregnancy began, really bad sometimes. I'll get you some Quickeze.'

She waddled out to the hall and came back promptly with a packet.

Macgregor thanked her and took two, chewing the chalky lozenges quickly. He belched again and excused himself. She giggled.

Macgregor sat listening as she chatted; he nodded, his mind storing every detail. It appeared that Danielle was well liked … Jill Elliot was not aware of anyone that had a grudge or any ill feeling towards her. She was, however, of the opinion that Danielle had met someone over the last few months.

'She paid attention to her appearance and wore nicer clothes, and had her hair cut and styled. A woman always notices these things you know,' she said, pulling a stray hair back up under the clip.

'Did she tell anyone his name? Did anyone see this person who motivated her into a new hairdo?' Macgregor asked.

'Not that I know about, maybe the other girl that works there, Sarah, she might know more. Sorry Inspector, it's been a few months since I really had anything to do with her. Patrick will know more I'm sure.'

Oh, I'm sure he will, thought Macgregor

CHAPTER TWENTY-SIX

Fowler was asleep, sitting propped up in the hard-backed computer chair, leaning against the wall of Macgregor's sparse office at the Batemans Bay police station, with his jumper a makeshift pillow and his feet up on the desk.

The shrill of the office phone woke him with a start, and he kicked over a cup of cold coffee that had been sitting in front of him. He grappled in the dingy light for the phone with one hand and with the other hastily tried to mop up the spill with a wad of tissues from a box on a shelf above him. Some files were on the desk and he quickly moved them out of the way, throwing them onto the floor.

'Hello, Sergeant Fowler speaking.' There was a pause and a slight echo as he heard a distant reply.

'Ah, Sergeant Fowler. This is the commissioner of the Brihanmumbai police, Central Bureau of Investigation. Hello, hello, is you hearing me please?'

The Indian accent was thick and guttural. Fowler glanced at his phone for the time, 11 pm. He had been waiting for this call to come in.

A week before, following a conversation with Lorna Paterson, Fowler had made general enquiries regarding Dr Panngesh's background. Lorna, Panngesh's theatre sister had told him that she had been concerned about Dr Panngesh and his practices; she said that she had also noticed that the certificates displayed in his office looked strange. She had studied them once when she had been in the office to collect patient records. Looking closely, she had felt they were odd, unlike the certificates of other consultants she had seen. The dates and names had been changed and cleverly concealed.

'You had to look really close to see the changes, but once you saw them there was no mistaking the altered details.' She also remarked that Dr Panngesh was hesitant to talk about his past, or his previous medical training and experience. He was secretive, unwilling to discuss or share personal information, which she found unusual for such a small unit of people working closely together.

Over time, this had given her concern and she wanted to talk with someone. The opportunity came when Fowler called her with news of Macgregor's assault, and subsequent recovery in hospital. She voiced her fears then.

Fowler noted her concerns and acted upon them, making enquiries to the Australian Medical Board. They had stated that Panngesh's credentials had been in order and nothing untoward had come to light. However, Fowler knew that Lorna would not make any of this up. He asked her to come to the police station, and she had agreed to make a statement. Although she was uncomfortable in doing so, she was also aware that in the past other surgeons had entered the country fraudulently and worked illegally.

Lorna recalled the Rockhampton case of a surgeon allowed to practise even though he had been disbarred in England and two other countries. He was charged with manslaughter, found guilty and subsequently acquitted on a technicality, after having worked illegally as a surgeon for a few years in Australia. Several patients had lost their lives. However, she was quick to note that Dr Panngesh had never caused harm to anyone ... that she knew about.

Fowler had made phone calls to India. He requested background and registration checks on Dr Panngesh, believed to have been registered in Mumbai, according to Lorna's statement and the medical license hanging on Panngesh's wall.

Fowler spent hours on the phone. With the five hours' time difference, it was difficult to get to the right people when he needed them. He contacted the majority of the medical schools in Mumbai and none was of any help. They were inconsistent with their files and listings of registered practitioners and surgeons.

The Indian Medical Council were equally as inefficient with obtaining and releasing any information, so finally he had been given the contact for India's Central Bureau of Investigation, and the commissioner's number in Mumbai.

'Seargent Fowlee? Is you hearing me please?'

'Yes, yes, I'm sorry I was asleep, it's 11 pm here. I'm Sergeant Fowler' he said, pronouncing his name.

'Ah yes, Sergeant Fowler, I have reports for you on Panngesh.'

Fowler stopped mopping up the coffee and listened carefully to the commissioner.

'You knows Panngesh is vanted for arrest here in Mumbai for fake, how do you say … fraudulent documents. He is vanted on bribery and corruption charges, working and operating as a surgeon. Panngesh, you knows, had bribed the medical council, for them to clear the mandatory screening test, yes with a lot of moneys, you knows over hundreds of thousands of rupees for getting a medical registration. So he can uphold his degree and certificates here in India, we have been on a big raid of this crime and now arrested several officials from the medical council who took these moneys.'

He coughed and cleared his throat, 'Sorry, sorry, I have cough yes? It's a big, big crime here, for many doctors are fake. Panngesh bought his medical degree from China you knows? Many buy from Russia or China and then bribe officials here to get past official screening test, Panngesh was, how you say, a big fish. He never did any study in Mumbai or India, he went to Australia, just before we wanted to arrest him, he must have alert, how do you say … tip off, from somebody in the medical council.'

Fowler listened intently, straining to hear through the echo on the phone. 'Go on commissioner, I'm listening.'

'Panngesh worked here for ten years with no legal certificates, he also has a cousin, Dr Patel, he is now also in Australia we also have a warrant for his arrest for illegal kidney surgery, you knows they sell many kidneys here for peoples with big moneys, many, many rupees?'

Fowler listened intently, focusing hard on what the

commissioner was saying, as it was quite difficult with such a strong Indian accent.

'Is that so, how very interesting, even unbelievable that he could get away with this for so long. Thank you commissioner, can you email me all the reports? If they're not in English I can easily find a translator. You have been most helpful.'

'Thank you, thank you, Sergeant Fowler. And yes we do use English for official reports. As you knows our motto ...' At this point he spoke in Hindi and rattled off something Fowler could not understand.

'Sorry, didn't catch that last bit,' Fowler responded, not quite sure if the commissioner had finished speaking.

'Ah yes! Sorry, our motto means "To protect the good and destroy the evil". I vill forward the reports and how ve must vork together to bring these criminals to trial.'

Fowler agreed with him, offered his thanks again, then said goodbye.

Cleaning up the last of the coffee spill, Fowler threw the sodden tissues into the metal, wastepaper basket sitting under the desk. He started to write an email to Macgregor, choosing this rather than a phone call; he was aware that Macgregor was going to the funeral of Danielle Dickson in the morning and he needed to get the facts straight in his head, knowing how pedantic Macgregor was. He sent the email outlining the information from the commissioner and that the reports would be sent first thing. I'll call him in the morning, he thought, as he grabbed the files from the floor, retrieving his jumper, and turning off the computer and desk light.

Walking past the desk officer he gave a wave that said 'I'm

out of here'. He had a report to write and wanted it to be ready for Macgregor.

He hoped he would also get some shut-eye before sharing this incredible new information. This was big news and all hell was about to let loose – he was feeling very smug over what he had uncovered and didn't want to mess it up. 'Panngesh isn't going anywhere. He thinks he got away with it!' he murmured to himself, leaving the building, 'And I can't wait to see that arrogant look wiped off his face. Isn't it?' he mocked.

CHAPTER TWENTY-SEVEN

t was still raining heavily as the last of the procession of mourners gathered around the gravesite at the old Dubbo cemetery. The cemetery was not far from St Mary's primary school, the school Danielle had attended as a child.

Filing out from the old church, once the funeral mass had concluded, a sea of black umbrellas bobbed along the narrow path to the gravesite. Mourners positioned themselves around the flower-adorned coffin; the rain relentless, fierce on the fragile, floral wreaths. Delicate petals began to fall away, dropping to the ground, leaving the florists' copper wires patchy and bare.

As Macgregor had waited at the back of the graveyard for the mourners to come out from the church, he sensed the loneliness of the place. He thought of the generations of mourners that had shed tears and paid their respects to the dead over many decades. He had wandered over to the solitary graves. Some headstones were broken and damaged, some so old the texts were illegible. Half-buried and leaning over, they looked sad and neglected, overgrown with weeds, moss and grass. A few dated back to 1863 when the first occupants had taken up residence in the township. Unlike the new lawn cemetery on the other side of town there were no urns with recently placed flowers or neat patches of trimmed grass. The caretakers of these graves had long gone themselves; a barren waste ground of forgotten people.

Macgregor headed back towards the church, his shoes drowning in the muddy puddles. He turned, hearing two black crows screeching as they fought one another over the carcass of a dead possum, tearing to pieces the remains, which lay strewn across the muddy path, ripping the belly open as a stringy line of entrails spilled out.

'Very few people are buried here unless there is a prior arrangement with the local parish priest,' Willoughby whispered to Macgregor as they stood at the back of the crowd. Wet and damp, the long, black, woollen coat worn by Willoughby was starting to emit a foul smell, as the heat from his body permeated through its fibres. Macgregor's shoes were still wet from the night before and felt clammy against his damp socks; the stitching on one had come undone even more, leaving a huge gap at the side of the shoe. Both had stood in the rain, waiting for over twenty minutes for the priest to finish the church service, knowing their presence inside would have been intrusive.

Father Christopher Harding-Pierce had just started the final farewell for Danielle Dickson. He was in his late sixties, of medium height, reddish blonde hair, and chiselled features with a strong chin. He stood clasping a black leather bound bible in his large, gnarly hands. To keep it dry he handed it to a solemn, grey-haired parishioner who held it under her umbrella as though it were a privilege to be trusted with its safekeeping. He spoke from memory, in a deep resonating tone. The priest's ceremonial vestments were black with a purple stole embossed with gold emblems. Macgregor thought this priest must be quite conservative as most modern and forward thinking priests wore white, symbolising hope after death: that the deceased had ascended into the Kingdom of Heaven. Black was to remind the Catholic flock that death was a reality and that prayer was the only salvation for forgiveness of the sins committed in life.

Macgregor stood scanning the mourners as the rain beat down noisily against the nylon umbrella given to him by Mrs Elliot the night before, which he now shared with Willoughby. A sudden gust of wind caught the umbrella and turned it sideways and then inside out. Macgregor grappled with it before finally pulling it back into shape. A few broken metal spokes protruded sharply.

Barbara and Andy Dickson stood at the front of the grave next to the coffin with relatives either side holding them up. Their drawn, ashen faces showed the full extent of the pain and distress they were going through. Many young people lined the pathways, school friends and local kids that knew Danielle, most red-eyed from sobbing; grief stricken and clutching comfort from one another. They were so young to have to deal with such trauma, thought Macgregor, so very young, and yet with road accidents, suicides, drug overdoses and the like, it was all too common to see young people united in grief.

Elliot and his heavily pregnant wife stood to the right

of the Dicksons. Suitably attired in black, raven-haired and handsome, Elliot showed little emotion on his tanned face, giving a nod to Macgregor when he caught his eye. Macgregor had not interviewed him the night before, even though he had waited for well over an hour chatting with Mrs Elliot. She gave him a smile and a soft 'hello' of recognition before turning back to face the priest.

Sarah Vincent, Elliot's assistant, stood to the left of the Dicksons, facing opposite Elliot and staring in his direction with a wry smile. She then glanced over towards Macgregor and Willoughby and knew she had been caught out staring at her boss. She coloured as she held her gaze on the coffin.

Mr Dickson let go of his wife's arm as he came forward from the crowd, and with a quiet whisper said 'Goodbye', gently laying a soft, cuddly tiger on top of the coffin, kissing it as he did so.

'We beseech Thee, O Lord, in thy mercy, to have pity on the soul of Thy handmaid, to Thou who has freed her from the perils of this mortal life, restore to her the portion of everlasting salvation. Through Christ our Lord, Amen.' The quiet murmured 'Amen' from the crowd was almost drowned out by the rain.

Father Harding-Pierce spoke solemnly on, disregarding the rain that was now dripping from his vestments and nose, his hair plastered in clumps against his head. Red, muddy puddles were filling in and around the grave. The priest then lifted his hand that held a wet sod of the red dirt. As the coffin was lowered into the ground, the sobbing and wailing almost drowned out the sound from his final words; he tossed the dirt onto the wooden box and sprinkled the remnants into the grave. The coffin slid slowly into the ground.

Danielle's parents followed the priest's lead, throwing white roses into their daughter's grave.

As Mr and Mrs Dickson turned to leave the graveside aided by friends, Macgregor saw a man at the back of the crowd. Half hidden behind a tree with dark glasses and wearing a hoodie, he seemed twitchy and on edge, glancing around.

What's he up to? thought Macgregor when he noticed him, 'Wearing sunnies on a day like this.' It was then that another strong gust of wind blew the hood down to reveal a mop of red hair.

'Christ all fucking mighty, it's the bloody kid from the zoo!' He barked to Willoughby, who now turned looking in the direction that Macgregor was heading. Willoughby saw Macgregor take off at great speed, splashing through blood- red puddles that now covered most of the graveyard's uneven ground.

Ryan Adams quickly realised he'd been spotted and ran for it. Lithe and half Macgregor's age, he bolted away quickly, jumping over headstones and the wrought-iron gates. By the time Macgregor stood where Ryan had been, the boy was well away and out of sight. Macgregor stood panting and soaking wet, trying to catch his breath. He had a stitch in his side and even though it was still pouring with rain and very cold, he was red-faced and sweating. Willoughby finally caught up; he'd called ahead to the station for a car and some uniforms, giving the details and location of the red-haired youth once he realised what Macgregor was doing.

Still clutching the phone and umbrella in his hand, he patted

Macgregor on the back. 'Mate, are you okay, you look ratshit! I've got uniforms on to it. Let him go. They'll catch him. Come on, the mourners are leaving, let's go and talk to that vet!'

They stood by the broken, wrought-iron gates as Macgregor caught his breath. Walking from the graveside, Father Harding-Pierce approached and stood next to them; he did not greet or acknowledge them and remained stony-faced. The parents of the dead girl were the first to greet the priest at the gates; they were completely drained and exhausted as they thanked him. Nodding in recognition at Macgregor, they left to be helped into a waiting car.

The priest consoled the mourners as they passed by. Standing erect and drenched from the rain, he stoically placed his gnarly hands on each one as they stopped to thank him and he offered words of comfort.

The last couple to pass the priest were Elliot and his short dumpling of a wife, her pregnancy still apparent under her dark overcoat. Macgregor approached the vet as he greeted the priest and with a sidelong gesture of his head said, 'Can I have a wee word, Dr Elliot?' He beckoned to him to move away from the priest and out of earshot.

The vet looked to his wife and then at the priest, completely disregarding Macgregor's gesture. 'Obviously, I would like to get my wife out of the rain and home Inspector. Can't it wait?'

'Aye, well get the lassie out of the rain and home, but we would like to speak with you down at the station later eh? About three o'clock? That suits me, what about you, Dr Elliot? Three okay for you?'

Elliot nodded with a humph as he walked away.

'Now don't go leaving town Dr Elliot, will you!' Macgregor remarked sarcastically as he and Willoughby watched them climb in to the black ute parked at the side of the road. They noted a pink sticker on the back windscreen.

Macgregor and Willoughby then approached the priest, noting that the last of the mourners had left.

'Can we have a moment of your time Father? I'm Detective Chief Inspector Macgregor and this is Detective Inspector Willoughby, we're investigating Danielle's murder. Was Danielle a regular churchgoer? Perhaps you can help us, tell us anything you think could shed light on her death?'

The priest held his gaze and with tight lips and furrowed brow, replied in a sombre tone.

'I knew Danielle very well, she was a very special girl, her family are devout Catholics and I've known her all her life.'

Before Macgregor could reply, the priest raised his gnarly hand and stared at them with a gesture that said 'silence'. He then abruptly turned, ignoring any response from the detectives and walked on through the wrought-iron gates to an awaiting car. The driver acknowledged the priest as he opened the car door for him to sit in the back.

'Inspector?' He called in an abrupt manner, as the side window glided down at the back of the black limousine. 'You're looking in the wrong place! These are good people, this crime has shocked us all, and we need time to grieve. Please leave us alone to heal,' he said closing the window.

'What did you make of that, Mike? A strange way for a priest to react don't you think?' Macgregor said watching the limousine drive off into the main throng of traffic.

'I thought he was very tight-lipped and weird. I hate all fucking priests!' Willoughby spat. 'My brother was abused by one; it did his head in, he's never been right since! And this one's no different to the rest of them.'

Macgregor had no idea about all this. He was a bit taken aback but quickly understood his pal's aversion to the Church. 'I think he knows something, he seemed very cozy with our friend Dr Elliot. Did you notice he had a strange hold over the congregation, I mean, even more than usual? Do you think he allowed the girl to be buried here for any other reason apart from being a devout Catholic?'

'Seeing as the last person to be buried in this hallowed ground was well over fifteen years ago, I'd say that was a big yes!' Willoughby replied.

'They're both hiding something,' said Macgregor. 'I might have to reform and start taking Holy Communion myself! As that old philosopher, Friedrich Nietzsche, is often quoted as saying, "After coming into contact with a religious man I always feel I must wash my hands," and he's not bloody wrong!'

'Well one thing is for sure, we know Ryan Adams is in the vicinity. Why would he show up at the funeral? His uncle is on the run, warrants are out for his arrest, he was taking a huge risk coming today. He must know we'd be looking for him,' Willoughby remarked.

'Perhaps he wants to get caught. You know, the old compulsion to confess.'

Willoughby turned and stared at Macgregor. 'Jesus. You're full of philosophical quotes today!'

Macgregor coughed, still squeezing his left flank from the stitch. 'Or could it be that Ryan Adams loved her, the girl's mother said they had dated when they were younger. Perhaps he wanted to say goodbye. It says a lot to turn up – I can understand him running from us, but why avoid the priest and the parents?'

'Yeah! That says he is bloody guilty,' Willoughby retorted.

'And did you see that flirty smile on Sarah's face?' Macgregor asked. 'You know ... the assistant from the surgery? I caught her eyeing off Elliot. She knows more. I think I'll need to pay that wee lassie a visit; we had a strange conversation yesterday. She said she knew Danielle was pregnant, she started to tell me about another girl ... Kylie, that was her name ... her sister I think, but she stopped mid-sentence, like she'd already said too much.

'I hope the uniforms track him down. I have a lot of questions for the little runt once we get him, and I'm hoping he'll lead us to Gunner,' Macgregor continued, as they made a dash to the Land Cruiser parked on the grass verge, just as another deluge began.

'Come on!' Macgregor said, 'let's get out of this bloody rain!'

CHAPTER TWENTY-EIGHT

Macgregor had received the email from Fowler. He suspected that Dr Panngesh was hiding something but nothing this big. He called Fowler from the Justice Place Police Station and discussed Panngesh's arrest. Codename: 'Taj Mahal'.

The Batemans Bay team would launch a dawn arrest and take him into custody, retrieving and impounding all relevant files and papers from his home and clinic, including his computers and laptop. This was a great result. Fowler had done well. Macgregor thought that it might just be the ticket to get himself back to Sydney.

He recalled how Lorna had tried to speak to him about Dr Panngesh, but in his pig-headedness he had casually dismissed her, his thoughts more aligned to the murder case and prime suspects. He made a mental note to call her later and take her for dinner, to congratulate her on her sleuthing abilities. A smart lassie that one!

He was missing her. He thought of the last night they had spent together. The lovemaking had been intense and passionate; she stirred an emotional response in him, a feeling of belonging; he wanted to feel that way again. The softness of her breasts, the curvature of her rounded buttocks. Her response had been quick, ready and eager to receive him. His arousal was beginning to show; he shuffled in his chair, adjusting his trousers, hoping no one else in the room was watching. Macgregor quickly forced his thoughts back to the reports on his desk and the conversation he had earlier with his sergeant.

He had made it clear to Fowler that Panngesh would be arrested for the charges outlined in the reports sent from the Mumbai commissioner: fraudulently obtaining licenses for medical practice; bribery to obtain false documents; illegally performing surgical procedures and treatments; illegally prescribing and giving medication; and assault.

Macgregor ordered that Panngesh was to be held in custody at Batemans Bay police station.

'He's a slippery fish and we dinnae want him doing a runner, he probably can pay for a big fat lawyer but hopefully the residing magistrate will not grant him bail,' he had said to Fowler. Macgregor had spoken to the local magistrate, who happened to be Fowler's father: Magistrate Hugh Fowler.

The hearing was to be arranged for the following morning in Batemans Bay Magistrates Court. It would then go to Sydney, as charges this serious would need to be dealt with by the Supreme Court.

Macgregor wished he were there to see the doctor's charges read out. He had asked Fowler to follow up on Panngesh's cousin, Dr Patel. A warrant for his arrest had also been issued.

He was sure Panngesh would eventually talk; he was the kind of man that was all out for himself.

'Sell his own bloody grandmother that one!' he mused.

He also asked Fowler to re-interview Ms Roseberry. She would know more than she let on the last time, and would be horrified to be caught up in all this mess. After all, her 'pristine' reputation was at stake.

Macgregor sent an email to his boss, Chief Superintendent Gavin Ross, in Sydney HQ, with reports on the pending arrest of Panngesh, and an update on the progress regarding the Dickson murder case. Ross was putting the pressure on about Gunner's escape; he wanted a result and so far there were no conclusive leads. The farmer's property where Gunner was sighted had been extensively searched with no signs of him. The surrounding bushland had also yielded nothing. Macgregor knew the bastard was hiding nearby. It was only a matter of time before they found him. Like a rat on a sinking ship, he would likely be flushed out soon enough!

Looking up at the whiteboard in the incident room, his two main suspects were Ryan Adams and Dr Patrick Elliot, the vet.

Both men had strong connections to Danielle, both had access to ketamine, the drug that was found in large quantities in Danielle's body. The vet had access to surgical equipment. Ryan Adams could have got hold of surgical equipment from the zoo in the animal medical facility. Red pen circled and arrowed each name on the board back to Danielle's photo.

The vet strongly linked in with CCTV footage, the bus driver's eyewitness account, and his working relationship with the girl, along with his uneasiness and unwillingness at the funeral to discuss matters. And the weird devil worship shit in his house, what the hell was that guy up to?

Or did Ryan Adams get jealous and kill her in some weird sadistic punishment? He had loved her when they were at school! Then there was the strong link with Gunner Adams, Ryan's uncle, and the Skull Brothers. Those connections were also no coincidence, 'And I don't bloody believe in coincidence!' Macgregor spat out loud, causing several uniforms to look up from their workstations.

Neither suspect had been interviewed. Ryan Adams had still not been found, although they were aware he was in the area. Local uniforms had gone back to his family's property at Devil's Hole Reserve, but more questioning and searching had revealed very little; a surveillance team had been in place for over a week without learning anything useful.

Macgregor finished his report quickly as it was almost 3 pm and the desk clerk had called through, telling him Dr Elliot was now in interview room three.

Macgregor grabbed a coffee from the shiny new espresso maker that sat on top of an old desk in the corner of the incident room and headed down. Knocking on the door of Willoughby's office he poked his head around the door. 'You in on this one Mike?' he called. 'The vet, in room three, I'm on my way there now.' Willoughby looked up from his desk. 'I'm sure you don't need me to hold your hand. I've got a lot of stuff to get through. You go ahead, I'll drop by later. Some results have come in from forensics, from Danielle's bag. I'm just going through it now.'

Macgregor acknowledged with a nod and sipped the cappuccino from the steaming, polystyrene cup. 'Let me know if anything interesting comes to light.'

He bounded down the polished wooden stairs, his stomach now growling, burning, the fiery pain building to a crescendo. An eruption of acid raced up the back of his throat; he grabbed the Quickeze from his jacket pocket and chewed, downing the chalky mush with the coffee. 'Christ! It's getting bloody worse' he cursed, reaching the bottom step.

Jasmine Wong, a criminal lawyer, sat with her client in interview room three. Small and slim, intelligent, mid-twenties and ambitious; her long black hair was tied in a neat ponytail with a clip. She was suitably power dressed in a navy blue two-piece suit, sitting with a straight back on the edge of the vinyl, padded chair, looking intently as Macgregor came in to the room.

'Ah! Good afternoon, Ms Wong. I see you have accompanied Dr Elliot, but you know it really wasn't necessary – after all, he is just helping us with our enquiries.' Macgregor pulled a chair out to sit opposite the pair. Macgregor switched on the ERISP machine (the electronic recorded investigation of suspicious person machine). He made it clear that Dr Elliot was accompanied by Ms Wong and that another uniform was in the room. He stated the date and time. He then asked Patrick Elliot to state his name, address, date of birth and occupation. He also made it clear to the vet that he had the right to remain silent but anything he said would be recorded and may be used against him in a court of law.

Elliot, still wearing his formal, black, morning suit, sat solemn and still, his handsome face unmoving, showing little emotion as he stared at Macgregor. Wong unfastened her briefcase and removed a folder; she opened it and addressed Macgregor.

'Chief Inspector, my client and I are deeply concerned at the harassment you showed towards him and his pregnant wife this morning ... at the funeral service of his late employee Danielle Dickson, and wish to make a complaint.' She stood, placing the file on the desk in front of him. 'You were seen harassing my client. We have witnesses.'

Macgregor laughed loudly and stared at Elliot as he bent across the table.

'Is that right, hen?' his Scottish dialect becoming stronger as the colour rose in his cheeks with the frustration that had been simmering in him towards Elliot.

'Well, well, well. Dr Elliot, are you hiding something? You have to bring Ms Wong with you to throw us off your scent? Would it interest you to know that we have CCTV footage that shows a very interesting picture involving a man of your description, driving a black Holden ute – the same car that you drive – on the morning Danielle disappeared? We also have a witness that saw a man fitting your description and vehicle picking Ms Dickson up from the bus station in Trafalgar Street that fateful morning. What do you say to that Dr Elliot? Where were you going with Danielle in that nice new shiny ute?'

Macgregor sat back down opening his own file, deliberately revealing the photos of the murdered girl's body. Wong remained standing, and the small powerhouse launched into another tirade.

'My client is not prepared to answer that or any other

questions. Unless you are going to charge and arrest my client, we will leave now. We would like to make this complaint to your superior, Chief Superintendent Gavin Ross.' Wong retrieved her briefcase and started to put away her file.

'Not yet, Ms Wong. Dr Elliot has some questions to answer and I said he is helping police with their enquiries, he may also be asked to stand in an identity parade so sit back down!' he demanded. He knew what they were both up to.

'My client will not be answering any questions. He has no wish to continue this interview. We wish to lodge this complaint, Chief Inspector!' Wong stood her ground.

Elliot interjected, continuing to stare at the photos now laid out on the desk.

'Jasmine, sit. I have nothing to hide. I'm happy to answer some of the Inspector's questions, but I will not be accused of having anything to do with Danielle's murder,' he said quite calmly.

Frustration showed in Wong's face as she looked at her client. Ready to protest again and slightly embarrassed, she took her cue from her client, remained silent and sat back down.

Macgregor looked up from his desk as Elliot slowly undid his jacket buttons and sat back with his hands clasped on his lap. He quietly asked Wong to take notes.

'So, Dr Elliot, do you admit to being at the bus depot and picking up Danielle Dickson on the morning of her disappearance?' Macgregor began.

Wong rose from her chair. The diminutive dynamo again interrupted.

'Inspector, that is a very leading question and quite intimidating to my client, please desist with this line of questioning.' She was quite flustered and her slight Chinese accent became more pronounced.

Elliot told Wong to sit down again, this time arrogantly pulling her down with his hands as they encircled her slender hips. The colour rose in her cheeks; she was losing confidence and credibility. Frustrated, she sat back down.

Composed, and after quiet reflection, Elliot replied.

'Yes … Chief Inspector I was at the bus depot, I did pick Danielle up. It's not quite what you imagine, she needed a lift, she said she had missed her connection to Canberra and called me to ask for a ride. I said I would take her as I had to pick up some medical supplies from the warehouse in Mitchell. I had already prepared for the trip and everyone knew I was going, she got into my ute but changed her mind within five minutes of driving out of town, I don't know why she changed her mind, she asked me to drop her off near Devil's Hole Reserve, a short distance from her parents' place.'

He remained unemotional and stoically sat unperturbed as Macgregor grinned a humourless grin in response to this answer to his question.

He stood and clapped his hands as if in applause. 'Really, is that the best you can do Dr Elliot? You're an intelligent and sophisticated man; come on! You can do better than that. That's bullshit!'

'Inspector that is what happened and I have nothing more to say on the subject.'

'Dr Elliot, may I ask why you did not reveal any of this when

I came to see you at your surgery? Is it perhaps convenient, now that we have you on CCTV, you need to embellish a nice wee story?' Macgregor was enjoying himself. 'Funny thing is Dr Elliot, it's not looking good for you. The last person to see this girl alive was you!'

Macgregor went on, firing on all cylinders now. 'What did you do to her? Where did you take her? Were you having sexual relations with the girl? Did she reject you Dr Elliot? Not getting any from the missus so hit on the kid eh? Is that how it played out Dr Elliot? How do you suppose her body was washed up on Surfside Beach?' Macgregor was in Rottweiler mode and this bone was juicy ... no way was he going to bury it!

Just as Macgregor was about to take another bite of this arrogant ass, a uniformed officer knocked and without waiting, came in to the room. He bent over and whispered in Macgregor's ear. Macgregor sat back and with a roll of his eyes said, 'Interview suspended at 4:13 pm due to the unforeseen circumstances regarding Dr Elliot's wife who has gone into labour ... and is now in the maternity wing of the hospital.'

He switched off the ERISP machine and with reluctance said, 'Dr Elliot, you can go. Your wife is in labour. We will conclude this interview tomorrow. If you desist, I shall get a warrant for your arrest, given the seriousness of these circumstances.'

For the first time during the interview, Elliot cracked a slight smile, and smirked a 'saved by the bell' glance at Macgregor. Patting Wong on the shoulder, he arrogantly got up and strode over to the door.

'Until tomorrow then, Chief Inspector?' he replied, still smirking. He gave a slight pat on Wong's bottom as he ushered her out the door, with a smarmy, 'Thank you for your help, sweetie.' Wong, embarrassed by Elliot's unwanted gesture, gave a clipped nod of acknowledgement to them both and walked out of the room. Macgregor blew out a long sigh once they had left the room.

'Arrogant, condescending, misogynistic, disrespectful prick.'

CHAPTER TWENTY-NINE

Dubbo RSL stood like a concrete beacon, a lighthouse drawing travellers into its warm and friendly interior. The biting wind had whipped up as Macgregor took the ten minute walk from Justice Place, still seething over Patrick Elliot's timely exit, and his treatment of Jasmine Wong.

'The bastard will be grilled tomorrow,' he said to himself, head down, fighting the wind and drizzle. Dusk was approaching, and with it, the temperature decreased rapidly. Macgregor had planned to meet up with Willoughby at the club and have a friendly game of poker with some locals. He was looking forward to it. Now for a hot shower and some grub. He would let the day fall away, first allowing himself the luxury of a glass of bourbon on the rocks. He made his way into the club and took the entrance to the hotel accommodation on the first floor. Not a very big hotel but it was central and convenient – the ideal place for him in Dubbo to get a bed for the duration of his stay. The newly furbished entrance area smelt of new carpets and paint. He went up the carpeted stairs, reached the corridor and headed towards his room. Room twelve.

Macgregor slid the plastic key card into the slot on the door until the light turned green and quickly pulled it out. It had taken a few times to get the hang of it; several times when he had tried, the light would stay red and he had to call the attendant at the desk for help. 'Bloody stupid things,' he murmured to himself.

He pushed open the door and with a hissing noise, the heavy door closed behind him. Removing his jacket and throwing it on the bed, Macgregor loosened his tie while undoing his shirt buttons.

His room was the standard 'three stars' with a queen bed. A door on the far left-hand corner led to the bathroom. A wood-veneer desk sat on the right when entering the room, with a lamp that had no bulb in it. He threw his briefcase on top of the desk. Knowing he had a lot of reports to write later, he decided he would make a start after the poker game.

An easychair positioned in front of the window gave a view of the main street. The only consolation was the bar fridge, which sat against the far wall under a shiny melamine benchtop. He wandered over, retrieving a glass from the cupboard as he hunched down to open the small fridge door. Macgregor's eye caught a glint of light, shining, reflecting off the surface of the benchtop.

He was suddenly seized with pain as a searing heat caught at his throat. Within a second, the skin on the left side of his neck was punctured as the tip of a large kitchen knife pressed into the flesh. He could smell the reek of halitosis and the overpowering acrid stench of body odour as his assailant dug the blade deeper into his skin tissue. A trickle of warm, sticky blood quickly soaked into Macgregor's white shirt collar. A throaty voice rasped with laughter, 'Got you now, fucker!' Macgregor kept very still, knowing that to move suddenly could be his demise. He tried to see his attacker's face reflected in the blade, but knew all too well who it was …

Gunner Adams held the blade to Macgregor's neck and with the other hand pulled at his hair, yanking his head back, extending and exposing his throat, his Adam's apple bobbing up and down vulnerably. Macgregor, now on his knees, desperately drew breath, pain also coming from his scalp as Gunner pulled hard on the recent scar tissue.

Trying to stay calm, but mentally assessing the possibilities, Macgregor tried to reason with him.

'Where have you been, Gunner?' He gulped, his mouth dry with fear. 'Why don't we have a wee dram eh? I was just going to pour one.' Macgregor knew that to engage him in conversation was probably the only way to stay alive.

'A drink with *you!*' spat Gunner, frothy saliva hitting the side of Macgregor's cheek.

The knife dug harder, tearing into muscle. 'Should of done you in when I had me chance at the fuckin' zoo!' Gunner hissed through a clenched jaw.

Any deeper and he has the carotid artery. I'm a dead man.

'Me fuckin' nephew stopped me!' Just as Macgregor was about to reason again, the resounding shrill and wailing of the bagpipes and drums of 'Scotland the Brave' filled the room as his phone sang out.

Gunner turned, distracted. As he did, the knife moved slightly away from Macgregor's throat. He took his chance, in what seemed an eternity but was less than a second. Macgregor grabbed the handle of a cutlery drawer that sat above the bar fridge. Pulling it open, he rummaged inside, and his fingers fumbled for what seemed an interminable time.

He found the metal-spiral corkscrew – a hangover from the days when most bottles of wine needed one – and in an instant had it snugly secured in the palm of his hand. He launched his right arm backwards, and rammed Gunner in the head, targeting his eye. He missed the target, but the agonising scream from his assailant told him he had hit flesh.

Gunner reeled back, dropping the knife. Macgregor quickly turned; getting up from his knees he looked at his handy work. The corkscrew was firmly embedded into Gunner's right cheek. It hung limply. With an almighty roar Gunner pulled at it, the metal spiral ripping out a large piece of his flesh. Blood poured from the exposed tissues as he yanked and threw the bloody implement to the ground.

Enraged, his eyes bulging, Gunner lunged at Macgregor. With beads of perspiration forming on Gunner's brow, their arms locked in some crazed, savage dance as they circled around the blood-smeared knife below them on the carpeted floor. They kicked at each other in attempts to win the knife, neither one prepared to unlock his grip. It was finally kicked to one side by Macgregor. Gunner's bloody face snarled as he lunged again trying to bite him, his open mouth showing filthy, rotten teeth. Macgregor, using all his strength to keep this madman at bay, raised his left leg, turned his foot so that it entwined around Gunner's knee, and in one final pull had Gunner off balance and crashing to the ground. Macgregor climbed on to Gunner's back; sitting astride he pulled and twisted Gunner's left arm back, seizing him in an arm lock.

Grunting and swearing, in intense pain, Gunner reached and grabbed the corkscrew from the floor using his right hand and in an instant had thrust in into Macgregor's left thigh. This time Macgregor reeled back, crying out in agonising pain as the corkscrew hit bone.

Fuelled with adrenaline, Macgregor made a desperate lunge and grabbed at Gunner, who was now standing. Quickly twisting Gunner's painful left arm again, he managed to secure him in a choke hold. They grappled and moved around the room like this; Gunner's head was locked tightly under Macgregor's arm as it squeezed his throat.

Gunner coughed and spluttered as they staggered towards the ensuite. With an almighty heave, Macgregor rammed Gunner's head into the ceramic bathroom sink. He heard a loud cracking sound. Gunner went limp; Macgregor released his hold and Gunner dropped to the floor.

Macgregor, breathing hard with exhaustion and pain, leaned back against the ensuite door, sick and faint, pressing on his thigh as blood poured from the wound. His left leg was burning, in pain, the corkscrew protruding from his trousers. He picked up a clean towel to form a makeshift dressing around it.

Blood oozed from Gunner's head, forming a red, sticky puddle as he lay still on the tiled floor, spluttering and gagging on his own secretions. Macgregor kicked at him tentatively with his shoe. Gunner remained still, his face turning blue.

'Fuck you, you're not going to die you bastard! I won't let

you!' he gasped, pushing Gunner over onto his left side to prevent him from choking.

Macgregor limped through to the bedroom, holding the bloody towel in place on his thigh. He retrieved his phone from his jacket and dialled triple-O. He fell back onto the bed; his leg burning and throbbing, his head spinning. Backup was on its way ...

CHAPTER THIRTY

t was just after midnight when Macgregor returned to his hotel room. His wounds had been treated at the emergency department. Limping, he climbed the stairs. X-rays and scans had revealed minimal damage to his thigh; he had six sutures, morphine injections for pain, and a large dose of penicillin injected into the area. Tetanus and a further shot of penicillin were given intramuscularly. Bloods were taken for possible cross-contamination looking for hepatitis and other bloodborne infections. His throat was very painful and bruised and a dressing was in place over the puncture wound.

Gunner was not as lucky. A scan yielded a fractured skull; he was unconscious, taken into ICU and placed on a ventilator.

The doctors had induced a coma and were preparing him for surgery to remove a large hematoma causing swelling and pressure on his brain. His prognosis was fifty-fifty, only time and surgery results would increase his chances of survival.

Macgregor had made his statement to Willoughby at the hospital and as there were no other witnesses. The police investigation concluded, as stated by Macgregor, that he was acting in self-defence. Macgregor didn't want Gunner's death on his hands but both agreed it wouldn't be such a bad thing for him to leave this mortal plane. Willoughby had called Chief Superintendent Gavin Ross with the news, and he saw the situation as a good result. Gunner was off the streets. Although Gunner was seriously injured, with an investigation pending, he did not seem overly concerned about his condition.

Uniforms had interviewed the hotel staff at the RSL – a cleaner named Sharon O'Conner had eventually confessed to letting Gunner into Macgregor's room. Shazza, as she liked to be called, had known Gunner before his long stint in Goulburn jail. She had been involved with him in a fiery on-off relationship over several years.

Sharon was in her early forties. She had dyed blonde hair that hung limply from a centre parting, showing dirty brown roots, and framing a face that looked sallow and worn. Still wearing her maroon RSL uniform, she had protested her innocence loudly. She yelled abuse at the uniforms when informed that charges may be laid against her. They accompanied her to the station to make a statement. Once concluded, she continued to yell and abuse the officers while protesting her innocence.

Gunner had made her open the hotel room, threatening to come back and, 'Beat the shit out of me and me fucking kids. He was doin' me fuckin' head in mate,' she wailed.

Willoughby wasn't as convinced of her innocence, as she did have prior convictions of her own, including theft, breaking and entering, and possession of illegal drugs. They held her at the police station for further questioning and possible arrest for aiding and abetting a fugitive.

Macgregor reached his room. The door was slightly open, a strong smell of disinfectant and bleach wafted from the inside. The forensics team had been thorough, had taken photographs, and marked, labelled and removed the knife and corkscrew for evidence, before the hotel staff had done a final clean. Exhausted and aching all over, Macgregor wanted to throw himself on the bed and sleep.

'What an asshole of a day,' he murmured as he went inside.

Closing the door, without switching on the light, he began to take off his clothes and shoes, dropping them to the floor. He had no willpower or strength to hang them up.

He lay back, naked, gently easing his leg into the cool, linen sheets as his head wearily fell back on to the pillows. Breathing out a long sigh, he closed his eyes, about to recount the day's events when a soft, slender hand met his shoulder. He turned, startled.

'What the!'

Isabella Kowowski's beautiful naked body slid over to his side, 'Hello John,' she said sexily tracing the tip of his lips with her well-manicured finger.

'Christ almighty lassie ... you scared the crap out of me! What the hell are you doing in my bed?' he demanded, pulling her hand down away from his face. He reached over to the nightstand and switched on the bedside lamp. The alluring Ms Kowowski, lay temptress-like on her side; long, dark hair fell around her face and shoulders, revealing her beautiful, full breasts. Resting her elbow on the pillow, she pouted, pulling back the sheets.

'John ... don't you want this?' she said in a sultry tone, allowing his eyes to wander over her voluptuous nakedness.

'Isabella, your timing is always way off!' he spluttered, unable to stop gazing at her.

Isabella moved closer, her warm and sensuous touch softly stroking his chest, her fingers making their way down across his abdomen towards his now engorged and growing manhood. She certainly distracted him from the pain he had been feeling from his injuries.

'I see you are happy to see me,' she whispered, grasping him again in her palm and gently kissing him on the lips. Macgregor thought of protesting. It had been a long and horrible day, he really just wanted to be on his own and fall asleep. Her face was inches from his, he could smell Chanel on her skin. Her soft, rounded breasts swayed above his chest, her sweet breath on his lips. She continued to cup, stroke and caress him.

It felt good. He moaned, ready to relinquish and succumb to her powerful sexual hold. He allowed himself the pleasure of her delicious tongue, playfully licking him from his lips down to his full erection.

Testosterone levels were high, and coupled with the powerful painkillers he had been given, he was done with fighting, arguing and struggling, as he responded. Isabella slid on top of his firm erection; striding her long, toned legs either side of him, she rhythmically circled her hips, as powerful contractions pulled him into her, lost in the moment of her intoxication and seduction. His hands grasped her curved and desirable buttocks as he thrust harder and further into her. His moist lips teased at her nipples. Isabella moaned and with a deep sigh released her desire, a gush of orgasmic contractions pulsating through her body.

Macgregor responded moments later with his own powerful release, groaning as he did so.

The ejaculation was forceful, all encompassing. Groaning and gasping, Macgregor lay back, still, exhausted, spent. Isabella lay back down beside him. Neither spoke. Macgregor rolled onto his side and quickly fell into a deep and heavy sleep. Isabella lay quietly, eyes closed as she too, languished in the afterglow of their union. Drifting into the space between dreams and wakefulness, she descended into the realms of sleep.

CHAPTER THIRTY-ONE

'Last call for passengers Kian Balakrishnan and Arjun Chandra, your aircraft has now boarded. Please make your way to gate fifty-one for flight AA7365 to Los Angeles, California.'

The two luxurious, first-class seats were finally occupied. The flight attendant smiled politely to the two Indian gentlemen as they quickly pushed the last of the luggage into the overhead lockers. 'I can help you with that, sir?' the flawlessly groomed blonde smiled as she moved to arrange the baggage in the compartment. She was eager to have all her passengers seated and ready for take-off. The captain was awaiting her final call from air traffic control for the commencement of the flight.

'No, no, that's not necessary.' With a perfectly whitened smile, the impeccably dressed Indian gentleman continued on with the task of squeezing the hand luggage into the small space.

The bulging baggage was finally forced into the tight space as the clunk of the overhead locker door fastened shut. The flight attendant turned smartly and made her way to front of the plane towards the internal phone, giving the all clear to the pilot.

Panngesh sat down calmly and adjusted his seat, clipping his seat belt in place; he glanced to his right and nodded to his companion Patel as they settled in for the long, thirteen-hour flight to Los Angeles.

He closed his eyes as the captain announced their departure, anxious to be underway. The engines began to roar and the plane taxied along the runway. The acceleration increased and the slight shuddering of the lockers stopped suddenly as they made their ascent. Smoothly, the plane rose high above the early evening sky, the sun going down, casting long shadows on the landscape below.

With a long sigh, relaxing more, he gazed down, looking out the window as the Pacific Ocean came into view. Small, white boats appeared to move slowly, leaving white, wispy trails and frothy sea-caps as the plane climbed higher into the darkening sky.

With the seat belt sign turned off, he unclipped his belt, the sumptuousness of first class allowing ample room and comfort. He pressed a button on the console and the footrest popped up. Stretching out, he slipped off his handmade shoes, one at a time.

The smiling flight attendant offered complimentary champagne; he accepted and lay back in the luxurious, navy, leather seat.

As he sipped the fine wine, thoughts of the last twenty-four hours filled his head.

Yesterday morning his world had been complete – the clinic, his patients, his illustrious lifestyle, property, cars and money. Oh yes, the money. Money that had allowed him these first-class seats, money that had allowed him to obtain the forged passports. He had kept them in his safe ready for, and if, the occasion arose when he would need them.

His world had almost been complete. The final icing on the cake – the offer to be on the medical board, a fellowship with the Royal College of Surgeons, a handwritten testimonial from the president, Professor White – all that hard work and grooming for nothing! GONE, in a day.

He fidgeted in his chair, gripping the wine glass tightly as he frowned. They had destroyed him when he had come so close to his dream, those fools, incompetent police. To think some stupid girl's death would bring about all this.

His informant had called him that morning from Mumbai, warning him that the Australian police had been in contact with the Indian Medical Council. They had found out about the forged documents and certificates, and were planning a raid any day soon.

The informant had been well paid, an investment well spent he reassured himself. Money could buy you anything – including people. With very little time to get organised all his papers and documents were still at the surgery. Papers he knew would incriminate him, but he had no choice but to leave, no time to lose. To go back to the surgery would have been catastrophic, with the police waiting for him ... a trap set. The humiliation. The phone calls had been hastily made to the airlines, using the false credit cards and passports, the ones tucked away in his safe for such an occasion. He had called Patel explaining the urgency and danger they were both in, and had told him to leave everything and drive to Sydney International Airport that afternoon.

Police would take months to find out where he had gone – if ever. The pre-prepared suitcase, always packed, ready to go, had sat in his large walk-in wardrobe, the expensive Louis Vuitton signature luggage with the classic logo. He had been diligent, he knew at any time he may need to leave at a moment's notice. Everything had gone like clockwork.

He cunningly had not driven his own car but used a taxi for the long hike to the airport; although he was sad to leave his classic collection of beautiful cars, it was a small price to pay for freedom.

Patel heeded his advice and also had hired a taxi to drive him the two-hour journey down from the Central Coast and meet him at the airport, his own surgical practice left in similar disarray. A faithful cousin and lifelong friend he had always remained loyal to Panngesh.

They had both come out of the dirt and filth of the Dharavi slums in Mumbai. The poorest upbringing had taught them to be streetwise. The sheer tenacity and determination to get out of the slums had taken them on a sordid path; one of corruption, forgery and criminal behaviour. They didn't owe anyone anything, what had society done for them as children? Nothing! It had left them to rot in the stinking filth and squalor of their surroundings. Everyone from his childhood had let him down, taken from him, deprived him; forced him to beg as a toddler on street corners, market places and in railway stations. Small thin bones, big brown eyes, dressed in rags, pleading to passing strangers and tourists for money and food, anyone who would take pity on the small child. His father waiting and hiding, watching eagerly, ready to snatch any offerings given.

Other children were not so lucky. Some children from his slum had had their limbs burnt with battery acid, their eyes gouged from now-hollow sockets – to attract more attention and money from sympathetic people who unable to keep walking past, who are forced to stop and stand in horror at the pathetic sight of these mutilated children before them.

This was the start of his strange and warped fascination with surgery. He remembered watching his own father remove an eye from a small, thin young girl no more than four years old. He had assisted in holding the child down. The screams still haunted him.

One small regret was he had had to leave his prize, model girlfriend behind. She was ignorant of his past so would be of no use to the police, giving nothing away that was of importance. She had been a useful item, a lovely ornament, but that was all. There were many ornaments out there; it wouldn't be hard to find another one.

Los Angeles would give him a new start, a new life indulging the rich and famous, with their never-ending demands for youthfulness. Yes, he would pander to their whims, take the money to start again, he could do it. Beverly Hills and Hollywood. He had enough money to open another clinic, create a lifestyle, find another ornament. His contacts had made arrangements for their safe and secure accommodation in Los Angeles, and a car would be waiting to collect them upon their arrival at LAX.

Timing was everything.

He raised the champagne to his lips and smiled as he sipped the fine, golden liquid.

'Your canapés sir,' smiled the pretty attendant.

CHAPTER THIRTY-TWO

Macgregor's phone vibrated on the nightstand in his hotel room. He awoke suddenly, still caught up in the dream he was having. In the dream he was wrestling a large grey wolf, its ferocious jaws seconds from snapping at his throat. The wolf had suddenly taken on the shape of a large green python, and the huge snake was about to sink its deadly sharp fangs into his neck. Turning quickly, his eyes darted to the phone, still vibrating and buzzing beside him.

It stopped. He let out a yawn, his neck hurt as he raised his head. He pressed his hand on the left side of the tender area; he felt a small dressing in place. Lying back on the pillow his mind raced trying to recall where he was ... the room was in darkness, except for a shard of bright light where the curtains had failed to close properly. His eyes adjusted as he looked around, it began to look familiar, the pain in his thigh jerked his memory banks into a sequence of events.

Gunner – the fight – Gunner's injuries – the hospital – his leg-stitches – PAIN.

His brain then triggered another thought, that of sex, Isabella, was it a dream?

He turned over quickly, the bed was empty, had the strong painkillers conjured up the whole experience?

He pulled the spare pillow over to his side – that was no dream, the lingering smell of perfume met his nostrils as he sniffed and buried his head into it. Recognition hit his senses. Chanel. She always wore that perfume. He sighed and thought about the repercussions this was going to have.

'My God man, what have you done, you stupid idiot?' he muttered to himself thinking how all of this was going to pan out. Yes, he had enjoyed sleeping with her but he knew how Isabella's mind worked. She would use this to get what she wanted from him, and Lorna, oh shit. 'I cannae face all that emotional stuff right now,' he said to himself. He picked up his mobile, and squinting through tired eyes saw five missed calls from Willoughby, he also noted the time. 11:15 am.

'Christ, all bloody mighty!' he said out loud, pulling back the bedclothes and revealing his nakedness – apart from the bandage on his thigh, which now was stiff and throbbing in pain. He had overslept. 'Overslept' being an understatement.

He limped over to the bathroom, clicked on the light switch on the wall, memories flooding his mind, an image of Gunner lying on the tiled floor, throat gurgling, his face turning blue. The pool of sticky blood, some of which had stuck to his shoes, the relief that the man had been caught and the anxiety at the thought of an internal enquiry looming.

He stood a little unsteady and, leaning against the wall, carefully aimed Percy at the porcelain, relieving himself of a very full bladder. Another fleeting thought streaked across his mind.

Operation 'Taj Mahal', the codename given to the dawn raid to take place earlier that morning at Panngesh's residence.

'Bloody hell!' he yelled, finishing and shaking the last few drops into the toilet bowl. He limped back through to the bedroom, clicking on the light switch on the wall as he passed it.

Sitting on the bed he yanked his clothes up from the floor, then stood hobbling, placing one leg in his trousers and trying to balance on the other as he attempted to get dressed. Finally, after some huffing and swearing, he succeeded. He grabbed his jacket and phone and tore out of the door, collecting his briefcase from the desk on the way out.

Macgregor limped down the carpeted stairs of the Dubbo RSL, clutching the phone to his ear. Fifteen messages on message bank.

'SHIT, SHIT, SHIT,' he exclaimed as he limped down one step at a time.

In agony, he headed along the footpath; he remembered he had left the prescribed painkillers in the room – too late to go back. He made his way to the Justice Place Police Station as quickly as he could, cursing most of the way.

Willoughby was in his office sitting at his desk, his large meaty hands clutching at an iPad. Beefy fingers bashed on the light, delicate screen; he too was cursing as he kept hitting the wrong touch keys, his fingers too fat and broad to fit in the small square boxes on the text screen. He was trying to write an email to his chief superintendent. In frustration, he threw the tablet on the desk. He looked up to see Macgregor approaching.

'Nice of you to drop in,' he said sarcastically. Willoughby had re-shaved his head; it had a shine in the centre as Macgregor looked down at him.

'Didn't you get my messages? Don't you bother to read my texts?'

'With your disastrous technique, how could anyone read them?' smirked Macgregor.

Willoughby ignored his comment, letting it slide as there was an element of truth to it.

'I reckoned you'd be late, given the antics from last night. Your leg, how is it by the way? The stitches and all?' Not waiting for a response, he blurted in exasperation. 'Fuck, John, it's nearly lunchtime!'

'Okay, okay, settle. I'm sorry, I had a late night, a late visitor from out of town ... unexpected.' Macgregor stressed the word, eyeballing him. Willoughby picked up the unsubtle clue.

'Wouldn't have anything to do with a certain newspaper would it?' he smiled.

'Miss Isabella Kowowski was here this morning, bright eyed and bushy tailed, glowing, you could say ...'

Macgregor cleared his throat, about to reply when Willoughby went on, 'Have you had a coffee yet?' Macgregor shook his head, still feeling a bit dazed. Willoughby relaxed a little, and standing up from his desk walked through to the main incident room, where he summoned a young uniform to fetch some coffee for Macgregor and himself. He came back and sat down at his desk.

'On a more serious note John, I rang and left several messages telling you that Gunner died at four this morning.' His face remained serious as he spoke.

'You know there will be an enquiry. Ross called earlier.'

'What did the big boss have to say?' Macgregor stared at Willoughby, taking this news in.

'Chief Superintendent Gavin Ross requested a press conference, it went out at six this morning, you were supposed to be there! All the media turned up, it was a fucking feeding frenzy, they were eating it up mate, they want to interview you, knowing your luck they'll turn you into a fucking hero!'

Macgregor sat down, his hand raking through the unbrushed hair, curls tangling in his fingers, still feeling discombobulated from recent events.

'What a bloody mess,' he sighed, and then looking at Willoughby, 'Did you ask the cause of death?'

'I think we both know what that was!' Willoughby spluttered.

'Yeah I know but still – it wasn't some fluky aneurysm or some genetic malfunction?' A crease formed in his brow. He knew as soon as he had said it that he sounded stupid, but he really didn't want to have Gunner's death on his hands. As much as he had hated the man and everything he had stood for, especially that of the 'suitcase murders' twenty years before, their relationship had come the full circle. He had wanted to kill him with every fibre of his body, but the reality was very different, to take a life and have memories of Gunner's grotesque face haunting him.

That, he didn't want ...

Macgregor sat staring out across the room, lost in memories. Twenty years ... he had been so enthusiastic in those days, probably wouldn't have given a second thought if Gunner had died. Willoughby interrupted his musings. 'I think a fucking crack the size of the Grand Canyon through your skull is pretty conclusive, Macca,' he went on, 'however, Ross seemed to be of a mind that you had done the community a service, the parents of the kids he killed twenty years ago were on breakfast television being interviewed this morning, claiming it as a karmic victory!'

CHAPTER THIRTY-THREE

Macgregor sat at his makeshift desk, in the corner at the back of the incident room. He looked up to see a junior female detective writing on the large white incident board; alongside the photo of Gunner Adams she scribbled 'Deceased' and the date with a red marker pen.

Macgregor shook his head, the memory of Gunner's distorted face still fresh in his mind, and went back to making phone calls. The list included calling Fowler, who had earlier left a message telling him that operation 'Taj Mahal' had failed as Panngesh and Patel had absconded.

He also had received several messages to call his boss, Chief Super Gavin Ross. He did not relish the call, knowing he was responsible for the death of Gunner and the failed attempt to apprehend Panngesh. There was also the unsuccessful attempt, so far, of tracking down the elusive, red-haired nephew of Gunner Adams. Ryan Adams was still wanted for questioning in relation to both Danielle Dickson's death and for association with his fugitive uncle.

Macgregor intended to call Jasmine Wong about her

client, Patrick Elliot, to request to have him back in for re-interviewing ... his first attempt yesterday had been cut short with Elliot's exit to the hospital for the birth of his child.

Macgregor's leg still ached. He rubbed his thigh, pressing against the wad of bandages. Gulping down the last of his coffee, his thinking was at last becoming clearer, with rational thought returning as the remnants of the powerful opiates left his system.

The first call he made was to Fowler. He had heard the recorded messages left on his message bank informing him that operation 'Taj Mahal' had been unsuccessful, and implying that Panngesh had absconded.

'Shit, shit, shit,' he muttered, dialing the number of his sergeant.

The phone rang several times before Fowler picked up. 'Fowler?' he barked.

'Sir?'

'Yes, it's me, listen laddie, it's been a hell of a night, I had an uninvited guest, Gunner Adams, he was hiding in my hotel room – let's say he wasn't too happy to see me – he had a knife to my throat, we got into a fight. I finally got the bastard in a headlock, I smashed his head against the bathroom sink, it wasn't pretty, he was unconscious when they took him to the hospital, he dinnae make it, he's dead!'

'Yes. I heard about Gunner, most of us at the station cheered when we got the news, scum like that don't deserve to live. Hope you weren't hurt too badly, sir. Did you get my messages from this morning? I also tried the station but they said you hadn't come in yet.'

'Ach, about this morning. I had intended to call you first thing, I did receive the messages but only heard them a short while ago, Panngesh must have got wind of us. What happened?'

'I don't know how he knew, sir, we had planned to go under cover of dark at three this morning and arrest him, we had the warrants, it was well planned. When we got to the house, the front door was open, not locked; everything seemed to be in its place, his cars parked in the garage. In fact, very little appeared to be missing, perhaps some clothes had been removed from his dresser as the drawer was left open, couple of empty coat hangers lay on the bed, but that was all.

'Oh! And a wall safe was open, but it was empty.'

'Sounds like he had an informant either locally or in India. Ach! Did you put out an all-points bulletin; cover the airports, domestic and international? The ports and docks? Oh, and that lassie, Miss Roseberry from the clinic – did you speak with her? You might want to have her brought in for questioning.

'Fowler ... are you listening?'

'Yes sir, I've already had contact with HQ. Information and photographs of Panngesh have been sent through to airport security, they are aware and informed of his identity, passport control is on high alert and the staff are being extra vigilant at check in.

'Ports and harbour authorities have been contacted, they are checking manifests and passenger lists on cruise ships and commercial ships. Nothing has come back to us yet, sir; no sightings of Panngesh. Unless he's using a false passport, sir, he can't get far.

'When we searched his home and belongings we didn't find any documents or a passport,' Fowler continued. 'We then made our way to the clinic. It was early but everyone was there and waiting for the doctor to arrive. The staff were busy, going about their duties, getting theatre ready and the patients prepped for surgery. No one had a clue as to the doctor's whereabouts or what was going on.

'Miss Roseberry was in shock when I took her into her office and told her about her employer. She did not believe it. She asked us why weren't we out finding him as he was needed for the list that day. I'm interviewing her later today. She had the grim task of informing the staff and the fifteen patients who were waiting, that the clinic and surgery was cancelled until further notice. She told them all to go home.'

'Good work, Fowler. Well we cannae do much more with Panngesh until he resurfaces or is caught trying to leave the country. Listen, once you have interviewed Miss Roseberry can you make tracks up here to Dubbo. There's a couple of leads I want you to follow. I've made a reservation for you at the RSL, it will only be for a couple of days. I still need to find Ryan Adams – you know – Gunner's nephew, the kid from the zoo, he's still around here but no one has flushed him out yet. We saw him at the lassie's funeral, he did a runner, uniforms are on to it. The kid won't be able to hide out for too long, it's a small town. There are a few more people that I want to have a chat with in relation to Danielle's murder, people that knew her.'

Macgregor looked around the room just as Willoughby was heading down the stairs, his stocky frame heavily stomping on each wooden step. Macgregor nodded, a silent gesture that implied, 'I'm on it pal, we'll soon have this case wrapped up and I'll be out of your hair.' The truth was far from it.

So far, he had nothing concrete to go on except for Patrick Elliot's admission of picking up Danielle from the bus station – it wasn't enough to convict him. He also had forensics go over the vet's car with a fine toothcomb. Nothing yet had come to light. One thing was certain however: the impending internal enquiry in relation to Gunner's death.

'Sir?' Fowler had been waiting.

'Sergeant Fowler, I think I've used up a lot of my favours around here, just call me when you get here okay? Before you leave, make sure you write up a full report and email it to me. Oh, and one more thing, have a chat with Panngesh's girlfriend, it shouldn't be too hard for you to find her. Just ask Miss Roseberry.'

'Yes sir. Sir? Talking of girlfriends, Lorna Paterson was in the clinic this morning, she asked after you, she said she hadn't heard from you and that she left messages but had not had a reply. I didn't tell her what had happened, what do you want me to tell her?

'Christ! Fowler, dinnae tell her anything! I cannae have that lassie scampering all over the bloody countryside tending to every cut and scrape. Tell her I'm fine and that I'll call her later today, have you got that?'

Fowler agreed and the phone clicked off.

Thoughts of Isabella stirred in him, flashes of her loveliness and the reality of her ruthlessness in equal measures crossed his mind. How that woman could give so much pleasure and cause so many problems. It would take a lot of careful handling to sort that one out. He felt guilty trying to rationalise his encounter with Isabella but knew he would have some explaining to do with Lorna. He would call her after work.

Macgregor thought about Panngesh and his slippery disappearance. The cunning Indian probably had several passports he could use. If he could get forged doctorates and medical certificates, then he had enough money to pay for high-end fake passports.

Macgregor set about making the next call.

'Good morning Ms Wong, Macgregor here, how are you?'

A silence met him on the other line.

'Ms Wong? Are you there? Can you hear me?' Still silence then a deep sigh.

'Is your client prepared for today? Can you please inform him that I would very much like to re-interview him this afternoon, here at the Justice Place Police Station, at your convenience?' More silence, then Wong's small voice. 'Yes, Detective Inspector. I am here, but as to my client, I am no longer representing him. He is no longer my client. Our association has ceased ... goodbye.'

With that, she abruptly clicked off the phone.

So the prick got to her, I thought she looked pissed off yesterday. Macgregor recalled how demeaning and chauvinistic Elliot had behaved towards the young lawyer. He was about to re-dial her number, then thought better of it – he would call Elliot directly. The arrogant prick would probably want to represent himself.

He dialed Elliot's veterinary surgery.

'The Animal Hospital, Sarah speaking can I help you?'

'Hello Sarah, this is Detective Inspector Macgregor, do you remember me? I would like to speak with your boss, Dr Elliot.'

'Yes Inspector, I do remember you, you got soaked the other day at the funeral,' she giggled, then went on. 'Dr Elliot is at the zoo today, he had to do a C-section on a gorilla, should be back by four, can I take a message?'

'Err, no, Sarah, that's okay, I'll call him on the mobile myself. Perhaps you and I can have a wee chat soon, eh?' Sarah stopped giggling and replied. 'Uh! Why would you want to chat with me? I don't know anything?'

'Oh, I think you might know more than you think, people usually do you know, just a wee chat about Danielle and her friends.'

'Danielle! Oh yeah, okay, well gotta go Inspector, see ya.' With that, she put down the phone.

That wee lassie is a little fountain of knowledge, he thought, looking at the last of the names on his list.

He took a deep breath, dialed the number, and made a final call, the one he least looked forward to doing.

'Chief Superintendent Ross? It's Macgregor.' He waited then heard the familiar Kiwi accent.

'Ah! Macgreegor ...'

CHAPTER THIRTY-FOUR

Cameron Fowler was on the last leg of his journey to Dubbo. The weather had changed from sunny and cool on the South Coast to overcast, and cold inland. Rain had just begun to fall. He had about fifty kilometres to go before he hit the township. He was feeling uncomfortable and stiff from the six-hour drive. His knees ached; he rubbed at them with one hand, the other on the steering wheel. He still had bouts of Osgood Schlatters disease, which he had as a young boy, 'growing pains' as his mum used to say. It gave rise to inflammation and pain in his knees and patella, aching when he went snowboarding or cycling. It was a fine balance he had learnt to live with. He loved his sports and tried not to let it interfere with his activities.

He hadn't stopped for a break on the journey, so decided to pull over for a leg stretch and for the call of nature. He jumped out from his RAV4 and noticed the car was covered in fine red dust. He wiped some of it from the bonnet with his hands, which he then rubbed clean on his jeans. He stared out across the long, flat plains, spreading endlessly out towards the horizon; he undid his fly, had a quick look-around checking for cars and stood next to a tree just off the highway. He had been busting to pee. And as he did so, he heard distant rumbling as thundery clouds rolled in. It would be dark and wet soon. He wanted to get to Dubbo before nightfall and hurriedly shook out the last few drops before redoing his fly.

He didn't want to be in Dubbo; he had a big weekend ahead of him, skydiving with his mates, and a party to go to on Saturday night. His girlfriend Hannah was on holiday with her friends in Bali for a week and he intended to let his hair down while she was away. Macgregor had screwed all that up for him. Although, if he could get the job done quickly, whatever it was that Macgregor had planned, he might make it back for the party. The skydiving would have to be cancelled; he made a mental note to call his buddy.

Friday friggin' night in Dubbo with the boss, he thought, sighing. What could be more boring?

He gulped at some water from the bottle sitting in the cup holder, turned the ignition and drove off. The day had been a long one; up before dawn for the early morning – unsuccessful – raid on Panngesh. Then the afternoon had weighed heavily with interviews and reports that had taken quite some time to write. Still, he had managed to grab an hour's sleep before the drive.

'What a day,' he yawned, rubbing at his eyes. 'Dubbo 22km' read the sign as he drove past. The rain was now coming down like stair rods; the warmth of the car's heater and the steady rhythm of his windscreen wipers were lulling him into a sleepy state he found hard to shake off. He knew all about microsleeps and how, in a second, you could career onto the other side of the road, head on into oncoming traffic; he had watched the video training sessions many times but had not actually experienced it for himself, up until now.

Turning off the heater and shaking himself awake, he opened all the windows of the car. A sharp, cold lash of rain hit his face; he held his head out of the window, allowing the downpour to wash over him. The cold air made him catch his breath. It did the trick. He felt more awake and energised. Leaving the front windows of the car open allowed the cold, icy, wet wind to blow through, hitting hard against his face. His mind turned back to the afternoon's events.

Alison Roseberry, Panngesh's efficient personal assistant, had returned to Batemans Bay police station in the early part of the afternoon, although he had hardly recognised her as he walked past her waiting in the foyer.

Her long blonde hair was loose, and gone were the Prada heels and tight-fitting, expensive two-piece. She wore a white t-shirt, warm top and tracksuit pants. Her make-up had been removed and she looked older and plainer.

Her eyes were red-rimmed; it was obvious she had been crying all day. She held a box of tissues as she was ushered through to the interview room and sat down in front of Fowler.

Still shocked that her boss, Dr Panngesh, had deceived her, and the entire staff, of his shady and murky past, when she had been so loyal and dutiful – she started to cry. Her car payments on the BMW alone were horrendous. 'Where am I going to get another job?' she wailed, blowing her nose into a wad of tissues. 'It isn't so easy in this small town,' she croaked again, clearly devastated that she'd lost the one job that could support the extravagant lifestyle she had become accustomed to. 'Oh, I'm finished!' she sobbed. 'Is it going to be in the newspapers?' With this thought resonating in her mind, she burst into more tears. 'Who would want to employ me after all this!'

She's obviously not concerned about her boss or any other member of staff, Fowler thought, rubbing his chin, and trying to get a word in. Every time he had tried to answer her questions, she had interrupted and wailed into her tissues; thinking solely of herself and her own circumstances, and how it would affect her standing within the community.

Fowler had tried to reassure her that he would try to keep her name out of the press. But it wouldn't be easy.

He surmised that she did in fact not know anything about her former employer's shady past and history. She was way more concerned with herself and her own future.

Getting nowhere, he concluded the interview. He stood to make his way to the door, handing her his card and saying to her that if she did have anything worth telling him to get in contact with him or the police station. She had snatched the card as he led her out to the main desk; she again burst into a flood of tears. She quickly put on some dark, Ray-Ban sunglasses. With her head bowed, she looked agitated as she ran out to the car park to her pristine, black BMW, and drove off. Fowler shook his head at the memory. What a drama queen! She was obviously well matched with Panngesh, like two peas in a pod those two, he thought as he drove the last few kilometres through the rain.

When he eventually contacted Panngesh's girlfriend, it was pretty much the same story and response; a lot of crying, only this time she had complained about who was going to make the payments on her penthouse apartment in town. Fowler had heard enough and decided to send a couple of uniforms to get a statement from her at her home. He couldn't take anymore crying from these prima donnas. He rounded the bend into the car park of the RSL club and spotted the hotel entrance. He parked the car and turned off the engine, then made the call to Macgregor.

'Sir? It's me, I'm here, just drove into the car park,' he said, reaching over to grab his grey duffel coat from the back seat. The rain still beat down heavily on the car roof and windscreen.

'Come on up, laddie, you're in room ten next door to me. Get your key and I'll meet you in the bar in twenty minutes, okay?'

'Yep, see you soon.' He tried to sound cheerful at the prospect of spending an evening with his boss.

'Great! That's all I need, Friday night boozing with Macgregor.'

CHAPTER THIRTY-FIVE

Macgregor was waiting downstairs in the smaller, quieter bar of the club, sitting in a tub chair, one of four, around a small round table at the back of the room, next to a large glass wall. The view looked out to an enclosed courtyard where smokers could take long drags on their preferred brand before heading back into the club. The annex was heavy with smoke and when the electronic doors opened, wafts of it would come through into the bar. It wasn't the best of views. He could still hear the incessant noise and constant bells, whistles and jingles coming from the array of gaming machines standing in rows lined up in the adjoining room.

He sipped at his drink, bourbon, swirling the glass in one hand. Refusing ice, he had asked the bartender to make it a double shot. He held his mobile phone in the other hand, thinking about the conversation he had just had with Lorna. Still upset about the Gunner incident she pleaded with him to let her come to Dubbo to take care of him. With a lot of persuasion, he had managed to placate her fears and reassure her that all was well. Apart from a sore leg and a nick to his neck – he was fine. He put the phone down and rubbed at his painful thigh soothingly. He had just taken two painkillers with a swig of his bourbon. Christ, that's all he needed, Lorna and Isabella head-to-head, coming to blows. He was aware that Isabella was still in town, and after their last, albeit exciting, encounter, he did not need any more dramas. He had carefully avoided her throughout the day. Six messages had been left on his phone, but he had neither answered nor replied to her requests. She wanted the scoop, an interview with him about the incident with Gunner. He was unsure where she was staying but hoped she wouldn't appear tonight in his bed. Not with his sergeant here.

He was glad that Fowler was coming. It gave him more credibility to have his own man on the team. He could also get him to do things without a lot of questions. He didn't have to explain, unlike the mob at Justice Place.

Early diners were making their way through to the Chinese restaurant within the club; chilli and garlic aromas permeated the room and Macgregor's stomach rumbled. 'Aye, I'll have a wee bite later with the laddie and bring him up to speed on the case,' he mumbled to himself. He remembered how much he liked Fowler; he had a good rapport with the lad even if his daddy was the local wig. He chuckled. He would make a good detective one day, but he wouldn't want the lad to get too big for his size tens.

Aye the laddie was smart no doubt about that.

Speaking of the devil, he waved as Fowler walked through into the bar area, wearing a navy woollen sweater and black jeans, anxiously looking around. He quickly spotted Macgregor sitting alone in the corner against the glass wall. A smile beamed across the good-looking young man's face as he walked over to where his boss sat.

'What are you having, laddie?' Macgregor asked, rising from the snug chair and heading towards the bar, the glass in his hand now empty, his phone placed on top of the table always aware he was still on the job.

'I'll have a Jack and coke, thanks, sir.' Fowler replied, pulling the heavy chair out to get his long legs in more comfortably at the table.

Macgregor got the drinks and sat back down, they clinked their glasses. 'Slange var,' said Macgregor. 'You hungry laddie? I've booked us a table here, hope you like Chinese, it's too bloody wet and cold to go looking for anything else around here, not that we'd find much anyway.'

Fowler nodded, he could eat anything right now – he could eat a horse the way his appetite was. They made their way through to the restaurant. The tables were in smart, uniform rows, with white linen table cloths, and neat place settings with chopsticks set against small red bowls. Brightly coloured, red and gold lanterns hung from wires strung across the walls. Traditional Chinese music shrilled in the background, and the place was filling fast as groups of locals headed to empty tables. The waitress wore traditional Chinese dress, and she politely showed them to their table.

Macgregor ordered the sweet and sour pork, Fowler the honey chicken; they had spring rolls to start and both chose to drink beer with their food.

Fowler was scooping up the last few grains of rice, feeling

a lot more human when Macgregor changed the conversation from cars, girlfriends and women in general, to work.

Macgregor brought Fowler up to speed with what was happening. Gunner's demise, and the impending enquiry into his death. Gunner's nephew, Ryan Adams, and his disappearance. He also spoke about the vet, Patrick Elliot, and his demeaning attitude to his very clever and sharp lawyer, Jasmine Wong, and about her sudden change of attitude. The strange collection of artifacts at Elliot's home, his pregnant wife, and subsequent delivery of the newborn. He went over the first interview he had with Elliot, and the witness from the bus company and his account of events. Macgregor then told him of the strange funeral service conducted by the obnoxious priest, Father Christopher Harding-Pierce.

'So laddie, tomorrow I want you to go and have a wee chat with a girl called Sarah Vincent. She works for Elliot at the animal hospital. Find out what you can about Danielle; Sarah knows a lot more than she's let on. I think she might open up a bit to you, with that handsome face, what lassie could refuse, eh?'

Fowler winced but knew Macgregor was probably right, his youthful appearance and manner had in the past allowed him to relate more with the young female offenders. He often had them eating out of his hands. Macgregor was old, crusty and grumpy, way too intimidating and scary for young people, which had its positive effects as well as negative ones. Fowler himself was a little afraid of the burly Scotsman, who could be very fierce at times.

'She'll no doubt be at the surgery with that elusive, arrogant

Dr Elliot. The prick keeps stalling his interviews with me. I tried to call him just before you got here, not answering as usual ... well enough is enough, tomorrow I will have that interview if I have to drag him there myself,' he said, downing the last of his beer. 'Another for you, laddie?' He raised his glass to get the attention of the waitress.

'No thanks sir, I'm good, I think I might hit the sack, it's been a long day.' Yawning, Fowler was unsure how Macgregor would take the refusal to drink with him. It was Macgregor's fourth beer – on top of a couple of bourbons – and to Fowler's amazement, he still appeared sober.

Macgregor shrugged his shoulders and put the beer glass down on the table, shaking his head to the approaching waitress. 'Fair enough,' he said, as both men stood and made their way from the restaurant to the foyer, then towards the entrance to the stairs and their rooms. They climbed the stairs, Macgregor wincing, every muscle in his leg ached with each step.

'Goodnight, sir, see you in the morning.'

'Aye laddie, breakfast at seven,' Macgregor replied abruptly as he slid the key card into the door and the burring green light clicked on.

He went inside, locking the door behind him as he loosened his collar and removed his jacket, yawning he lay on the bed and quickly fell asleep.

CHAPTER THIRTY-SIX

Cameron Fowler skipped breakfast. He'd decided against having another meal with his boss; last night was enough for him. Macgregor could be quite overbearing at times and they had little – if anything – in common apart from work. Most of the polite conversation had been taken up the night before. He made an early start and headed out to interview Sarah Vincent, Elliot's assistant. Macgregor had given him the address.

From what he had gathered, she was a bit of a manipulator and had been unkind in her statements about her colleague Danielle regarding their time working together at the animal hospital. Macgregor thought she knew more than she had let on, being very cagey in her responses when questioned; and she had also made some comments to Macgregor about knowing Danielle was pregnant but had failed to give any more details. Macgregor was suspicious and wanted all the information Fowler could pry from her. He knew he had hit a wall and she had clammed up, which is why he requested his sergeant to do this interview. He ran his hand through his fair hair. He hoped his good looks, affable personality and youth might get her to open up.

Fowler desperately wanted to regain recognition and success after the last failure regarding the futile raid and arrest of Panngesh and his cousin Patel.

The fact that they were long gone and had probably left the country by now had frustrated him; nothing had come back from HQ regarding any sighting of the two men. He was this close to having achieved a major conviction and was feeling deflated. The opportunity to shine and shore up a few brownie points were his if he could have a breakthrough on this murder case. It would boost his reputation and confidence.

The flat was in Church Street, not far from his hotel and he decided to walk the five minutes or so. Rugged up in his thick grey duffel coat, a bright tartan scarf pulled up around his face, he breathed hard in the cold morning air. His hands were tucked snugly into his pockets, staving off the biting wind. It was really cold; he never knew winter was so cold this far out west.

Sarah's flat was above a group of shops not far from Justice Place Police Station. There was a laundrette directly below her place and it was open at this early hour, barely 7 am.

Large bulky dryers turned in unison, joined by the droning, mechanical whirring and thumping sounds coming from the washing machines; their users sat on hard, wooden, bench seats, watching in a glazed semi-hypnotic state. One younger guy stood leaning against a dryer, rocking backward and forward with a single earpiece in place, hooked up to his phone. He mouthed incomprehensible words to a beat with his silent song, as he tapped his foot on the tiled floor. He was wearing pyjamas with a cord pulled around his middle over a t-shirt; a long, fleecy, dressing gown trailing around oversized; and dark brown, furry Ugg boots. A thick, woollen, rainbow-coloured beanie covered his long, blonde, limp, dreadlocks which were tangled among dangling pompoms. Gee, you wouldn't see that too often, Fowler thought, giving a nod of recognition through the window. Condensation dribbled like rain down the large windowpane from the warmth of the dryers hitting the cold glass.

He knew the feeling. Many times before he had been in that same position, getting in early before the crowds; with all the wet weather recently it was impossible to dry anything. He smiled, thinking of the lovely, shiny, new washer-dryer he had bought a few months ago. How easy it was now: get up, load the machine, set it to what you needed and leave. Warm, dry clothes ready when you got home. He never worried about ironing, his mum used to do it all, so now he just hung his shirts on a hanger and the warmth of his body pulled out any creases.

Fowler walked past the other shops – an accountant, a real-estate agent, Vinnie's store – the charity shops were popping up all over town due to the increased rents business owners were having to fork out. They were all closed at this early hour as he quickly made his way to the rear of the building. He climbed the dozen or so concrete stairs and walked along the semi-enclosed verandah.

Number three wasn't too far along; there were only eight doors, all facing outwards, overlooking the back of the building onto the car park. The door to Sarah's flat was purple, a very dark purple, and leaning against the wall stood a weary looking bicycle with a flat front tyre and a wicker basket over the handlebars. He checked the door and could only find a broken buzzer on the doorframe. With frozen and numb fingers, he pushed the rubber knob protruding through the broken plastic cover and waited.

Fowler could hear the sounds of the radio or TV coming from within. He waited and then pushed the buzzer again. Still no answer, so he knocked firmly and called her name.

Sarah Vincent came to the door, opening it slightly, with bleary eyes, drowned in a wash of black mascara and eyeliner. She squinted and looked him up and down, 'What, uh, who are you?' she croaked, obviously worse for wear. Possibly from the night before, thought Fowler. Her voice was raspy as she coughed and cleared her throat.

'Hi, Sarah Vincent? I'm Sergeant Fowler. I've come to ask you some questions in relation to your colleague Danielle. Is this a bad time?'

Sarah, suspicious of any one calling at this ungodly time, gave him the once over. Fowler pulled his tartan scarf down from his face and flashed his handsome smile. His damp blonde hair clung to his forehead. He looked more like a movie star than a policeman; his girlfriend Hannah often said he was the spitting image of Chris Hemsworth, famed for his role as the comic hero, Thor.

Sarah liked what she saw and immediately tried to pull her own hair into some semblance of order, pushing it back from her face, while rubbing beneath her eyes with a licked finger in an attempt to remove last night's make-up with saliva.

'Can I come in please, Sarah?' he said, showing his ID.

She glanced at it momentarily, then opened the door. 'Oh yes, please, do come in,' she said with sudden, forced formality, showing him into her small living room as she put out her hand to offer him a seat.

'Give me five will you, make yourself at home, I'm late already and need to get dressed.' She hastily retreated through the heavy beaded curtain hanging in the doorframe leading to another room.

Fowler entered the small living room. It was warm and he could feel the radiating heat coming from an oil heater in the centre of the room. He looked for a chair and was left to chance his fate with either a half-filled, red beanbag ensemble propped up against the wall or a broken-down sofa that had seen better days. He chose the sofa. He sat down and quickly sank back into it as his weight pulled him down into the centre. The springs had gone and not much was keeping it together. He looked around the room, pulling himself forward to regain a more comfortable position. A small, flat screen TV played the ABC's Rage program, an eclectic mix of hit songs and accompanying videos from the last three decades. He had forgotten it was Saturday morning; he often watched Rage himself. There was a small CD player on a coffee table over on one wall, next to a large oval mirror with lots of beads strung around it. A pile of clothes lay neatly in a corner. He gazed around the walls and noticed several posters; dark, moody images of werewolves, skeletons, skulls, headless corpses and bloodsucking vampires. He winced.

He remembered Hannah had been into the whole Bella and

the Twilight theme; many younger and some older women loved the Twilight movies. The rivalry between the vampire, Edward and Jacob, the werewolf ... how he had sat through hours of the ongoing saga, the endless debates as to who Bella would end up with.

Thank God Hannah has moved on from all that! he mused. The small bookcase to the side of him held some well-thumbed, dog-eared romance novels and magazines; there was a copy of *Witchcraft Monthly* nestled among a collection of lipsticks and hair clips. The room smelt heavily of incense, Nag Champa if he wasn't mistaken. He remembered his friend Justin used the same one.

Whoa this is a bit random he thought, thumbing through the Witchcraft Monthly. The front cover showed the face of a beautiful girl, an illuminating crystal ball in her hand, her hair in braids with a wicker crown adorned with flowers. The special feature depicted in this month's issue was 'Covens to Crypts'.

Ten minutes or so had passed when he reached for his laptop and notebook, which lay on the other side of the sofa, as Sarah came back into the room. She had changed into her work gear, a pink tunic top covered with images of caricature puppies. Her face was now free from the black panda eyes and make-up, and her hair had been pulled back into a neat ponytail. Cameron had to look twice as she took on a completely different appearance – young, fresh-faced, with large innocent-looking eyes.

Oh, how we are deceived by looks, he thought, smiling flirtatiously at her.

For the first time in the last few days, Macgregor had felt

good about getting up and going to work. Today is the day! You prick Elliot! He spoke to the craggy reflection in the bathroom mirror as he continued shaving. He was going to nail the bastard, he was also pleased to have Fowler here working with him, on his side, it made him feel more in control.

Renewed energy and anticipation grew with each scrape as the sharp blade shaved away his greying stubble. He carefully avoided the scabby puncture wound on his neck.

He would drag Elliot's skinny, tanned arse back to the station and go for the jugular. Fowler can follow up with the assistant Sarah Vincent and the uniforms should have some feedback on Ryan Adams and his whereabouts by now. So many loose ends, he tutted, lots to do. He winked at the aging face staring back at him.

Dressed, wearing a new, crisp, white shirt, Macgregor headed down to breakfast. As he approached the dining room, he became aware that Fowler wasn't at the allocated breakfast table. The small Chinese waitress welcomed him, showing him to his table. A pot of hot, freshly brewed coffee was waiting for him, the sweet smell filling his nostrils as he pulled out the chair and sat down.

'I'll give the laddie a call,' he muttered to himself, then thought more about it. Maybe not, he was dead beat after that big drive coming here, aye and he did have that night time raid to deal with. More contemplation followed as he poured the steaming coffee. 'Ach well, let the laddie sleep in, I'll give him a call in an hour.' Rubbing his hands together, he prepared to home in on the coffee just as another waitress brought a large plate towards him. The Big Brekkie: a plate loaded with bacon, eggs, sausages, hash browns, tomatoes, mushrooms and two chunks of thickly sliced toast oozing with melting butter.

Ah just what I needed. He tucked in ravenously.

With an empty plate and his belly full, Macgregor stretched back in the chair, getting more comfortable as he eased his belt out a notch, eager now to look at the morning newspaper. He scanned it quickly, the front page, a full page image of the murdered little girls, golden-haired angels, smiling sweetly, holding hands in front of a Christmas tree. In one corner of the paper a small insert picture of Gunner, slashed across the photo in bold lettering, 'THE MONSTER IS DEAD!' Turning over to the article the subheadings read, 'Happy but still not satisfied with the justice system'. There was a quote from the murdered girls' parents and questions being asked, 'How did Gunner escape from a maximum-security prison?' Macgregor had asked that himself and believed that Gunner must have had an insider helping him. HQ had still not released details to either the press or the public.

Well ... they probably had but only to the higher echelons of the police division, he thought. *I'm certainly not in that club!* With nothing concrete to go on, the press had made up their own assumptions by creating diagrams of potential escape routes and other possibilities as to how Gunner got out of Goulburn Correctional Centre. The press were hungry and desperate for information. Isabella would be out for blood today Macgregor mused, turning the page. *I'd better keep a low profile.*

He continued reading: more Dubbo dramas, domestic violence, break-ins and car thefts.

'Lucky to be Alive': a house fire with an elderly man found unconscious. He had gone to bed leaving on an old electric bar heater; it had fallen over and caught fire, setting his bedclothes alight.

Boring, boring, boring. Nothing shedding any new insights for Macgregor. He closed the paper and stood up. His stomach was now feeling the impact of the Big Brekkie, rebelling against the large intake. He let out one large belch; he self-consciously covered his mouth with a serviette and looked around but the place was empty. He should have taken his antacids before breakfast.

Damn it! I'll suffer all day now!

Willoughby was in his office as Macgregor approached. 'And where is boy wonder?' he chuckled, seeing Macgregor on his own.

'Aye well, the laddie was tired, just cutting him a bit of slack, he did have that early raid in the Bay. You ken what these young guns are like, sleep all day if you let them.'

Willoughby laughed, thinking of his own twin boys at home. They slept until lunchtime, sometimes longer, if Hilary didn't go in to wake them up. Macgregor undid his overcoat, shaking off some of the light drizzle he had encountered leaving the warmth of the RSL. The water drops hit the floor as he hung the coat up to dry on the stand in the corner.

'You want coffee?' Willoughby asked sipping from a polystyrene cup, noticing Macgregor rubbing his hands together, trying to instigate warmth into his cold, blanched fingers.

'Ach no, not at the moment thanks,' he said as another belch raced up the back of his throat, quickly closing his mouth as he tried to constrain it. His chest jerked in response as he swallowed hard. 'Well, what's new?' he asked, opening his briefcase and retrieving files.

Willoughby had his computer screen open and brought up an email. He opened it, reading aloud the senders' names: 'Aviation Intelligence, the Australian Security Intelligence Organisation and the Australian Federal Police Agency.'

Macgregor listened intently, brows furrowed. Willoughby began to read the email giving Macgregor the gist of it.

'Intelligence officers had been closely observing CCTV at Canberra and Sydney airports of all outgoing passengers. They were looking for the two men fitting the description given by Macgregor's team, that of ... Panngesh and Patel. Working from the time frame given by Fowler they had found nothing. However, they decided to backtrack and look through previous tapes, painstakingly sitting through reams of CCTV footage, nearly nine hours of it, checking all passengers fitting the profile. When, bingo – up pops two characters running very late to gate 51 in Sydney for a first-class seat to Los Angeles. They were spotted leaving more than seven hours before the raid. When they checked the passenger list the names came up as possibly the two fugitives.

'Kian Balakrishnan and Arjun Chandra. Quite creative weren't they!' Rolling his eyes, Willoughby went on.

'So anyway, they were almost halfway to LA, when your sergeant was barging his way into Panngesh's house. Seemingly, they had got through check-in with forged passports, admittedly very good forgeries, but the visa security numbers did not correspond with passenger names or passport numbers. The alert didn't show up in the system until they had arrived at their destination at LAX and by then, it was too late, as they'd left the airport.'

Macgregor took a deep breath and sighed, 'Fuck it! The bastard got away, I hope the LAPD are on to them. So have you heard any more?'

'Not yet, mind you they could have got on another plane, be in another state, driven anywhere, all we can do is wait and see what our Californian brothers come back with.'

Willoughby closed the email, smiled and went on to say, 'On another note, Ryan Adams was seen buying a pizza last night at Domino's. It's along Amy Lane in town. They have security cameras in the shop. The delivery guy was setting out to pack his scooter with pizzas when in walks Adams just after 10 pm – the red hair caught his eye. There is footage of him in the shop waiting for his Meatlovers!

'The pizza guy didn't do anything about it until this morning. He had been watching TV when the morning newsfeed showed our police plea, with our very upstanding Chief Super Gavin Ross in full regalia, requesting anyone with information to come forward or call Crime Stoppers. They had photos of Adams, I guess the red hair jogged his memory.'

'Didn't think he would be too far away, have uniforms gone out?' Macgregor interjected.

'Yes they're doorknocking again, someone must know something. They'll squeal eventually. He was getting a bit cocky going out in public like that. Well. He can't hide forever.' Macgregor bundled his work under his arm and made his way to the incident room and sat at his makeshift desk. Looking at the whiteboard, it hadn't improved. Nothing new had been added.

He turned on his laptop to check his emails.

He re-read the one that Willoughby had just discussed. Nothing he could do about that but wait.

One email from Isabella, very formally asking for an interview; that day, at his convenience. No way, *José*. Forensics had come back with some information from Danielle's overnight bag. They had found a very waterlogged, A4 sheet of paper lodged at the base of the bag, typed on in red ink. The damage was quite bad and the forensic team was in the process of deciphering it.

He scanned through a lot of updates, internal staff meetings, nothing worth reading. He decided to catch up with the more pressing matters of phone calls.

Macgregor called Fowler first and waited as the call went unanswered, straight to message bank. He left a message for him to call him back, telling him that he was at Justice Place but would be leaving soon to go and re-interview Elliot. He gave instructions for him to go to the animal hospital and have a chat with Elliot's assistant Sarah, assuming that the lad was still sleeping and hadn't been up and about. If she wasn't working then to track her down and interview her.

His next call was to Elliot's mobile, no answer there either; he decided not to leave a message. He would go and find him, then accompany him back to the station for more questioning. This time the prick wouldn't get out of it.

No baby, whether primip or primate, would stop him this time!

An email came through. The preliminaries to the enquiry into Gunner's death would be held in Sydney next week, a meeting with the big wigs and the coroner.

Dreading doing it, he started preparing the report for his boss on Gunner's demise. With the hearing next week he really needed to get it up to speed, but it was a pain of a report and he really didn't feel in the mood. Ross had been breathing down his neck about the whole messy business and wanted it all tidied up and neatly packaged. Macgregor checked his watch. By the time he had finished, it was nearly lunchtime; he tried Fowler's mobile again, still no answer.

Christ all bloody mighty where is that laddie? He called the RSL hotel. The front desk answered and informed him that housekeeping had already been in to clean Fowler's room and there was no one in it. Macgregor asked them to look for Fowler's RAV4 in the car park; a few moments later the desk assistant came back. 'No sir, no RAV4 in the car park.'

'Fuck it, that's all I need! Well I hope the laddie is out doing some bloody work!' he grumbled.

His leg ached from sitting for so long and it was feeling very stiff. He decided to go out, grab a sandwich and get some fresh air. His mind had been on the Dicksons and he wondered how they were doing. He was thinking of paying them a visit. He had referred them to grief counsellors as he knew they were taking their daughter's tragic death very badly, especially Mr Dickson. Danielle was their shining light in a somewhat gloomy existence; all their hopes and dreams had been for this very loved daughter. It made him feel more determined than ever to find her killer. The visit to them would ignite the fire to fuel the anger he already felt towards Dr Patrick Elliot. Firing on all cylinders he would then pay the arrogant vet a visit.

Macgregor's mobile shrilled just as he was putting his overcoat on, 'About bloody time, Fowler' he said, talking to his phone. The caller ID was a private number – not Fowler.

'Err, hello Chief Inspector Macgregor.' He recognised the accent of the small, nervous voice speaking quietly into the phone.

'Chief Inspector, it's Jasmine Wong, I, I have something to tell you, I think you should be aware of my previous client's activities ...'

CHAPTER THIRTY-SEVEN

The drive from the Dicksons gave him time to think. He was shocked once again by the appearance of the middle-aged couple, they now looked so much older. Both were struggling, living day to day on autopilot, only just getting through. They pleaded with sunken, dull eyes; had any arrests had been made? Macgregor didn't want to give any false hope, and never did, but on this occasion he felt he needed to offer some comfort, some glimmer of hope that the police were on track to find the person responsible for their daughter's brutal murder.

Macgregor sighed, thinking how he might react in the same position. He knew he would be completely devastated, totally lost if anything happened to his boys – well, they were men now – but all the same, a son is always your boy no matter how old he is. He knew he would be angry and reckless once his emotions had let loose if any one of his boys had been attacked in such a brutal manner.

His mind wandered to the unusual call from Jasmine Wong. She had been uneasy when she called him, but had wanted to make Macgregor aware of some of Elliot's 'peculiar activities'.

He had asked her what she meant; she was slow and uneasy to open up about her previous client and hesitated before speaking. Wong had wanted to get back at Elliot, that was obvious, smear his reputation and bring him down, following his humiliating and demeaning attitude to her at the police station interview. Macgregor listened intently as she divulged the information.

Wong explained that she had heard about Elliot's involvement in a very private and select group that held regular secret meetings. She knew there were other prominent local people involved. She wouldn't say who they were but said cryptically, look to the Devil's Hole!

In frustration, Macgregor racked his brains. Okay, every piece of information that he had, that in any way related to that place: Devil's Hole Reserve.

Gunner had killed two little girls twenty years ago, putting their tiny bodies in a suitcase that had floated down the Macquarie River. The same river that ran alongside Devil's Hole Reserve. Gunner had lived on a property nearby.

Elliot's house, The Old Presbytery, wasn't too far from there. Elliot had said that he'd dropped Danielle off at Devil's Hole Reserve in the last interview, he said she requested to be dropped off, not long after he'd picked her up from the bus station in town on the day she went missing. The red-haired Ryan Adams, an old boyfriend of Danielle's, had close family connections to Gunner. The family lived in a ramshackle property not far from the reserve.

It all appeared so transparent, yet he was unable to make any further connections, Macgregor rubbed at his forehead.

What the hell was missing here? What is the connection? Uniforms had come back empty-handed after several, thorough searches had been made at the reserve that comprised a large clearing and a picnic ground in bush style parkland that backed onto the river.

He placed both hands back on the steering wheel as he pulled up and parked on the grassy verge outside the front of the animal hospital. Macgregor switched off the engine, got out of the car, and walked over to the entrance. The surgery was closed. Macgregor wanted to make sure that Elliot wasn't there before he ventured out towards the zoo. The sign on the door gave an alternative number to call in case of emergency, the name of a veterinary surgeon that lived locally. 'Coincidences. Huh … I don't think so. My gut's never wrong!' Macgregor said aloud, still trying to work out the connection to Devil's Hole. He got back into the car and started the engine, driving off from the verge onto the road, passing the signs to the zoo and turning onto the Obley Road. Pulling into the main entrance of the zoo, Macgregor parked the Land Cruiser and looked out of the window into the car park. Once again, it was nearly closing time. With the sun setting, darkness was falling quickly. Macgregor's memory of his last visit here stirred responses in him, flashbacks; he flinched, with clenched fists gripping at the steering wheel. His mind triggered memories, recalling the pain from Gunner's violent blow to the back of his head. The eeriness of the place in the darkness, the cry of the howler monkeys, the feeling of impending doom. He shook himself as he took a deep breath. 'Well, not this time!'

Thinking rationally knowing Gunner was dead, anxiety and

fear were still plaguing his mind. The thought that someone might be waiting and watching him gave rise to a heightened awareness of any threats or movements around him.

Getting out of the car, the shrilling, shrieking, eerie sounds of the animals again alarmed him, rattling his already jangled nerves. He had never suffered from anxiety, but now his heart beat faster, his breathing quickened. He could feel the adrenaline rush as he quickly made his way to the main office by the entrance gates. Relieved to be inside the warm room, he breathed a huge sigh. Unaware that he had been holding his breath, he turned to speak to the pimple-faced attendant behind the information desk. Pimple Face answered his enquiry regarding the vet's whereabouts with, 'Dr Elliot finished hours ago and hasn't been back all day.' Macgregor thanked him without further questioning.

Back in the safety of the Land Cruiser, he tried calling Fowler once more ... still no response.

That's not like the laddie, not to call me back, he's usually very prompt and keen to let me know what he's been up to, he thought. It didn't sit well with Macgregor; his mind searched for all possible reasons as to why the sergeant was not contactable, by phone or at the hotel. No one had seen him at Justice Place either. He grabbed his phone and made a call to the desk sergeant back at the police station, checking for updates from Fowler. No one had seen or heard from him. Macgregor asked for a patrol car to go out and look for his sergeant and his RAV4.

He reassured himself, thinking it was probably something very trivial. Fowler's phone was lost or broken; he had missed connections or been playing phone tag. Pushing these thoughts to one side he thought about Patrick Elliot, the arrogant bastard was told to be available. Where the hell was he?

Driving back on the highway, Macgregor turned on the radio for some distraction. A familiar song came through the speaker; the gravelled, whiskey laden voice of Buddy Baxter's lyrics filled the car. The bluesy singer was finishing the last chorus:

Deep down in the Devil's hole
Sinners burn
Deep down in the Devil's hole
Oh dear Lord come and save my soul
Once you've made that fatal deal
Oh dear Lord there ain't time to heal
Sinners burn!

That's the same song I heard before, Macgregor realised. *Hearing it twice in a week, that's odd!*

He strained, listening intently while turning the volume up, waiting for the DJ to say who had requested it. The program was run by the local community. He missed the name, the DJ only referencing the request as from 'our regular caller'. Another song came on and Macgregor turned the volume back down. The distraction had caused him to miss the turning to the town and he found himself in the direction of Elliot's house. At least all bases would be covered if he paid a visit to the vet's home.

He turned into the driveway to the Old Presbytery. The

gargoyles and the looming dark structure gave an even more haunting look, devoid of lights to illuminate the inside. Macgregor remembered that Elliot's wife was in hospital with the new baby. He could see that no one was home and didn't want to hang around this mausoleum. He turned his car around and headed back onto the highway.

It was very dark now and as the lights in the town came on, his thoughts came back to Fowler. Where the hell is he? Why hadn't he checked in? No response from the station either.

Another attempt at Fowler's phone – still no answer. Macgregor's internal alarm switched to 'ON' and his stomach knotted inside.

He called Dubbo RSL again and got them to check the room and the car park. Still no sign of Fowler.

He went back to Justice Place. It was almost 7 pm and Willoughby was about to leave the building, having just shrugged on his thick overcoat, when Macgregor arrived. 'You look like shit mate!' Willoughby said, looking concerned, 'Look like you just lost your wallet.' He laughed, trying to force a smile from the dour-faced Scotsman.

Macgregor looked serious, with a furrowed brow, clearing his throat.

'It's Fowler. He's missing!'

CHAPTER THIRTY-EIGHT

Macgregor woke up suddenly, the shrilling ringtone of 'Scotland the Brave' bagpipe music coming from his phone. It vibrated its way along the bedside cabinet. He reached out, grasping for it, just as it toppled to the floor and fell silent. The beeping sound instantly alerted him to a text message left by the caller. He rolled onto his side and with his outstretched arm, fumbled and groped around the base of the cabinet until he retrieved the damn thing. He'd had a restless night, not getting any sleep until the wee hours, on constant alert for any new updates on his missing sergeant.

Missed call: he scrolled to messages, a text from Willoughby.

He sat bolt upright, rubbed his eyes, looked again at the screen ... re-read the text and started to rationalise what he was reading, What the ...

'John you better get here now! Looks like another murder!'

Macgregor's brain was in high gear, in tandem with the speed at which he tore along the Newell Highway. The road was quiet this early on a Sunday morning as he headed for the location given to him; he could see the patrol cars in the distance, lights flashing red-blue. Other vehicles were parked along the side of the road including the white mortuary van, easily recognisable with its tinted black windows.

Macgregor felt anxious, the God-awful fear that the body discovered could be Fowler. His acid reflux was in full throttle, burning an already inflamed oesophagus as it violently erupted from an empty stomach. Willoughby had not disclosed any other details. Macgregor slowed down as he neared the crime scene and parked alongside Willoughby's Subaru.

Macgregor's Land Cruiser leaned in towards the embankment; the road was slippery, wet and muddy. Police cordon tape flapped around in the wind, as a white plastic tent was being erected around the body. The forensic pathology team had arrived and a local GP was kneeling inside the tent, presumably certifying the body. Road closures on the side of the road were being set out and uniforms blocked either end with their cars.

Long pale toes were the first thing Macgregor saw– he did not want to look any further. This might be his sergeant. He then forced his gaze past the yellowish feet; he saw the long, sallow, lean legs of a male with minimal muscle bulk; he then continued to look further up the cold naked torso.

The narrow-frame shoulders gave an indication of an older male. Macgregor took a deep breath and gazed upon the head, a face he recognised ...

The gaping, waxy mouth and balding skull were features of a man he knew.

It was Bryan Johnston. The cabinetmaker and handyman. Macgregor had been playing poker with him for the last eight months. Not since that last game had he seen or heard from him.

Macgregor's brain tried to make sense of this, the relief that it wasn't Fowler, the confusion of seeing this man like this. His brain didn't compute.

'What the hell is Bryan Johnston doing here in Dubbo? Lying naked in a ditch?'

The forensic pathologist, Douglas Solomon, broke the inspector's concentration.

'Ah Macgregor, nice to see you again, they called me in. I happened to be in the vicinity, my brother owns a farm just outside of town – we always have 'Christmas in July' together,' he said jovially. Solomon, who was wearing white overalls and blue latex gloves, went on.

'As we are looking at a similar MO to our Lady of the Bay, I thought it prudent to be,' he paused, attempting a concerned smile as he pushed his glasses up onto his nose, 'here for the initial forensic assessment.'

Macgregor, still stunned and trying to make sense of the situation, turned to Solomon.

'What do you mean similar MO?'

Solomon nodded to his assistant, who carefully turned the body over. Solomon bent down onto his knees; with medical forceps he gently opened an incision about ten centimetres long, directly over the left kidney area, pointing out that the kidney had been removed. With his gloved hands he then moved lower down the back of the body and pulled Bryan Johnston's flabby buttocks apart, at the same time requesting his assistant to shine a torch over the area. He then carefully removed from the anal canal two dismembered testicles with the long toothed forceps. Macgregor had failed to notice that they were missing when he had first looked at the body.

'Jesus Christ, what the hell!' Macgregor spluttered. He almost lost his footing as he reeled back.

He felt nauseous with acid reflux, the lack of sleep and trepidation of the possibility that the body was Cameron Fowler's. And now this. He took a deep breath and swallowed back the acrid bile rising in the back of his throat, trying hard not to vomit. He turned his head away from the shocking scene before him.

Solomon stood up, beckoning his assistant to come over as he dangled the fecal-covered flesh from the forceps in the air. The assistant untwisted the cap of a specimen jar and, using the long forceps, Solomon tapped at the edge of the container as the gnarled hairy skin and flesh plopped into the formalin solution. He raised the container to look on as the two testicles floated around in harmony with the swirling motion.

'When I say similar, I mean both the deceased in question have ligature marks around the throat, in keeping with strangulation as well as the removal of the left kidney. If you observe the genital region, you will see no bruising is present indicating that when the testicles were removed blood had stopped flowing, meaning life had ceased.'

Macgregor couldn't help but stare at the mutilated genitalia.

Solomon went on to explain in his usual know-it-all manner. 'This chap has been dead for at least ten hours. Rigor mortis is still present and the lividity would be consistent within that time frame. There would have been significant bruising and blood loss if he were alive at the time of removal of the kidney, but no bruising, meaning it was removed after death. I'll have these findings concluded at the autopsy, but I'm sure we'll also find large quantities of ketamine in the blood stream. There is also a small puncture wound within the right cubital fossa, that's where the ketamine may have been injected or infused.'

Solomon tapped the container, with a smug look on his face. 'We'll see,' he chirped, talking to the floating testicles.

Willoughby entered the tent. He had seen Macgregor's car pull up but had been on the phone to HQ and his boss, Superintendent Gavin Ross, updating him of the situation. He pulled Macgregor aside.

'Macca, you look like death, come out get some air.'

Formalin fumes had filled the small tent. Macgregor had gone from a shade of deathly white to a sickly green.

Willoughby grabbed at Macgregor's arm and pulled him out from the stifling, noxious atmosphere.

Macgregor took a deep breath, getting some colour back into his face. Several deep breaths later, with disbelief, he spoke.

'I knew him, Mike. I played poker with him, remember I told you about the poker cronies that I meet up with once a month, well he's one of them!'

'You're sure? What's his name? More importantly, why is he here if he lives in the Bay?'

'His name is Bryan Johnston, he's retired, he's in his late sixties, he does a lot of handy man jobs in the Bay, he used to be a cabinetmaker. I just cannae fathom what the hell he is doing here? This far from the Bay, lying in a fucking ditch with his balls up his arse!'

Willoughby snorted a suppressed laugh and then apologised.

'Sorry mate, it's just a bit funny the way you came out with that!'

Macgregor rubbed his hands through his unruly hair, sighed, still feeling relieved that it hadn't been his sergeant in the ditch.

'Christ all bloody mighty.' Staring back at Willoughby. 'I mean, I knew the man, but we weren't that close, we talked poker strategies – what the hell are we dealing with here, Mike?'

Willoughby climbed up the muddy bank of the ditch. Once on terra firma he held out his hand to Macgregor and pulled him up. They stood looking down on the activities in and around the white tent.

'Who found the body?'

'Cyclist riding past, training for one of those bloody triathlons, he set out at dawn and stopped a few metres away to pull out a stick that got caught in his wheel. He's been all shook up since he came across the body. He called us straight away. An officer that was just heading into the station picked up the call and came out. That's him over there.' Willoughby motioned to the cyclist, now hunched over sitting on the side of the road as the constable in front of him finalised his statement.

Both men walked along the edge of the embankment. 'Still no sign of Fowler ... Mike, I'm worried, I asked the kid to be here, what the hell is going on? His father is on his way here, he's our local magistrate. What am I going to tell him? What a fucking mess!'

Willoughby patted his mate on the back. 'Come on mate, let's get back to the station, there might be some news on Fowler. At least this wasn't him,' he said, nodding at the white tent.

Macgregor looked on as a gurney was carefully wheeled down the steep embankment. One of the forensic team zipped up the black plastic body bag before it was lifted onto the stretcher.

Macgregor climbed into the Land Cruiser, and looked on at the scene unfolding before him. A cluster of black crows were circling and hovering above. The small beady eyes furtively watching, waiting …

CHAPTER THIRTY-NINE

'They found him!' Willoughby put the receiver down hard, he had been in the incident room briefing his team when the call came through from the desk sergeant.

Macgregor stopped doodling on the small Post-it notes in front of him. All his neurons snapped back into consciousness as he raised his eyes, waiting for Willoughby to elaborate.

Willoughby picked up on the glare and quickly responded.

'They have Ryan Adams in interview room two, uniforms picked him up twenty minutes ago. Seen loitering around the graveyard at St Mary's church.'

A cheer rang out from the rest of Willoughby's team. Macgregor stayed silent, and stared at his colleague grimly. For a second he thought that Fowler had been found; all day he had been on edge, adrenaline pumping with every chirrup of a mobile or landline phone.

Macgregor let out a deep sigh and stood up, making his way to the stairs.

'You coming, Mike?' More of a command than a question.

Willoughby nodded in recognition as he quickly finished

briefing his team, a renewed enthusiasm now filling the room.

Ryan Adams sat awkwardly in the chair with his head down, wearing a black tracksuit that looked too big for his slight frame. He appeared thinner and smaller than when they had last seen him on the day of Danielle's funeral in the church graveyard. A dirty, white, Nike t-shirt hung from bony shoulders; worn, muddy trainers tapped nervously on the tiled floor. The hood of his jacket was down, revealing a mass of tangled, red hair. He looked tired and anxious as Macgregor and Willoughby entered the small interview room. A female officer had given Adams a can of coke and as he sat, his right knee shook vigorously, knocking against the leg of the table.

Adams gulped from the can of coke too quickly and spilt some of the contents down his front and onto the table as the two detectives approached him.

'I ain't done nuthin,' he blurted. 'I hid because of me fuckin' nutjob uncle,' he declared, watching them warily.

Macgregor and Willoughby pulled out two chairs that were sitting in front of the table and sat directly in front of Adams. They remained silent.

'I had to hide, didn't I? Now he's dead ... I, I, can tell yous.'

Macgregor sat in silence, directing his gaze at the young man's face.

Willoughby spoke first, reaching for the ERISP recorder, his big meaty fingers fumbling to press the button, cursing as he eventually switched it on. He cleared his throat and in a loud and abrupt tone spoke into the machine detailing the date, time and those present within the interview room.

Macgregor broke his silence as he pulled his chair forwards

towards the table. Leaning on his elbows, he looked directly at the youngster.

'Okay Ryan, can I call you Ryan? Or do you have a nickname laddie?' Adams looked up, knee still jiggling and shook his head 'Na, I'm just Ryan to me mates.'

Macgregor smiled and nodded in agreement. Soft tactics. 'You were a good friend of Danielle's, right?' Adams glared back. Macgregor could sense in the boy's eyes a look that said 'no, more than that'.

'Take your time Ryan, tell us what you know about Danielle and the last time you saw her eh?' He spoke softly to the boy, his lilting Scottish brogue soothing. The good cop to Willoughby's bad cop.

The two detectives sat listening as Adams explained how on the day Danielle went missing, he had been walking along the Newell Highway not far from his own home. He was heading into town when, 'I seen a black ute pull over on the other side of the road.' He had recognised Danielle as she got out from the ute. Adams went on to tell them that the bloke driving the ute had got out from his side to lift a bag from the back. The bloke handed her the bag but had held onto her arm tightly as he pulled her close to him and kissed her. Adams had watched as the bloke looked like he was pleading with her to get back in the car. She had pulled away from him and continued walking, carrying her bag over her shoulder as she headed towards Devil's Hole Reserve. When asked if he recognised the bloke, Adams said he hadn't; he was also unable to remember the ute's number plate. He said he had been on the 'bong' the night before and was stoned that morning.

Adams said he had called out to her as he crossed the highway; she had turned and upon seeing him had waved but continued walking. The bloke had driven off, so Adams ran up to her and asked where she was going, and if he could help her by carrying the bag. She stopped, looked at him said, 'You'll never understand! Ryan, leave me alone, I have to meet a friend and I'm late,' and continued walking.

Adams at this point stopped recalling the event, stayed silent, and looked pensive as he stared at the wall behind the detectives. Then, as if a spell had been broken, he turned to Macgregor as a large tear rolled down his cheek.

'So, this friend, did she give a name, Ryan?' Macgregor continued on, not wanting to break eye contact with him. Another tear rolled down his sallow cheek. The boy had cracked; no wonder, thought Macgregor. He's been hiding, living rough, no money, deserted his job, an appalling lack of support from a criminal family, and a bastard of an uncle that wouldn't think twice about killing him.

Adams sniffed, wiping away the tears with the back of his sleeve, his voice cracking with emotion and sadness. 'Na, she didn't say, just that she was meetin' someone and didn't have time for a chat.'

Adams continued to look directly at Macgregor, avoiding Willoughby's stare. He cleared his throat and sniffed again.

'She looked happy but, you know, like she was excited like, and she looked really hot.'

Willoughby interrupted. 'Okay, enough of this bloody Hallmark moment, did you fucking kill her? What was it, Adams – jealousy get the better of you? Had to have her one more time! Couldn't stand another man touching her! We know you two were an item.' The detective spat, glaring at the slightly built young man in front of him.

Willoughby leaned forward, his large frame dominating the table, his presence intimidating. Just as he and Macgregor had planned on the way to the interview room.

'I never touched her, she was me fuckin' angel! I loved her!' he screeched, as a huge sob burst from his throat and tears flowed freely down his cheeks.

Macgregor took his turn at the pantomime playing out before them.

'Okay Ryan, here ye go laddie.' He handed him a wad of tissues. Macgregor had given the nod to the female uniform to retrieve the box from the shelf.

'Is that the last time you saw Danielle, that morning on the highway?'

Adams nodded, blowing his nose hard into the tissue, red-rimmed eyes welling up again.

'Then why didn't you come forward and tell us, why run from the funeral when you saw us there?'

'I wanted to say goodbye to her, tell her I loved her, and that I was sorry that I hadn't been there to protect her. I had to find the fuckin' bastard what had done her in!

'I never touched her, I hid because of me fuckin' shithead uncle, if he hadn't fucked things up! I was scared.' He swallowed hard, unsuccessfully holding back the emotion that was engulfing him.

'What the fuck happened at the zoo Adams? Or is that another bloody tear-jerker story as well?' Willoughby interrupted, delivering the next line of the production.

'I didn't do nuthin'. I told ya, me fuckin' uncle came to the zoo to find me, I was shit scared. I had no idea he had done a runner from jail – he was mad like, he had that look in his eye, like he was gonna kill someone. If it hadn't been for me, your mate here would be pushing up fuckin' daisies!' He blew his nose harder into the tissues.

'I got there just in fuckin' time, I'm tellin' ya, I pulled the fuckin' branch outta his hands, he was gonna kill ya, he wanted me to help him, like, escape you know? I gave him all me cash I had, he threatened to hurt me if I went to the cops, so I ran an' hid from him too. I had to, he's a fuckin' nutcase. He would've bashed me fuckin' brains in.'

Adams took a breath and wiped his face with his sleeve again.

'Now he's dead, I wanted to tell yous, but it looked bad, like I was guilty or somat.'

'You gave us the fucking run around! Do you know how much time, money and resources we have used tracking your skinny arse down? Wasting our fucking time!' Willoughby shouted, saliva hitting Adams in the face.

Adams sat very still, exhausted, shoulders hunched. The battle lost, he felt defeated but at the same time relieved. Now he was safe, free from running and hiding any more; he let out a long sigh.

'What happens now?' he said quietly, directing the question to Macgregor.

Macgregor picked up the phone.

'It's Macgregor, in interview room two, can you organise a

lunch for the laddie in here? Aye, room two, and by the way, send in a uniform to take the statement from him, thank you sergeant.'

CHAPTER FORTY

He opened his eyes narrowly ... it hurt to open them. It felt like sharp spikes were sticking out from each socket, scratching the surface of the lids as he blinked. Through blurred vision, he glanced at the shadows dancing around in front of him. The shadows rose and fell, animated puppets in some grotesque caricature landscape.

Strange wailing and singing came from these shadows, high pitched and indecipherable sounds. The back of his head throbbed as he tried to move, but he couldn't, he was stuck. It felt like concrete was weighing him down, trapping his legs. Legs that failed to cooperate to the commands of the brain's neurotransmitters, synaptic failure.

What is happening?

He remembered a dream he had like this, trying to run from some evil force but couldn't move, as if paralysed. The harder he had tried to run, the more he was unable to do so, his legs embedded in heavy stone, cold as marble.

Images came to mind of a hypnotist, a show he had watched on television, a volunteer from the audience had gone on to the stage. At some point during the show, a particular song was played and the poor sap would quickly obey a command that had been given earlier by the hypnotist. Although appearing to be awake, he was still completely under the influence of hypnosis. Unable to move and literally being glued to the spot, his legs firmly stuck to the floor, as the audience roared with laughter. The volunteer ridiculed for the audience's amusement and entertainment.

With this strange sensation of heaviness in his legs Fowler thought maybe he too was in the show.

He tried to sit himself upright as the heaviness overwhelmed his body.

I can't move, why is it impossible for me to move?

Fowler's thoughts quickly tried to detangle the situation.

Panic crept in as he asked himself, Where am I? Why can't I move? Am I asleep?

No ...

The pain in his head told him he was very much awake. The painful, bleary vision and feelings of detachment to the real world made him think perhaps he had been in an accident.

No ...

He sensed he wasn't in his car, no engine sounds or gasoline smells, or the familiarity of his car.

He tried calling out.

Help!

His mind gave the command but his mouth did not open, he was unable to control or coordinate any movement, his vocal cords desperately trying to form the words, but still no sound came. Complete silence.

Drool slowly dribbled from the side of his mouth as he attempted to swallow, his throat parched and irritated.

Move, move, move! he signalled to his brain, willing his arm by his side to move but still nothing happened, the cold numbness remained.

Again he opened his eyes, pushing back the pain, trying to see through the bleariness. Where was he?

The darkness was interrupted by soft amber glow and the dancing shadows.

Panic and fear took hold as adrenaline quickly flooded his veins. The sudden realisation of where he was and what it meant. Impending doom trickled like an icy finger down his spine, sparking the synapses of each vertebral neurone into action, but still the heavy limbs and muscles lay motionless.

His heart beat wildly in his chest and his breathing quickened, coming in deep gasping sighs as sheer terror replaced the dream-like state.

A faint whimper came from his raw and painful throat as he lay against hard, cold stone.

The shadows continued to dance and shriek as his eyes rose and fell with the silhouettes. Slowly his eyes closed as his mind lapsed back to the deep unconscious abyss, where he had desperately struggled to gain control.

CHAPTER FORTY-ONE

Monday morning. Macgregor had been anxiously sitting at his desk at the Justice Place police station since 6 am. He was extremely tired; he had little to no sleep the previous night. The dark-coloured, heavy bags under his bloodshot eyes told their own story. Coffee had been his only nourishment that morning. His stomach was now on overdrive with the constant fire-dance leaping up and down his already inflamed oesophagus. Acid flames were reaping havoc on the delicate membranes and lining of his gut as he waited for news of his sergeant's whereabouts. Patrol cars had been out all night searching, combing the area, as uniforms went door-to-door knocking within a twenty-kilometre radius. It had been established that the last known sighting of Cameron Fowler was at the Dubbo RSL hotel. There was still no news of his sergeant and nothing else had been reported.

Macgregor waited for the arrival of Fowler's father. The magistrate had driven without stopping from Batemans Bay and had come directly to the Justice Place. He had left from

Batemans Bay courthouse once the information about his missing son had reached him.

Willoughby led Magistrate Henry Fowler through to the incident room. Introductions were politely made as Fowler sat down at the desk in front of Macgregor. Willoughby had been bringing him up to date with all the relevant information pertaining to his son's disappearance and the case. Fowler held a steaming coffee and placed it on the desk in front of him, untouched.

Willoughby gave a nod and a wink to Macgregor behind the magistrate's back as if to say, 'Well, I'll leave you to it then,' and without saying anything, turned and walked towards his office.

Macgregor had worried about the meeting, it's never easy when a person goes missing but more so when it's a colleague close to you in your everyday working life. It was difficult dealing and speaking with anxious relatives and he was unsure as to how it would go. He had never had a discussion with his sergeant about the position his father held in the local community. Macgregor was unsure about how the man would react or how he felt about him – as a detective, never mind as a man. Macgregor had had little contact with the magistrate back at the Bay apart from the usual police procedural work, but never in a social capacity.

For the first time in a very long while, Macgregor felt unsure of himself, in unchartered waters. Overwhelmed by the situation, obligated to speak with Fowler to reassure him, to tell him that everything possible was being done to find his son.

That feeling he was responsible. That he had failed his

sergeant, that he had failed as a boss, as a mentor, and in some ways, as a father.

Fowler wore a look of weariness and anxiety as he sat in front of Macgregor. His face also showed great love and concern for his son and, as one father to another, Macgregor could understand his pain. Macgregor relaxed a little. Henry Fowler was similar in age to Macgregor, fifty-ish, and with a full head of thick, grey hair. He was tall and although heavy-set he didn't have the paunch belly of most middle-aged men. His normally formal attire had been replaced with casual jeans and a navy sweater. He carried a black raincoat over his arm which he hung over the arm of the chair.

Macgregor found Fowler to be a humble, courteous and respectful man. The articulate and softly spoken magistrate listened intently to what Macgregor had to say, his hands twisting and untwisting the belt of his raincoat as it hung over the arm of the chair. Most magistrates he had had dealings with in the past had been arrogant and rude. This man in front of him was just another anxious and distressed father as Macgregor relayed the circumstances leading up to his son's disappearance.

During the interview, a phone call came through for Macgregor. He politely excused himself to Fowler as he took the call, listening intently to the person on the other end of the line. Macgregor didn't say much. With the occasional 'Aye' and 'I see' he scribbled some notes on some paper in front of him. He ended the call, thanking the caller. It was information regarding CCTV footage that had been collected from within the CBD area at a traffic lights intersection. Macgregor sat back in his chair took a deep breath, and looked at the magistrate.

'It's your son, sir. They have CCTV footage of him in his car at the traffic lights at the intersection just off Argyle Street, from Saturday morning. They are formatting the footage and it's being scanned and emailed, they are sending it through now.'

He waited for a reaction from the magistrate. Henry Fowler sat, not saying anything. He looked dazed, lost in some hazy dream.

Macgregor stood and suggested that they both go through to Willoughby's office and view the footage and pictures in more privacy.

Henry Fowler remained seated, still discombobulated as Macgregor stood by the doorway waiting for him.

'Sir, this way sir, please.' He raised his right arm suggesting he follow him.

Fowler quickly snapped into awareness. 'Yes. Yes of course,' he replied quietly, leaving his coat and coffee behind as he stood and followed Macgregor though to Willoughby's office.

Willoughby had asked a uniform to fetch another chair and the three men sat, squeezed together, their backs to the wall behind Willoughby's desk. Willoughby opened the email and several attachments and quickly the black and white grainy images of the traffic lights at the intersection on Argyle Street came into view. Frame by frame they watched as vehicles slowed, stopped and waited for the lights to change. The footage had been marked with the time of Cameron Fowler's sighting.

The three men watched as Fowler's car came into view.

The familiar RAV4 pulled up to the lights, he was in front of a minivan that was slowing down behind him. The time was 08:07 on Saturday morning.

The image was grainy and dark with the looming dark clouds as rain lashed across the screen.

A uniform interrupted the men and Willoughby snapped. 'Yes, what is it?' His impatience was getting the better of him. He felt uncomfortable in the middle of the two other men. He liked his space.

The young constable answered. 'Sir, sorry sir, it's the photographs that were requested, I've come straight from the lab, I was told to bring this directly to you, sir.'

Willoughby moved forward from his chair, his knee touching Macgregor's leg as he snatched the large white envelope out from the young constable's hand.

Macgregor interjected, 'Thank you, laddie.'

He was acutely aware that they had the magistrate with them. Willoughby had failed to remember.

The envelope was hastily opened as Willoughby's meaty fingers fumbled then pulled out several enlarged images, pictures taken from the footage that was still playing out on the screen. One picture showed a clearer image of Cameron Fowler behind the wheel, approaching the traffic lights and next to him, a female, recognisable by her hairstyle, a neat ponytail, as she glanced sideways out the car window.

Macgregor stared at the image. 'I know her. Sarah Vincent. Dr Patrick Elliot's assistant from the animal hospital. Fowler was told to go and interview her on Saturday morning.' The pieces slid quickly into place as he excitedly said, 'He must have left before breakfast that morning, he didnae show at the restaurant and I was there at seven, he must have gone straight out to interview her.'

He stood up, making his way around the chairs, heading to the door and out of the office. 'Where are you going, John?' Willoughby asked as he stood, with a look that said, 'And what do I do with him?' His head tilted towards Henry Fowler.

'I'm going to find my sergeant, that wee madam, and track that bloody vet down!'

CHAPTER FORTY-TWO

'Uniforms came back with information on Bryan Johnston, he had been working as a driver for the Western Plains Zoo, going between here and the coast to Mogo Zoo for the last few months. He had apparently made quite a few trips to the coast, delivering supplies and exchanging equipment. He drove a white transit van, we haven't found it yet but uniforms are onto it. Oh, and Douglas Solomon called, He said that the autopsy showed that Johnston's body was full of ketamine and his left kidney, like Danielle's, had been removed, as well as his testicles, as you would remember.' Willoughby cleared his throat at the gruelling memory of the man's hairy testicles floating around in the jar of formalin.

'Solomon suggests it's probably from a satanic ritual, a sacrifice, both victims with the same MO, both with the left kidney missing. Why his balls were removed he wasn't sure, he said he had researched similar cases in the US, some satanic nut jobs over there. Well it's that, or we have a fucking serial killer!'

Willoughby had received the call from Solomon just as Macgregor had raced out from Justice Place that morning.

'Oh, and another thing – the forensics mob came back with some interesting results on the soggy paper found in Danielle's overnight bag. Mate, it's very weird, there are all sorts of rules and rituals for a satanic mob that must meet somewhere around here, but you need to read it for yourself. There's also a connection with the zoo, Bryan Johnston, the vet and Danielle, and possibly that girl Sarah Vincent. I have my sergeant and a patrol car at the zoo with a warrant to search right now. Where are you?'

Macgregor was on the Newell Highway not far from Patrick Elliot's house and not far from Devil's Hole Reserve. He had pulled over to the side of the road; it was foggy and getting darker, the sky heavy with dark grey clouds.

'I went to Elliot's surgery, it was all locked up as expected. Arrogant prick has gone AWOL. I'm on my way to his house, his wife must be home by now. Uniforms went to the hospital earlier looking for him but the staff said his wife had already been discharged. Elliot would have to be home with her. I also went to Sarah Vincent's residence, she wasn't there. The place was locked up, her bicycle was outside the front door with a flat tyre. I'm thinking she asked Fowler for a lift, to take her to work at the animal hospital, maybe even to the zoo ... with the flat tyre and the weather it's not hard to put two and two together. Fowler must have gone there early Saturday morning, the time line works with the CCTV footage.'

'We have a warrant for Patrick Elliot's arrest, a patrol car is out looking for him. John, don't go alone! There are some weird fucks out there,' Willoughby said, concern in his voice for his friend.

Macgregor's mind switched gears, 'What exactly was on the

paper from forensics?' His stomach grumbled as he belched, an internal inferno in a state of eruption. He wished now that he had stopped for a bite to eat, to soothe the flames.

'Too hard to explain, a whole lot of devil worship stuff. When are you getting back to the station?' Willoughby asked.

'I'm not coming back until I find Fowler!'

Macgregor finished the call – at last they were getting somewhere. He put down his phone; it flashed 'Low signal' then went blank. He picked it up, pressing the buttons and keypad, nothing, still blank. 'Fuck it! Bloody weather!' He threw the phone down onto the seat next to him. He was thinking about Bryan Johnston as he pulled into the muddy driveway of Patrick Elliot's gloomy house. The place looked empty. *Poor fucking sod, what the hell did you get into, Bryan?* His mind was recalling several poker games he had played with the dour-looking man. Always thought he had no balls when it came to making the best call on the cards.

He parked the car and got out, the muddy path still holding large puddles of blood-red water.

He walked up to the imposing stone entrance. The boots and umbrellas sat in the same place as he remembered, along with the snarling gargoyle shoe-scraper. He lifted the large doorknocker and let it land heavily against the wooden door. The vibration and noise echoed within the vestibule. He lifted it again and hit the door harder this time; no noise from within, no wailing of a newborn. Silence, empty.

He stood back, took a few paces to the left, and peered through the large, front bay window. Through the heavily draped facade, he could see the gloomy room he had recently been in when interviewing Jill Elliot. The grotesque gnarling statues glared back at him. Winged creatures seemed to stare from every corner.

He called out, 'Hello ... any one home?'

Silence ... the wind had picked up and it was bone chillingly cold. He pulled his coat collar up around his neck. It was Mike's coat, the one he had borrowed and still hadn't given back to him. Macgregor continued to follow the muddy path to the back of the house, trying to avoid the larger puddles, yet still managing to splash the red muddy sludge onto his shoes and up the legs of his trousers.

The back of the property was extensive, with several outbuildings and old barns. Tyre tracks led into one of the barns and Macgregor assumed that to be the one that Elliot would garage his vehicles in – it was certainly large enough to hold three or four at a time.

The doors were made of corrugated iron held together with a secure padlock. He pulled at the chain as he tried to peer through the crack, a slit about an inch wide, where the doors wouldn't close properly due to age and damage. He could just make out a vehicle inside the barn but there was no light. He wandered around the side of the barn, and something colourful caught his eye, flapping in the overgrown shrubs to the back of the walled garden. He walked over, and stopped, recognising the material – tartan, a scarf – the scarf Cameron Fowler had been wearing. The CCTV footage had shown him wearing it. The younger generation had a funny way of wearing scarves these days and Macgregor had noticed it on the image he had seen that morning. He carefully removed the scarf from the tangling shrub and folded it neatly, placing it in his coat pocket.

As he walked back towards the barn, he spotted and pulled at a short metal bar lying in the undergrowth. It was a broken star-picket fence post that had fallen to the side of an old wire fence. Armed with the metal post, he approached the locked barn doors. Macgregor pulled the metal post through the loop of the sturdy, thick chain that hung by about two inches down from the padlock. He then secured it through the dangling chain by twisting it around and around as tightly as he could. His fingers were cold and blanched, they ached as he applied the pressure. He wished he had worn gloves. With an almighty yank on the post he pulled down hard on the chain. The entire padlock and bolt fell to the ground, the padlock still intact within the chain.

Macgregor stepped back, kicking the chain and padlock out of his way with his muddy shoe as he pulled back on one of the corrugated metal doors. The screeching of rusty metal along the worn door tracks noisily echoed from within the barn. He stopped, quickly glancing around – waiting to see if the noise had disturbed anyone. He held his breath, listening for signs of activity.

Several black crows took off from an overhead branch of a large gum tree, cawing as they flew to a safer and higher spot.

Macgregor continued with his quest, and seconds later, the door was open wide enough for him to walk through. Macgregor's eyes adjusted to the dark interior of the barn.

It was here! As he had suspected.

Cameron Fowler's RAV4 sat in the middle of the barn surrounded by old rusting farming implements, tractor tyres and oil drums. As he approached he could see that the car was empty. The wheels and arches around the tyres were muddy. The doors were closed. He pulled the scarf out from his pocket and used it to cover his hand as he pulled at the handle on the driver's side. It opened, creaking as it did so. He got in and sat down, scanning and searching the vehicle for anything that might tell him what had happened to his sergeant. He bent down, his arm stretched out to feel around the floor. He carefully opened the glove compartment to feel inside, using the scarf as a makeshift glove – not wanting to contaminate a potential crime scene. He then did the same with the door pockets and console. Nothing of significance. Macgregor turned to view the back seat and the rear of the car's floor. In a corner, on the floor just under the passenger seat, he could see the corner of what looked like a brown leather wallet. Macgregor stretched, squeezing his arm under the seat with difficulty, his fingers were painful; he grappled and clawed at the object until eventually he grabbed it. He opened it. Fowler's photograph smiled back at him from a driver's licence as Macgregor scanned the contents: some cash, credit cards still in their allotted slots, his girlfriend's sweet face in a photograph at the back section of the wallet. Nothing appeared to be missing.

The only thing missing was Fowler. He placed the wallet and the scarf into his pocket.

A further feeling of uncertainty hit him like a brick wall, a growing fear suddenly realised. The probability of finding Fowler alive was less and less likely with each passing hour.

It was dark as Macgregor stepped out from the barn and closed the screeching door behind him. The sky was heavy with low cloud formation; a storm loomed in the distance.

He hurriedly squelched his way back to the car, avoiding the muddier parts of the path, his shoes now caked in red mud.

His car offered some shelter as large rain drops hit the roof and windscreen. Any moment it would be bucketing down. Macgregor turned on the engine and put the heater on full blast. The temperature outside had dropped significantly, and it was icy cold. His fingers were numb and showing signs of bruising. He sat blowing onto his hands, generating warmth and encouraging circulation back into what felt like raw flesh. He reached for his phone. He had to call this in to the station. Fuck it! Still no signal; he threw the phone back down onto the passenger seat.

Macgregor could only imagine what was happening to Fowler. *Kidnapped? Tortured? Or worse? Dead!*

He didn't want to think about the way poor Bryan Johnston had ended his life. He pushed his foot down on the accelerator desperate to get back to Justice Place.

Pulling out from the driveway onto the road, he turned on the radio. He wanted to hear news or updates. The local radio station was still tuned in. The DJ was rabbiting on about some local farmers opposing an industrial estate that had been purchased, land they had been using for the last forty years for the weekly markets. His mind was still caught up in Fowler's situation.

Where the hell was Fowler? Could he get to him in time? What the hell was Patrick Elliot doing and more to the point, where the hell was he? What did his assistant Sarah Vincent have to do with any of this?

His mind was going round and round searching for answers,

trying to navigate through the recent events, the facts. 'Always stick to the bloody facts John!' he swore to himself.

Lost in his thoughts, he didn't take any notice of the song being played over the radio, until the second verse.

Deep down in the Devil's hole
Sinners burn
Deep down in the Devil's hole
Oh dear Lord come and save my soul
He's gonna know you're ready to sell
Way down deep in the fires of hell
Sinners burn!

The unmistakable voice of Buddy Baxter. That song …

Macgregor turned the heater off, the fan making way too much noise as he turned the volume up. The song ended with the DJ once again happily chirping on about the request coming from 'our regular caller'.

Macgregor pulled over to the side of the road and stopped the car. This time he was going to the source.

'Sinners burn, in the fires of hell! I can bloody well think of a few who are ready to sell their souls!' he swore out loud.

He quickly turned the car around and drove off, his tyres screeching and sliding on the muddy embankment as he accelerated.

At speed, driving along the Newell Highway, through sheets of heavy rain, he suddenly slowed down as he approached the slip road, pulled in and stopped at the sign. 'Devil's Hole Reserve'.

CHAPTER FORTY-THREE

Willoughby had managed to persuade Henry Fowler to go back to his hotel. Exhausted and anxious, Fowler had yielded to the suggestion to get some sleep. He had booked into the Dubbo RSL. The man was extremely stressed and Willoughby felt uncomfortable having him hanging around the police station in such a state. Everyone was feeling anxious and on edge, most of the younger team knew Cameron Fowler and liked him.

Fowler's father, on the other hand, a pleasant enough man, had the entire team walking on eggshells. It didn't help that he was also a magistrate and made them feel that they were being scrutinised. He was alert to every ring of a mobile or landline, hovering over desks and listening in on calls.

With reluctance then, he gathered his raincoat and his overnight bags. He turned as he was leaving and pleaded with Willoughby to contact him immediately when any information came through about his son.

Willoughby reassured him that everything was being done that could be done and he would be the first to let him know if and when any information came to light. He had not been feeling that hopeful about the situation but had put on a brave face to appease the magistrate. He was doubtful about Fowler being found alive. As in most cases of missing persons, if they weren't found within twenty-four hours, it was usually a recovery of the body rather than a rescue mission.

Patrol cars had been dispatched to the zoo and search warrants issued. A detective sergeant had gone to interview several of the employees including the other vets that worked there. The zoo's surgery had been searched, and although ketamine was found in the anaesthetic cupboard, it was circumstantial rather than conclusive evidence, not linked to the ketamine that had been used on the two victims. The same applied to the surgical instruments found in the zoo's operating room. Uniforms had taken whatever they deemed as evidence. Many items were bagged and labelled, including laptops and computers.

The rope used to strangle both victims was more difficult to ascertain. Willoughby thought that most likely any rope that had been used to strangle the victims had been discarded and destroyed.

The manager of the zoo, Phil Albright, was not impressed and pleaded with them to keep the newspapers and the media away. This was going to cause a lot of headlines and he worried about the impact to visitors and the benefactors that had made contributions to fund and care for the animals.

A detective sergeant and several uniforms had also gone to Elliot's surgery. It too had been gone over with a fine-toothed comb. Once again, ketamine was found in the drugs cupboard, but that wasn't unusual, as it would be used in any animal hospital. There was still no sighting or trace of the vet or Sarah Vincent. Nevertheless, again, all evidence that was deemed suspicious was gathered, bagged and labelled. Willoughby knew that this evidence may be circumstantial, and it could not be proved beyond reasonable doubt that it had been used in the murder of both victims in a court of law.

The door-to-door knocking had been unsuccessful. No one had seen or heard anything untoward that Saturday morning at the Dubbo RSL or within the vicinity of Sarah's residence. Traffic had been minimal that morning and without incident.

Fowler's car was still missing and uniforms were still out in force searching within a twenty-kilometre area of the local paddocks, farms and bushland.

Willoughby hadn't heard from Macgregor since leaving earlier that day and knew all too well what he was like when flying solo. It was worrying, considering what recently happened to him at the zoo.

That man can get himself into some deep shit!

He rubbed at his forehead. The start of a migraine, it had been building all day and what a hell of a day. He popped a couple of painkillers with some cold coffee from a polystyrene cup. He had no choice but to stay on at the station. Willoughby had left several messages, the last one over an hour ago. It was dark outside and still no message or reply from Macgregor.

It worried the hell out of him. He didn't want the embarrassment of having to tell Chief Superintendent Gavin Ross that Macgregor had also gone missing. He knew he would have to start writing up his report regarding the similar

MOs of Danielle Dickson's and Brian Johnston's murders. With nothing concrete to go on apart from the interview of Ryan Adams, it made him feel anxious and look completely incompetent.

What a bloody mess!

He rubbed his eyes, they were tired and his vision bleary; the pain in his head had intensified. Straining to focus, he persisted in reading the report. The words jumped around on the screen of his computer with white flashes haloing them. The usual telltale sign of his impending full-blown migraine. He wanted to review the findings from the forensics team. The soggy sheets of paper that had been found in Danielle's overnight bag had been deciphered. Some of the words were missing but the forensics team had been able to put together a lot of what it had said. He admired their dedication and the intelligence that went into such work.

He re-read it. It had been written in red print.

Rules for the Coven
Page 2

New members must be chosen very carefully, as it is not easy to establish the trust and unity required for a coven. Remember, allowing a person into your coven is much easier than getting them to leave if serious problems develop that cannot be reconciled. Be selective, and above all, listen to the advice of the Demons. Everyone in the coven should be getting the same message. Covens cannot replace members easily like churches.

Satanism is for the strong!

When working within a group, energy takes on a different sensation and format in contrast to working alone. It is very important for the High Priest to be able to handle the energies, infuse them with his will, and send it towards the chosen goal. These abilities come with persistent and consistent devotion to Satanic power.

Willoughby kept reading, the painkillers slightly alleviating some of the tight band that was pressing around his head.

A gap within the next paragraph, it had been indecipherable, too difficult to interpret, but then it went on to say:

Dancing can take form in a spiral, as this symbolises the Serpent and pattern of life. When enough energy is raised, the dancing should then form a circle to begin the working of the sacrifice.

As long as it is directed properly, each member has their own means of letting go of the energy. Some members might fall to the floor or ground, while other's arms will extend upwards, while some members chant or sing.

Everyone in the coven should be able to speak openly concerning anything to do with the group.

Things kept silent will manifest in a negative way, destroying the unity of the group and its energies!

Every member of the coven should always be present in any of the rituals.

All or nothing applies here.

Storms are a boost to any ritual as the electricity in the air gives the ritual an added increase in energy. Working out of doors provides the same. Wooded areas are best, but it is extremely important the coven is not intruded upon or disturbed in any way.

'What a load of nutters!' Willoughby spoke out loud. 'What kind of bloody idiot believes all this crap? Wankers!'

Time and time again his team had searched the woods and Devil's Hole Reserve and found nothing, not even a hint of a fire or a used barbecue. In the wintertime, and with the recent rain, the local beauty spot had very few – if any – visitors.

He continued on reading the last paragraph from the report.

The entire group can perform a special bonding ritual in the name of Satan, to help with unity and the merging of energies. With this, the entire coven should be dedicated to Satan.
Never forget, working for Satan is your primary focus.

'Weirdo's! More like a fucking orgy!'

Willoughby printed a copy of the findings and closed down the computer. His head completely succumbed to the pain as the migraine peaked. The painkillers had ceased working, unable to numb the vice-like grip that had taken hold. With his hand pressed against his forehead, he got up from his desk to close the office door and turn off the lights. He went over to the front window, which gave a direct view onto the main street and looked out at the heavy rain; it was bucketing down as he pulled down the blind. This was the only way to alleviate the agonising pain and help him get through the next few hours. He had suffered migraines throughout his life but more so when he was stressed. He lay down on the couch in the corner of his office. The dark and quiet space offered hope of some temporary relief and he closed his eyes

CHAPTER FORTY-FOUR

Macgregor switched off the engine of the Land Cruiser but kept the headlights on full beam. It was dark and the pouring rain made for poor visibility. He got out from the car and made his way over to the main area of the reserve, sloshing through large deep puddles. The moon was hidden behind the dark low clouds. It was pitch black across the grassed area. The pathway was very muddy and he slipped a few times but managed to stay upright. The headlights from the car cast long black shadows through the trees as they loomed in the darkness. He could just make out the picnic area and the tables, and an outline of a barbecue.

It was eerily quiet, with only the sound of rain hammering on the ground. The treacherous flow of the Macquarie River from the recent torrential downpour had breached its banks, the inky black water rushing past making its way around the sharp bend.

He stood in the middle of the grassy clearing, peering through the rain at the desolated area. The reserve was completely empty. The only sign of life was a large fruit bat that swooped stealthily past him, making him cower for several seconds.

It became obvious to him that no one was here, or had been here.

Where the hell are they for Christ sake?

Macgregor quickly made his way back to the car, exasperated. His mind desperately tried to make sense of it. He climbed into the Land Cruiser, cold, soaking wet, his hair dripping with rain. He grabbed an old rag from the back seat and shaking the rain from his brow rubbed his face and head dry. The Buddy Baxter song still on his mind, he hummed the song trying to remember the words.

It's all in that bloody song, I know it is!

The words came back in a flurry; he raced through the verses:

Deep down in the Devil's hole
Sinners burn
Deep down in the Devil's hole
A one way ticket, there's no return
Oh dear Lord come and save my soul
Once you're down, way down that track
There's no way you're coming back

Deep down in the Devil's hole
Sinners burn
Deep down in the Devil's hole
A one way ticket, there's no return
Oh dear Lord come and save my soul

He's gonna know you're ready to sell
Way down deep in the fires of hell
Deep down in the Devil's hole
Sinners burn
Deep down in the Devil's hole
A one way ticket, there's no return
Oh dear Lord come and save my soul
Once you've made that fatal deal
Oh dear Lord there ain't time to heal
Deep down in the Devil's hole
Sinners burn!'

Macgregor's realisation dawned as he repeated, 'Deep down in the Devil's hole, one way ticket with no return! Oh Lord come and save my soul!

'Jesus Christ they're at the bloody church! That priest! Father Harding-Pierce! That obnoxious prick! With his bloody cold and slimy hands!' he said aloud, remembering how he felt the need to go and wash his own hands after shaking the priest's.

All the synapses in his brain clicked into gear with great clarity. His mind was in overdrive, a whirr with everything now piecing together. The Buddy Baxter song and the meaning behind it. The signal from the radio station to the others involved in the group. The satanic objects and books he saw in Patrick Elliot's home. The paper that had been found in Danielle's bag that Willoughby had read pertaining to the written rules of the satanic group. Macgregor thought of the victims and how they had been murdered with the sacrificial removal of their kidneys. The last phone call he had with Jasmine Wong. His mind snapped back to the funeral of Danielle and the strange burial service at the old graveyard, a graveyard which hadn't been used for many years. Macgregor recalled how Father Christopher Harding-Pierce had been deliberately obnoxious and obstructive when they had gone to interview him and talk about the murder of the young woman.

With renewed enthusiasm, Macgregor turned on the engine of the Land Cruiser, pulled out from the reserve's slip road onto the main road, and drove back into town.

The church ... he had to get to the church!

His muddy shoes kept slipping off the accelerator pedal, causing the car to slow and slide when re-accelerating.

St Mary's stood on the hill just on the outskirts of town, the large grey-stoned church, the bell tower silhouetted against the dark heavy gloom of the storm, cracks of lightening in the distance lighting the sky as the storm rolled by.

Macgregor pulled in on a grassy verge at the rear of the graveyard. The rusting, spiked, metal fence was just high enough for him to straddle over. It was wet, cold and slippery as he heaved his leg up between the spikes to climb over. He stumbled forwards as his trouser leg caught in the spike, and he heard a large ripping sound as the material shredded. He fell over onto the ground on the other side, the trouser leg flapping in the wind as a searing pain hit him. Macgregor looked down to see a large ragged gash on his shin as the blood gushed down his leg into his sock and shoe.

'Fuck it!' He made a feeble attempt to stop the flow of blood as he pressed on it with his torn trouser, but it continued to pour.

No time to worry about that now, he continued searching for the rear door to the old building. He remembered seeing the small arched door when he had attended the funeral.

As he limped along the old stony path that led to the rear entrance of the church, he noticed several small, leaded, lattice windows. They were no more than six inches high and ran along the bottom of the church wall, close to the ground.

A soft amber glow of light shone through as Macgregor knelt down to peer inside.

The glass was old and dirty, many years of grime and algae had grown over several of the panes. Macgregor rubbed at the glass, scraping off the dirt with his fingernails. He could barely make out what he was seeing. He pressed his face at an awkward angle to catch glimpses of shadows and movement. The pouring rain pounding his face and blurring his vision.

He pressed his ear to the glass. Yes!

Voices?

No!

Singing? No!

It was chanting!

Macgregor carefully stood up as his leg throbbed.

With as much speed as he could muster, he made his way to the arched door.

Breathing hard, he reached the small wooden door. It had an old metal latch bolt; with adrenaline flooding his veins he pulled the heavy latch up. The latch made a loud metallic clunking sound as he released it.

He held his breath.

Christ! Think, John, no back up, no bloody phone contact and God only knows what the hell was going on inside.

He thought of Fowler and the possibility of what could be happening to him. Without hesitation, he pulled the door open. As he entered the small lobby he quickly ducked, avoiding hitting his head on a stone mantel. The height within the entrance was limited and obviously not designed for a man over six foot. With his head bent forwards, he slowly adjusted to the dim light and saw before him a narrow, stone, spiral stairway that led down beneath the main body of the church. The chanting sounds were more audible as he quickly made his way down the stone slab stairs, careful not to slip with the mud clinging to the soles of his shoes. He noticed his sock was bright red but the flow seemed to have stopped. The pain in his leg intensified as it seared its way along the front of his shin.

Macgregor reached the bottom step; a long, arched and narrow stone tunnel led towards the amber glowing light. He had to keep his head and neck bent over as he limped his way along.

The voices had stopped chanting. A high-pitched screeching wail echoed along the stone wall followed by more wailing as a chorus of deeper male voices hummed in a resonating tone.

Macgregor limped to the end of the narrow passageway.

He stopped where the wall ended and turned left into another, larger area. Slowly, he peered around the side of the wall. Candles filled a large arched room. The walls were painted in a deep dark red; the stone ceiling was vaulted, dancing shadows jumping from arch to arch.

A circle of people dressed in long, black, hooded robes held hands high above their heads as they chanted and hummed, moving in a clockwise direction, barefoot. Within that circle was another smaller circle, ten or so naked women moving in an anticlockwise direction, danced as they held hands. Their bodies writhed and skipped as they chanted and wailed, their heads adorned with thorny wreaths and flowers as the wailing increased. It wasn't in English nor any other language Macgregor could recognise.

He stayed behind the entrance wall as he peered around. This time he noticed, within the circle of dancing naked women, at the centre, stood a large, heavy, stone slab. The slab was surrounded by neatly tied bundles of plants, bushes and tree branches. A small, red, velvet pillow had been placed at the head end.

Macgregor pulled back as the chanting suddenly stopped, as did the dancing. He carefully peered around the wall again hoping nobody would notice him. One of the naked dancers came out from the centre-circle as she made her way to the top end of the stone slab.

Macgregor recognised the face. Sarah Vincent!

She giggled. Macgregor remembered that giggle; he had heard it before, when he had spoken with her at the animal hospital, it was a sort of nervous laugh. Her small, naked frame skipped as she picked up the recently decapitated head of a goat that had been sitting in a large, silver-coloured bowl. She held the goat's head high above hers, its dull black eyes staring emptily as she threw her hair back and allowed the blood to trickle down the front of her body. The blood ran between her breasts. She then chanted with her eyes closed as another robed figure came and stood in front of her, and with a finger, smeared and circled her breasts with the sticky blood and marked her with a symbol that looked like an upside down crucifix.

Macgregor held his breath. Bloody hell! he thought, as he subdued – as much as he could – the urge to wince, not only at the sight before him but also from the pain in his leg.

The group stayed silent as Macgregor peered again. A thick heavy curtain hung behind the stone slab, and through the curtain, the priest emerged, Father Christopher Harding-Pierce. Sarah moved to his side as he came forward, and with outstretched arms, he bellowed a command to the group in a heavy monotonous tone.

He stood solemnly, dressed in a long red robe, with the hood down. On his head, he wore what appeared to be deer antlers, his face was smeared in blood. He turned, and raising his arms in a gesture of command summoned his savior. Satan.

From a belt that hung loosely around his middle, he pulled a large curved knife from a highly decorated sheath. He started chanting as the group re-initiated their humming, wailing and dancing. He held the knife high in the air, the reflection of the candles glinting across the room and into Macgregor's eyes.

Sarah approached a small wooden table, picked up a silver goblet and held it high above her head as the priest, with eyes closed, uttered a prayer to Satan. The table also held an assortment of bowls and dishes and a thick, short, rope. Macgregor noticed that one of the dishes held a hypodermic syringe.

Moments later, two robed figures emerged from the middle of the heavy curtains carrying a man's body and laid him on top of the stone slab.

Macgregor could see the toned, lean, naked frame of Cameron Fowler. Fowler's limp and rag-doll-like body was slumped as they put him down. He was alive! Macgregor could just make out Fowler's chest slowly rising and falling. He was also unconscious, most probably drugged the same way as they had drugged and killed Danielle Dickson and Bryan Johnston.

Macgregor had to act, and act fast, another few moments and Fowler would be slaughtered.

He had no gun nor any weapon on him and thought the best course of action would be the element of surprise – to run at them yelling as he did so. He searched the room looking for any other escape. NO! Only one way in and out, unless there was another door behind the curtain but he doubted it – that was at least one good thing. He would have to grab the knife from Harding-Pierce and hope to hell that the others in the group wouldn't mob him.

As Fowler lay motionless, Harding-Pierce moved to the side of the stone alter, motioning to the two robed figures that had carried Fowler in. They rolled Fowler on to his left side. The priest held the knife firmly in his hand. His eyes bulged, glazed with excitement, a look of madness in them, the veins in his face standing out, pulsating, as he loudly recited a satanic verse. With saliva drooling from the corners of his mouth, he raised his voice with each verse; the saliva fell, hitting Fowler's face, but his body remained quite still.

The priest raised his arm, poised, the knife firmly in his palm ready to deliver the sacrificial incision.

'AAAAAAHHHHHHHHHHHHHHHH!'

Macgregor raced out from behind the wall and rushed at the priest, the robed figures still lost in their chanting, unaware of the detective as he charged.

Harding-Pierce turned, his eyes gleaming, the lust for blood pulsing through every cell of his body.

Macgregor lunged at him, pulling him down and away from Fowler's limp body. They both fell to the floor, the priest turned, staring into the eyes of Macgregor.

'You!' he snarled, the knife still firmly in his hand. The dancers, suddenly aware of the commotion, gasped and stood back as the two men grappled on the floor. The robed figures stopped chanting and circling as they too now noticed the commotion. Some of them ran from the room.

Others stood watching. One robed figure came forwards and took down his hood. It was Patrick Elliot, his face growing red with anger and hostility as he leapt on top of Macgregor and started punching him. Macgregor's only advantage was that he had shoes on. He started kicking wildly at the vet as hard and as violently as he could. The priest held the knife towards Macgregor's chest as the two men struggled. Macgregor holding the handle of the blade as far back as he could from his body, straining every muscle to keep the knife from entering his flesh.

As Macgregor lay kicking at the vet he toppled over the small table and the bowls and contents fell crashing to the floor. Macgregor was still desperately trying to keep the large curved knife away from his body, holding firmly onto the handle of the knife, pushing with all his strength against the maniac priest. The priest loudly called upon Satan to give him strength. Macgregor turned to see Elliot had now gained a better position to attack him. The vet had straddled the detective, he sat on top of him avoiding the heavy kicking blows from Macgregor. The detective continued to kick wildly into the air, adrenaline masking the pain of his recent injuries. The vet pounded into him, kidney punches, every blow coming harder and faster.

Macgregor searched for anything around him that he could use to defend himself. With his hand stretched out on the cold stone floor, he grappled, searching for a makeshift weapon.

His fingers hit a sharp pointed object and it stung; at once Macgregor knew he had pierced his index finger with the sharp point of a needle. He quickly grabbed at the needle and syringe, careful to turn it around until it was firmly in his hand, and with one quick lunge, he stabbed the needle into the arm of Elliot, plunging its contents into the forearm muscle. Macgregor was damn sure he knew what was in it and hoped his attacker would quickly succumb to the contents of the drug, ketamine...

Within seconds, the vet reeled back, and in anger gave one final blow to Macgregor's head before swaying and falling on the floor, lapsing into unconsciousness. Macgregor kicked at the vet again, pushing him away with his foot as he tried to maintain the force necessary to keep the knife-wielding, mad priest from cutting him.

Exhausted and not sure how long he could sustain his

strength, Macgregor suddenly heard the sound of loud voices yelling.

'Drop to the floor!'

It was the police.

Lights and torches filled the room as uniforms darted in and around the group, armed with guns and tasers. The robed figures immediately obeyed the yelled commands. Some were handcuffed as they lay on the floor, others were forced against the wall with their hands behind their heads. The priest's eyes darted around as a gun was held to the back of his head.

Willoughby's big, bald, shiny head and grim face peered down at Macgregor's face and he winked as he said in his distinctive abrupt tone,

'Drop the knife, you fucking weirdo! NOW!'

Two uniforms grabbed the knife from the priest, cuffing him as he was dragged to his feet. They then helped Macgregor up. His leg was still oozing and he had lost a fair amount of blood. When he stood he felt woozy. He leaned back against the stone wall, breathing hard, pain resonating through his ribs and kidney areas. Through gritted teeth Macgregor quietly worded a 'thank you' to Willoughby.

Willoughby shook his head and bellowed, 'You're a fucking nutter Macca, must you always go it alone? Do I always have to save your arse? You don't answer my calls, I left a hundred fucking messages! Nothing! Not a bloody peep! I had to get IT to track your phone, you have no idea what a headache you gave me!' He then sniggered, knowing this wasn't unusual for his friend to do.

The satanic group was led out from the church, with curses

and blasphemous retorts made to the accompanying officers. The naked females were offered blankets as they were led away, the wailing and crying echoing through the stone narrow passageway. Sarah Vincent stayed calm, her giggle returning when asked to put on clothing as she smiled defiantly, staring at Macgregor.

Harding-Pierce, cuffed and also defiant, was led out to the awaiting paddy wagon, still invoking Satan as he was dragged away. The madness glowed from his blood-rimmed eyes. Ambulances arrived and paramedics brought a stretcher in for Fowler. They carefully placed him on it, covering him in a warm blanket and assisting his breathing with airway clearance and oxygen. The paramedics spoke with Willoughby, they said that although Fowler was heavily sedated, dehydrated and was suffering from hypothermia, by all accounts their first impression was that he would recover well. He was young and strong.

They would most likely keep him in the hospital for observation and until he fully regained consciousness.

The second stretcher brought in was headed towards Elliot, lying listless on his back, unconscious, his breathing noisy and laboured; he had totally succumbed to the powerful effects of the drug Macgregor had injected and was oblivious to his predicament. The paramedics secured an airway and into the back of his hand inserted a cannula that was then hooked up to an infusion of normal saline. They then hoisted him on to the gurney, wheeling him out to the awaiting ambulance.

Willoughby assisted Macgregor out of the church. Macgregor limped slowly along the muddy footpath leaning heavily on his pal. Willoughby told him not to drive, he then opened the rear door to the awaiting patrol car.

'Better get that seen to at the hospital mate, big day tomorrow, I'll call you later.' He nodded at the gash on Macgregor's leg, which was again oozing, the blood beginning to congeal around the top of his sock. Macgregor bent forward to sit in the back of the police car, wincing; he protectively held his right side as he moved, the muscles in his chest burning with every intake of breath.

Willoughby closed the car door and tapped on the roof of the car. Macgregor turned slowly, easing the window down, and rather than speaking, he gave the thumbs up to his pal. He looked out at the graveyard, the rain was still pouring down. He watched as the somewhat ridiculous charade of robed figures were led into waiting police vans.

Thank Christ it's over!

CHAPTER FORTY-FIVE

A shard of light trickled through a gap where the curtains had failed to close. Particles of dust danced as they settled upon the carpeted floor. Macgregor lay in bed reflecting, recalling the events over the last few days. Rubbing at bleary eyes, he turned over carefully, moving his leg slowly as the stiffness and pain started to bite at his shin. The clock said 9:27 am.

It had been a tough few days – fifteen sutures to his shin, another round of antibiotics – he was definitely becoming a regular at the local hospital, he even remembered the nurses' names.

He felt relieved, the whole Devil's Hole nightmare was being pieced together. The discovery and uncovering of the satanic cult in action, the arrest of the priest, Father Christopher Harding-Pierce, and also Dr Patrick Elliot, for the murders of Danielle Dickson and Bryan Johnston. Dr Elliot, the vain vet, had religiously been dying his hair black. Macgregor had suspected as much, but it was evident now since his arrest; the roots had started to grow, a bright ginger-red strip ran along the centre parting of his hair. As a Dubbo local, the vet didn't want his natural red hair linking him to the notorious Adams family, whose close ties with Gunner Adams would have been devastating to his position and status within the town.

Kidnapping and assault charges were brought against the vet's assistant, Sarah Vincent, who was also charged as an accomplice and accessory to the murders. The other members of the group had been interviewed and some had charges made against them. Dubbo was certainly making news, the media would be having a field day!

Macgregor decided to visit the home of the Dicksons. In a sombre and courteous manner he delivered the news that they had caught Danielle's killer. He had promised he would deliver the information before any media got hold of it. They were shocked and grateful at the same time. Stunned, and in utter disbelief that their own valued priest could be responsible for such violence. The pain ran deep in Mrs Dickson's eyes as a staunch Catholic and a regular churchgoer for most of her life. Clinging to her rosary beads dangling from her hand, she said that for the first time in weeks she would be able to visit her daughter's grave and weep for her beautiful child. Mr Dickson sat slumped in his chair, the half-empty whiskey bottle within arm's reach, staring blankly at the television screen. Closure was so important to all victims of murdered loved ones.

The last few days had brought more discoveries regarding the priest and his difficult and troubled youth. As a young child, he had been taken into care, following horrendous abuse and neglect from his father and other members of his immediate family. A criminal family, well known to the police, with a background in violence, drug dealing, illegal weapons, arson, soliciting and theft. The list was endless.

As a young boy and following many unsuccessful attempts of fostering him into 'normal' families, he was eventually brought into care and sent to live with the Christian Brothers.

St Augustine's orphanage in Geelong in Victoria was notorious now as the home of pedophiles and brutal men who had been in charge of young boys over fifty years ago.

Christopher Harding-Pierce had from a vulnerable age suffered at the hands of a notorious pedophile. This man had sexually assaulted him over a period of seven years and had beaten him daily, threatening to end his life if he were ever to tell anyone. This man, this 'Christian Brother', whose brutality was made public through a trial and public hearings – resulting ultimately in his incarceration in prison – had sexually abused over fifteen boys during the sixties at the Geelong orphanage. The 'Brother' was well into his seventies now and had still shown little remorse for his actions when a local journalist had interviewed him as part of a documentary.

Harding-Pierce went on to say how he had been guided and encouraged to become a priest by some of the 'good' Brothers and enter into the Catholic Church. He stated how it had made him feel safe, a way to escape his unfamiliarity with the outside world; after having had little contact with the rest of society, it was an environment he understood. Growing up in the orphanage was the only real home he had known. However, there was always a dark and sadistic need deep within him. He relished the power and control over his worshippers and delighted in the occult group he had kept hidden for years. The satanic rituals and the powerful hold he had over the members of the group satisfied the increasing evil compulsions within him. Compulsions that had begun much earlier in his life. As a young child living with his neglectful and dysfunctional family, he had enjoyed torturing and strangling small animals.

Macgregor had sat listening as the priest recalled, without remorse, his reasons for the ritualistic killings of his victims. When questioned about why he had removed a kidney from each victim the priest answered in a cold, matter-of-fact tone, quoting passages from the books of the Old Testament, the ones that follow the Pentateuch – the first five books of the Bible – mostly from Jeremiah and Psalms – Genesis, Exodus, Leviticus, Numbers and Deuteronomy. According to tradition, the books were written by the Israelite leader, Moses. Macgregor had scanned through the passages and googled a summary from a religious paper.

The human kidneys are cited figuratively as the site of temperament, emotions, prudence, vigor and wisdom. In five instances, they are mentioned as the organs examined by God to judge an individual. They are cited either before or after, but always in conjunction with the heart as mirrors of the psyche of the person examined. There is also reference to the kidneys as the site of divine punishment for misdemeanors, committed or perceived, particularly in the book of Job, whose suffering and ailments are legendary.

It explained a lot about the priest's obsession with religion and Satanism and ultimately, his behaviour. But it was no excuse for the violence or the pleasure he had taken from performing those terrible acts.

It also didn't explain why he had removed Bryan Johnston's testicles and had them shoved up his anus, unless he was literally saying, 'UP YOU! ASSHOLE!'

Other victims of the same orphanage had suffered but none of them had gone on to become killers. Macgregor wasn't taken in by his sad and unfortunate history. He had seen the madness in the luminescent glare of his eyes and knew the wiring in his brain was messed up long before the violence and abuse from the orphanage had started. A true, narcissistic, psychopath, showing no empathy towards his victims and no remorse for his actions.

Patrick Elliot's love of satanic objects and the occult had led him into the direct path of the priest. He had found in the priest a kindred spirit and became a true devotee to him and the satanic group. Elliot had been carried away with the illusion of the satanic power and the mystery of it, mesmerised by the priest's sermons on Satanism. His skill with the scalpel and knowledge of human anatomy had led to a symbiotic relationship, each dependent on the other for their mutual desires. Elliot had access to powerful drugs and he would often use them on unsuspecting younger women, allowing him to act out his fantasies of having the sex that he craved with nubile women. Watching them dance naked in the rituals fuelled his lust, but he went further, by impregnating not only Danielle Dickson; he had also fathered a child with Sarah Vincent's sister, Kylie Vincent. Her sister had left Dubbo not long after giving birth, made possible by the cash Elliot gave her in an attempt to 'pay her off' and conceal the baby from his wife.

He had wanted to do the same with Danielle, 'pay her off', only she wanted more. She was in love with him and begged to be with him. Elliot had given her false hope and had lied, telling her that he loved her too, convincing her to meet him at the Devil's Hole Reserve that unfortunate last day of her life to 'work things out'. However, Danielle had decided to pack and leave home early that morning. She had called Elliot on her mobile from the bus station, asking him to pick her up. She had been feeling unwell, nauseous. Carrying a heavy bag she was exhausted by the time she had reached the bus station. Elliot had, in a panic, called the priest, asking for advice, knowing his wife was almost due to give birth. The girl's pregnancy would have devastating consequences. It was easy for the priest. He would simply arrange to have her eliminated. The priest engineered the entire plan, which had gone well until the discovery of her body on the beach.

Bryan Johnston, the poor sap, had tried to blackmail the vet, which then impacted directly with the priest. Elliot had asked Johnston to dispose of a large dead ape, as he had done many times previously, and been well paid for each time. It was the usual practice to cremate the larger dead animals at the Western Plains Zoo, however the furnace was dysfunctional and out of use. Elliot had asked him to drive to another furnace at Mogo Zoo for the disposal of the animal. Johnston had become suspicious by the vet's nervous behaviour and unwrapped the securely wrapped plastic sheeting in the back of the transit van to find that it was the body of a young woman, and not an animal. Once discovered, he quickly assessed his position and decided to use this situation to his advantage. Johnston thought he could make some big bucks by blackmailing Elliot. Instead of taking the body and leaving no trace, in a drunken state he had carelessly dumped her body from Batemans Bay bridge into the flowing Clyde River. The body had wound up on Surfside Beach three days later, coming in on the king tide.

Johnston had been summoned by the priest to discuss why he had lied about the disposal of the body, so he made his move and said he would go to the cops if they didn't cough up more cash. They had previously paid him a large sum of money, but he went back and demanded even more cash, threatening to spill the beans ...

Well, he wasn't that good a poker player, everyone could read his tells. He never really had the knack of knowing just what he was dealing with.

Bryan Johnston became the next sacrifice to Satan and ultimately met his maker – minus his testicles.

Cameron Fowler had recovered quickly and told how he had gone to interview Sarah Vincent that morning. She had asked him to drive her to Patrick Elliot's to pick up some supplies. They had gone together to collect his car from the car park and drove to Elliot's house at the Old Presbytery. It was when he went to get the supplies from the barn that Sarah had injected him with the ketamine. He had collapsed, quickly succumbing to the powerful sedative. He could only surmise as to how they moved him to the crypts in the church;

vague memories still haunted him. All good apart from some bruising and grogginess, he was soon discharged from hospital. Cameron Fowler was driven back to the Bay – his car, the RAV4, had been impounded for forensic evidence – by his father. Magistrate Henry Fowler had stayed by his son's bedside throughout his ordeal.

Macgregor stretched and made his way to the edge of the bed. He stood gingerly, putting a little weight on the damaged leg and limped over to the desk where his phone was charging. He was about to unplug the cord when it bellowed 'Scotland the Brave'.

It was Lorna. He hesitated before answering.

'Hi lassie I was just thinking about you. I'll be back in the Bay in a few days, how about I take you out for a braw candlelight supper?'

He waited for a response – a few seconds of silence – then a deep sigh. 'What part of sleeping with another woman is okay, John?

'I know you were sleeping with Isabella Kowowski!' Another deep sigh.

Macgregor interrupted, 'Och Lorna, ye cannae think ...' Lorna cut him off sharply with a rapid response.

'I'm so disappointed John. Why?' A silent pause then, 'I can't see you any more, or talk to you! It's over!'

She hung up and left Macgregor speechless, unable to voice his defence, which he knew he never had. Guilty as charged.

Hells bloody bells, shit! I didnae think that was going to happen!

Macgregor started to re-dial then stopped; she had sounded

upset, sad, but resigned. He doubted he could reassure her or wangle his way out of this situation. He always knew the possibility was there, and although he hated deception, he had been hoping that he had got away with the indiscretion.

He sat back on the bed with his hands combing through his unruly hair. That's all he needed, just when he thought he had a fairly good chance of a more permanent relationship with Lorna. The possibility was there and yet he had once again fucked it up!

Macgregor, leaned back against the wooden headboard and sighed. He scanned the four dull walls. He'd had enough of Dubbo, the case, and living in this shoebox of a room. He wanted to be home and never hear about the Devil's Hole again. He thought he would never hear himself say it but he did miss the Bay. He missed the uncomfortable furniture in his small boring flat, missed his empty fridge, and was very keen to catch up with his cronies for a good game of poker. He needed to get back on his own patch. The sooner the better!

That's it, damn it! I'm leaving, today! Willoughby can sort the rest of this shit out, I'm done here. To hell with the inquiry into Gunner's death.

Chief Superintendent Gavin Ross had summoned him and Willoughby to a hearing in Sydney the following day. Flights had been booked, cars to the airport arranged.

To hell with them all!

He walked over to the small-mirrored closet, opened the sliding door and pulled his tweed jacket off the metal hanger; he picked up the crumpled and creased trousers from the floor and pulled them on. A clean shirt would have to wait as he pushed his arm into the rolled-up sleeve of the shirt. He stared out the window, watching as one black crow swooped down on a lone sparrow. It pecked at the sparrow's head forcing it to the ground. Blood-smeared feathers stuck to the pavement as the tiny bird relinquished a morsel of food from its beak. The crow gave one final peck to its tiny head, and it stopped moving. Just like people, he thought, violent and selfish. It's a bird-eat-bird world.

He pulled the other sleeve on, unrolling the cuff as the phone beeped an incoming message.

He picked it up and scrolled to message inbox. 'See you later John, it is still room twelve, right?' Macgregor smiled.

Timing was never your thing, Isabella ...